The Nabi

Printed in the United States of America.

ISBN 978-0-692-68328-6

Published by DeWayne Jordan Hampton
Fayetteville, NC

Subject Heading: AFRICAN-AMERICAN—CHRISTIAN/CHRISTIAN—FANTASY/CHRISTIAN—SUSPENSE

Scripture quotations also taken from the King James Version of the Bible.

Prior Works by DeWayne Jordan Hampton/Jordan Hampton

THE MENTALITY TRILOGY

The Mentality

The Corruption

The Purification

Scripture Quotations

"Very truly I tell you, all who have faith in me will do the works I have been doing, and they will do even greater things than these, because I am going to the Father."

John 14:12, TNIV.

"No, in all these things we are more than conquerors through Him who loved us."

Romans 8:37, TNIV.

"I can do all this through Him who gives me strength."

Philippians 4:13, TNIV.

ACKNOWLEDGEMENTS

This book, by some of its early readers, has already been called the greatest work I've ever written, and to deny others the part they played in inspiring it all would only paint me as a fool. First and foremost, I have to thank my Lord and Savior Jesus Christ for enabling me to speak His truth and infuse it with my own work. I strongly believe that I can do nothing without Him.

Secondly, I would like to thank my mother and father for giving me life and teaching me how to pursue what I love with fervor.

I would also like to thank my close friends who are the reason why the bond between Aiden and Eran exist in this book.

To my teachers in high school and college, you all have done me a great service that I will never be able to repay.

To my spiritual father, Pastor Warren H. Stewart Sr., you have been an incredible mentor to me over the last few years and have encouraged me to strive after what God wants me to be.

To SSGT Slavens and TSGT Dicicco, thank you for the many things you taught me during my time in your flight in Basic Military Training. You two are truly invaluable, and because of you I know that the Air Force is in good hands.

To Flight 395, my flight, I am proud of each and every one of you and thankful that I had the opportunity to get to know a good amount of you before we all parted ways. I pray that your experience in the Air Force is everything you hoped it would be and more. God bless.

To Flight 396, my brother flight, thank you for giving us some good competition and raising the bar for us to push beyond the standards of our limitations. It is a blessing to know you.

All of you have played such a vital role in the creation of this book, and I will never forget what you left me with.

Chapter One

He sat in the sanctuary silently as the preacher spoke. He watched the people carefully, but couldn't help but allow the Word that was being spoken in his hearing to minister to his Spirit. He needed it, that empowering message, that reassurance that he was on the right path, that restoration to his soul. The sermon, though powerful and inspiring, did little to sooth his troubled mind and even less to make him forget about that horrible night twelve years ago. He looked down as he pressed his milk-chocolate hands together and bounced his knee in distress at the memory. It haunted him in the worst of ways, how he'd failed that night, and though he did his best to distract himself with the words of the preacher, with the stained-glass windows, with the shouts of praise and worship as the pastor in the pulpit lay into his sermon, he found that he simply could not escape. The preacher continued in his theological soliloquy with unbridled passion.

"In addition to understanding that we don't fit in those circumstances, we must acknowledge that we are numerous," he spoke with fervor. "Once again we look at verse 14 and we see that the people of Joseph don't list any issues with the land. Their grievance isn't as much about their inheritance as much as it is about themselves. They didn't say that this land is too small, too poorly stocked, too raggedy or anything like that. What they said was, 'We are a numerous people.' In much the same way there's just too many of us trapped here, and I'm not talking about the ministers and deacons and apostles and pastors and what have you," he said with an air of dismissal that made Aiden's eyes refocus on him, "I'm talking about the people like me, who have been mistreated, who have been discriminated against, who have been mocked, who have been emotionally destroyed, who have been rejected, who have done wrong, who have gotten into fights, who desperately need and desire a Savior from the harsh realities of this world, the ones who are all lumped into that same category of 'broken and defective.'" The words of the preacher only added to the echo of the man's past, but it was only when his mind revisited the shadows as they swallowed *him* that he acknowledged the truth behind what was being said, and more than that admitted to being just as broken as anyone else.

His face distorted as he restrained tears. *Get it together, Aiden*, he urged himself. His head sank again as the rapid images of that night cycled through his consciousness. He could hear the sinister laughter and helpless screams of fear and agony as clearly in the distance as when they first penetrated his ears, and though he sat in a clean church amid hundreds of worshippers who donned their best fragrances and outfits, he could smell nothing but hellsmoke and see the pain in the hearts around him. The preacher spoke of moving forward, of understanding oneself in the trials of life, and with every word uttered those within earshot opened up their mouths and shouted in agreement with looks of conviction and sincerity written about their countenances.

He had to leave soon, because even though his Spirit could take it, the age-old wounds on Aiden's heart had yet to heal. The minister continued as Aiden stood.

"We must remember that the Promise is possible, my brothers and sisters! Remember that 'He who began a good work in you will carry it on to completion until the day of Christ Jesus! Just because you don't feel like you're there right now doesn't mean you won't get there. You have to be confident in the Lord, confident in who *He* says you are, and lastly you must be confident in where you're going! Remember that your life has a purpose! It's up to you whether or not you act on it!" As Aiden moved to the center aisle and toward the double doors that would be his exit, he could feel this inner rejuvenation reach its completion and the reassurance of who he was began to set in and assuage his inner turmoil.

He couldn't allow himself to feel any such despair over the events of the past. It would be a slap in the face of the man he'd failed, his brother in arms and brother at heart. It perplexed him that he cared so much, even to this day, or that it even resonated with him that he was alone. He'd only known the grounds of an orphanage in his youth. He was neither the brightest child, nor the strongest, but fought desperately to prove himself otherwise. In the end, he only earned the scorn of the children around him and the ire of the adults who provided his care. He had always been alone, and he'd never once imagined himself wanted by anyone. He felt even now that he was adrift in a vast ocean with nobody to throw him a line to save him. At least nobody left. But that was irrelevant. He knew full well how badly he'd failed, but it was that failure that drove him to defend others with his life and ensure that he never failed like that again.

He walked along the sidewalk as he wrestled with his thoughts. His hands were balled tightly at his sides as he passed through the streets of Edgehaven, Arizona and admired the skyscrapers around him that shielded him from the harsh summer sun. He stopped at a corner as a car sped by in the opposite direction, and smiled as he continued for his destination. It was red, *his* favorite color, and though the boisterous sound of the powerful engine faded into the noise of the rest of the city, just the vitality of the color was enough to replace Aiden's depressing memories with those of happier times.

"Hewer, Eran," he heard their military training instructor call. In his mind, he was transported back in time to the earliest days of Air Force basic training in San Antonio, Texas. He could suddenly feel a humidity that he'd all but forgotten and a sense of shared terror as he and the rest of his flight stood under the overhang just outside their dorm.

"Sir, Trainee Hewer reports as ordered!" Hewer responded. The rest of the flight stood perfectly still, head and eyes straight forward as the MTI began to chew him out over his initial PT test scores.

"What I don't understand," Staff Sergeant Driver yelled, "is how you could look so stinkin' strong and then go out there on that workout pad and prove me wrong like this! How stinkin' lazy and unmotivated do you have to be?" Hewer barely twitched when Driver stood face to face with him and yelled, "Stop moving around! Stop stinkin' moving around! You lock your body at attention when your superior addresses you, tracking?"

"Tracking, sir!" Hewer did his best to calm his nerves, but Driver continued to apply pressure to the psychological grip he had on the young trainee.

"You wanna be the first one on the bus home, don't you, Trainee?" Hewer rapidly shook his head, which only made Driver yell all the more. "No! Did I say you could adjust? Don't stinkin' adjust! Get it together, Trainee, and bring these stinkin' scores up! Dismissed!" They watched in sheer terror as the MTI walked away, and filed back into the dorm from the overhang. Hewer shook, from a combination of terror and anger, and walked back to his wall locker in total silence as others laughed and rejoiced that they weren't the ones who disappointed a man with the reputation as the best instructor at Lackland Air Force Base. Aiden watched him carefully; curious as to what course of action he should take. He'd never had a friend before, but he knew an opportunity when he saw one. He walked over to Hewer and sat in the seat adjacent him, but as always, he was completely ignored.

"Are you alright," Aiden questioned. Hewer's eyes narrowed as he glared at the white linoleum tiles of the floor and tightened his fists on his kneecaps. He remained silent, and in his humiliation and sorrow, Aiden stood with his eyes now locked on the floor as well. "Well, if you need anything, I'll help in any way I can," he assured him. "It isn't like I have anyone else to talk to." He started to walk away when Hewer looked up.

"Wait," he implored. Aiden turned around swiftly and was unable to mask his excitement at the prospect that he could finally have a new friend. Hewer stood there with a camouflage cap in his hand and a somber scowl firmly in place. "You were about to leave your hat. One of us being the example for today should be enough, don't you think?" Aiden smiled silently as he took back what was his, and walked away with a cheery façade and a flurry of negative emotions. Hewer sat back in his chair and mulled over the look on Aiden's face. *Those eyes*, he thought. In those eyes was the same look of solitude that he'd experienced all his life, a sign that kindred spirits did in fact exist within the flight.

The next day started at 5:45 a.m., as did any other, and in the trainees' rush to prepare themselves for morning physical training, Aiden stewed in his sour thoughts and figured himself an idiot for making the attempt to be accepted. The years he spent in the orphanage taught him that nobody would ever accept him, no matter what he did or how hard he tried. He was destined to be alone, and coming into a profession where people depend on you isn't the same as joining a social club. His shadowy brown eyes urged him to seek some manner of companionship, but he resolved as he washed the shaving cream off his well-defined jaw line that he would do no such thing, and would live out the rest of his days in the reality of his isolation. He attempted to gather his belongings but dropped his shaving cream on the floor.

He stooped down to pick it up, but when he turned around he saw Hewer there before him with an apologetic smile in place. Aiden's expression was cold, though his eyes still shimmered with the hope of one day finding a friend.

"May I help you," he asked with a bite of sarcasm. Hewer's smile disappeared as he stared into Aiden's eyes and saw that same loneliness he shouldered. His brow furrowed as the mood intensified, and suddenly time seemed to be of little concern.

"Listen," he began calmly. "I wanted to apologize for blowing you off yesterday. I wasn't in the best mood after Driver got done ripping me a new one."

"Obviously," Aiden said matter-of-factly as he pushed past Hewer. In silence they endured PT, in solitude did they fold and put away their laundry, and the atmosphere in the dining facility around chow grew even icier than usual, though they sat on opposite ends of the room. Aiden's determination to safely dwell behind his self-erected walls wouldn't be done away with so easily. He fancied himself a fortress of impenetrable outer defenses, and the opportunity that Hewer had to make a difference in Aiden's life had already passed. He was committed to block him out just like everyone else, to beat the others to the punch in regard to his isolation so that nobody could see his pain or add to it.

What he didn't account for was the initial mail call that took place later that night. He heard Driver call out name after name.

"Amos," he started. It was the first name on the list, and as the rest of the trainees passed his letter back to him, Driver continued. "Bridges," he continued, and passed out a thick package. "You and a wingman stay behind when I dismiss the flight. I have to watch you open that to make sure you can have it. Brown," he continued. As he made his way down the list, Aiden could feel his heart nearly pound its way out of his chest, and though he grew with anticipation, with the hope that someone on the outside remembered him and sought to reach out to him, he sat perfectly still in the back corner of the room, distanced from his so-called brothers in arms. "Brown," he repeated with another letter to pass back. "Brown. Carter," they passed a large envelope to the trainee just in front of Aiden. *They're getting closer,* he thought with profound excitement.

"Coleman," Driver continued and proceeded to repeat the name three times. The stack of letters grew smaller and smaller, and with that eagerness in Aiden's heart erupted a desperation like he'd never known. "Davis," he called. No answer was given and no hand was raised. "Trainee Davis!" With the sudden eruption of volume a semi-bulky trainee shot a hand straight into the air and the others passed his mail to him. "Wake up," Driver called angrily, and the trainee sank into himself in embarrassment. "Forest!" Driver's attitude was in rare form now, and the other trainees found themselves with a renewed motivation to respond to his call quickly. The previously mentioned names were repeated a few more times before a new name was called. "Hewer! You all have five minutes to read what you have before details and lights out. Dismissed!"

Time seemed to stop for Aiden. No, it didn't surprise Aiden Zane that he'd once again been proven to be alone, but for once, just once in his life he'd hoped that things would be different. His gaze sank to the floor as he heard his flight mates cry over the sweet words written to them by their families and joined them in their weeping, but whereas they wept out of joy, it was the bitterness of sorrow that tugged on Aiden's heart.

It was the formation of his first friendship and only true rivalry, the first relationship in his entire life that pushed him to be truly better than he was. It seemed so distant to him now, and as he entered into his apartment complex in the present day, his mind still wandered around in the past.

He could remember the painful experience of walking into the same white-walled Day Room for the second mail call. He moved to his corner, only to find that Hewer was seated right next to his established spot. Aiden scowled, but quickly collected himself as he sank into his position.

"What are you doing back here, guidon bearer? I thought you were always supposed to be at the front of the flight with your fancy little stick," Aiden shot. Hewer just smiled and watched the other members of the flight as they laughed and joked together. Aiden narrowed his gaze on the rank insignia chart on the other side of the room in an attempt to distract himself from his evident loneliness. It was the same routine as the last time in that Staff Sergeant Driver had walked in with a disgruntled expression and a massive stack of letters with the occasional package mixed in.

"When you hear your name, raise your hand so I can pass it back," commanded the MTI. "Amos!" Tears began to well up in Aiden's eyes as he dismissed the call. *There's no point in even paying attention*, he figured. *I don't mean anything to anyone.* A tear streamed down his cheek that attracted the attention of the man who sat at his side, but instead of comfort,

Hewer briefly feigned a cough to mask the smile he found difficult to restrain. "Zane," called Driver with a letter in his hand. Aiden paid no attention to the sound of his name, which only drove the instructor to repeat the call with increased volume. "Zane! Wake up! I'm stinkin' talking to you!" Aiden, in all shock, slowly lifted his hand into the air and watched as the members of the flight passed back mail that was apparently his. He couldn't believe it. He'd finally been thought of by another person, finally gotten his first letter, but the years of solitude that led to that point crushed the joy of the moment. *It's probably a mistake,* he thought as he sulked in the corner. The letter came to him and reluctantly he took it, just so he could see if it was truly meant for him.

He opened it, and to his surprise it was a handwritten note that bore his name. He began to read and as his eyes indulged in every word, he could feel his broken heart begin to mend.

To Aiden Zane,

My son tells me that you spend most of your time alone. Forgive me if I'm a little too forward, but I don't think that's any way for a man to go through such a trying time as this. You may not think it, but there are people who do care about you. They may not present themselves outright, but in time they'll come into your life and never leave because of how remarkable you are and how important you are to them, and if you'd let me, I'm more than willing to be the second. I think my son has already beaten me to the position of first. If you ever find yourself in need of civil conversation, I would be more than happy to talk to you as regularly as I can.

Your friend,

Eva Hewer.

Aiden's tears dripped onto the page as he grasped it in his hand with unnecessary force. Hewer placed a hand gently on his shoulder and Aiden quickly turned to face his comrade. Though he initially felt embarrassed to be seen crying in front of him, the warm expression in Hewer's icy blue eyes told him that he needn't be.

"If you need anything, I'll help in any way I can," said Hewer. Aiden's eyes widened in surprise at the reiteration of his feeble attempt at making a friend, and then narrowed as his own overwhelming sense of joy caused the tears to flow more profusely. The heartbreaking image of his new friend in tears compelled Hewer to hug him and comfort him like nobody ever had.

Aiden, fully returned from his pool of memories, stood on the balcony with tears in his eyes as the sun began to set, and watched the people on the street below tend to their ordinary lives. He wondered if any of them shared in his loneliness, and with a cringe he receded into his dwelling to shed his secondhand suit and don his signature jeans and blue t-shirt. He looked around and released a melancholy sigh. The dingy steel-colored walls, archaic television and indoor collection of lawn furniture for a seating arrangement filled him with a sense of hopelessness and rage that all but compelled him to return to the bustle of the world without. He worked hard to make a living, and yet this pitiful excuse of a home was all he could afford. Still, it was better than life on the street. He wandered the sidewalk in search of an inexpensive meal as the stunning mix of reds and yellows that danced in the late afternoon sky grew cooler and more vibrant with every moment that passed.

The colors, along with the light breeze that reduced the temperature from scorching to comfortable, calmed his senses and brightened his otherwise pensive day, and with little hesitation he lost himself in the tranquility of the moment.

"Get out of the way!" The shout snapped him out of his momentary calm, but before he could assess where it came from he was knocked from his feet to his back. His head snapped against the concrete sidewalk, and out of pain he briefly closed his eyes. He opened them in a rage, prepared to reprimand the clumsy fool who carelessly toppled him, but that feeling of anger and readiness to shout swiftly subsided when his eyes reopened.

A young woman of a smooth vanilla complexion that brilliantly contrasted with his chocolate skin and seductive blue eyes that glimmered in the fading sun lay pressed against him on the pavement. She brushed the longer side of her uneven bob out of the way of her face as she turned to look behind her and quickly regained her legs.

"Sorry," she shouted to him as she ran through the crowds of people to get away from something. He still watched the girl dressed in a black and purple frock as she fled, and by the time he stood again, he was shoved out of the way by a man in a black fedora and torn leather trench coat. As Aiden stood there and watched as the man chased after the young woman, he could see the drooling black demon with monumental horns as gray as ash that protruded from the man's back like a spiritual tumor. It laughed as it compelled the man to give chase to the girl, and with a groan, Aiden knew to follow at a distance so as not to be detected.

He slipped into an alleyway off to the side with the intention of heading off the path of the pursuer. He walked hastily around a corner into another lengthy alley and clasped his hands together.

"Lord God in Heaven I beseech you, clothe me in your glory and your power. Use me as a vessel to do your will. Amen." His body began to glow and in an instant the t-shirt and jeans he'd donned before his departure from that lackluster shack of an apartment were transformed into a black collared ministerial shirt with black slacks. A blue hooded robe of considerable length manifested on his body, and a holy blue blaze took to his shoulders that showcased the very power of God Almighty. Aiden closed his eyes and heard the screams of the woman in the distance. He could see the man as he pinned her against the warm brick wall of a building and spewed profanities at her, and he felt every bit of the desperation and fear that exuded from her tearful eyes.

Aiden's anger burned hot, and the man possessed slapped the girl to the ground and unbuckled his pants. Aiden's vision shifted to the street sign that read, "Norville Avenue," which was a mere three blocks over. Without caution, Aiden charged through the alleyway with incomparable speed and vaulted the trashcans and stationary cars that blocked his path with the utmost ease. He came to a busy street, but charged through traffic as if there was none in the hopes of reaching the girl before the events of the vision took place. He heard the girl scream in the distance, and though it hurt him in ways he couldn't describe, he pushed himself to move ever faster.

Aiden arrived, just as the fiendish criminal pushed her to the ground and moved those accursed hands to his belt.

"I really wouldn't do that if I were you," Aiden spoke up with his fists balled at his sides. The criminal turned to him and quickly pulled a gun out of his inner breast pocket.

"Don't move," said the man, but it wasn't the mortal that Aiden fixed his gaze on. It was the demon that had him bound. Aiden took a step forward and the man fired at the center of Aiden's forehead, but the fires on his shoulders created an aura of heat so strong that the bullet was incinerated long before it reached him. Aiden walked through the cloud of smoke that the bullet left behind to the horror of the man and the amusement of the demon. "How did you—" the man began, and Aiden lifted his right hand.

"'No weapon formed against me shall prosper,'" he responded. The gun melted in the hands of the would-be assailant, which drove him into a rage, and the demon that loomed over him expressed the utmost joy at the sudden spike in his vessel's negative emotions. The pawn charged Aiden, but with his hand uplifted once more, Aiden completed the verse, "'and every tongue that rises up against me shall be condemned.'"

"You son of a bi—" the criminal started with a fist upraised, but before the completion of the curse he found himself incapable of speech or movement. He resisted in vain as his mouth pulled his lips within its confines, and while he struggled to regain control of his body, Aiden turned his attention to the now distraught demon that hovered in his presence. Aiden lowered his hand to his side and closed his eyes. In the next instant, they shot open and radiated a solid azure hue that pierced the shadow offered by his hood. While his body proceeded to apprehend the criminal, his Spirit appeared beside him in a lighter, almost shadow-like version of the alley to face the bulky creature.

"Well, well, well," spake the beast, "you're just full of tricks, aren't you? I didn't expect something of an inferior breed to cross over into this world." Aiden smirked.

"You're about to see a lot more than that," he confirmed, and without warning he darted for the monster opposite him. The beast brought its claws to a point and hurled its massive hand toward Aiden as he drew closer, but with a second to spare the latter being narrowly spun to the right of the supernatural drill and continued his advance. Before the demon could respond, Aiden had already placed his palm flat on the chest of the barbaric imp, and with a smile he watched shock overtake the now immobile monster. "Go," he whispered, and the flames on his shoulders encircled the demon and pulled it downward, back to Hell from whence it came.

Aiden's Spirit rejoined his body in the natural world, but the use of this divinely given power proved too much on him, as he immediately had to take a knee. The young woman now sat up and watched the blue coat and dress attire evaporate into a glimmering blue mist, and when she took notice of his face she gasped in disbelief. Aiden glanced up at her and smiled as her face went from shocked to disappointed before he slipped into his unconscious beside the criminal he'd handled before.

Chapter Two

Images flashed in his mind again. The smoke, the screams, the darkness, the separation, and the sense of despair it all brought to his heart made him squirm in the hospital bed. He could see Hewer's face and feel the fear as he did his best to hang onto Aiden's arm.

"Don't let me go," he begged as he slipped a bit further into the darkness below. A distant grumble alerted the both of them, and simultaneously they looked into the blood-red sky.

"I'm not going to," Aiden comforted. He grabbed his comrade with the other hand and pulled him up to the portion of the roof upon which he stood. Whatever that was that growled from the atmosphere was the same otherworldly force that broke the building apart and created the black abyss below. There they stood, alone and unarmed, and watched as some sort of battle waged deep in the earth below. The foundation of what was left of the building shook, and in a sense of alarm Aiden reached for his only friend, but he was too late. The building began to crumble beneath their feet, and before they could jump to a more stable platform, both of them were pulled into the darkness below. "Eran!" Aiden shouted it as they fell.

He cried the name again out of fear, but just as before, he'd received no response. The darkness that swallowed them became blacker, until he could no longer see the red lights of the sky above. *Alone... again...* he thought in despair. His body met the ground below with a sickening thud, and the shock of the dream snapped him out of the memory and back into the questionable reality. He placed a hand on his throbbing head in an attempt to stabilize his vision, and looked around the room to see a bouquet of flowers on a tray at the foot of his bed, lightly kissed by the fading lights that shone through the window. His heart suddenly sped with deep anxiety as he recalled his Sunday.

Church... food... I got knocked down by a—, he thought, and the image of the lovely young lady came to the forefront of his mind. He panicked as he scrambled to get out of the bed and knocked a copy of the newspaper down to the floor from the adjacent nightstand. His eyes instantly met the front-page headline: THERAPIST SAVED BY PASSERBY. His bare feet hit the cold floor when a faux cough emanated from behind him.

"I don't think it's such a good idea for you to just jump out of bed like that," came the voice of the young lady from before. Aiden turned around to face her with a solid scowl. "Calm down, big man. I only returned the favor for you helping me out the other day."

"The other day?" Aiden took the paper in his hands and scanned for the date. He'd been unconscious for two days. "I see… So what is it you want from me?" The woman's eyes narrowed in agitation.

"Not too trusting, are we? Listen, I was only looking to help. There's no need for hostility," she insisted. Aiden looked into her captivating eyes, and though they teased him his seriousness remained intact.

"I didn't need your help," he said bluntly. She held her hand to her chest, appalled at his reaction. "Thank you, though."

"Well forgive me if I think lying face down in the dirt for forty-five minutes is a cry for help. Next time I see you just passed out in the middle of a dark alley with a criminal right next to you, I'll be sure to just leave you to your nap," she shot back. She folded her arms and took a seat in the chair beside the door, much to Aiden's confusion. He proceeded to walk towards his clothes and pulled off the hospital gown. She couldn't help but admire the athletic build of her savior, but quickly recalled that she was mad at him and looked in the opposite direction.

"I was only in that condition because I was trying to protect you," he retorted. She placed her hand over her mouth in sarcastic surprise before she stood up again and walked over to him.

"I'm sorry, I didn't know I needed a man to rush to my aide like some storybook damsel in distress. I didn't even ask you to come save me, idiot. YOU put yourself in danger like that; I didn't ask you to do anything for me," she fired. Aiden's eyes narrowed.

"There's no need for name-calling," he told her softly as he sat once more upon the bed.

"Oh, I'm sorry," she snapped with attitude, "did I hurt the hero boy's feelings? Well maybe you should give a little thought to what you say first, and then you won't end up hurting yourself." He remained silent and redirected his attention to the streetlight that flickered on the other side of the window. *Watch your mouth, boy,* he heard them taunt in his head. *We take care of you here; you don't talk to us like that!* He could see the disdain in the eyes of the attendants at the orphanage, but given the current situation, Aiden did his best to push those memories out of his head.

"I apologize for being so inconsiderate," he muttered as he slipped on his socks. The woman who stood on the other side of his bed looked at him with softened eyes and sighed.

"And I apologize for calling you an idiot," she told him honestly as she took out her phone and sent a brief text message. "Please forgive me, I don't typically act that way." Aiden said nothing and only looked at the newspaper headline from before. He looked at her and analyzed her attire.

Her hair was just as perfect as it was when they'd met, and her black and purple garb from before had been exchanged for a white dress with black accents and a small, simple diamond and onyx necklace. Her stunning appearance proved enough to incite hesitation on his part, but he corrected himself and stood to his feet.

"What is this," he asked solemnly. She smiled as she pushed the lengthy side of her bob out of the way of her eyes and took the paper from him.

"That," she began with a noticeable lack of enthusiasm as she handed the paper back to him, "is what happens when you tell the paramedics and the police that the unconscious man to the left saved you from being raped by the unconscious man to the right." Aiden's eyes went wide with fury, and he slammed the paper to the floor with authority.

"You—" he started to yell, but then realized his volume was unnecessarily high and brought his tone back down. "You told people about who I am?" She giggled at his sudden nervousness but waved off the comment. Of course, had he bothered to read the article over the headline, he would have known that she barely revealed anything about him, and that the hooded figure reported in the paper was a completely separate entity as far as the media was concerned.

"Relax," she urged him with a smile as her opportunity presented itself. "I didn't tell them about your little secret. I only told them that you saved me from being defiled by a criminal. But," her tone suddenly shifted from jovial to serious with the utterance of that word, "I'm going to need to know some things about you if you want me to keep it that way." He could see in her facial expression that she was in no mood to kid around.

“Fine,” he breathed in compliance, “I’ll tell you whatever it is you want to know, but not here.” He applied his shoes and moved around the bed and straight for the door.

“Ah, Aiden, I can’t wait.” He stopped with his hand on the knob and stared at her in utmost confusion.

“How do you know my—”

“I went snooping through your wallet when the paramedics brought you here. At first it was to figure out who you were. After that, though, it was out of the selfish desire to satisfy my curiosity,” she confessed and extended a hand. “My name’s Maya Hadarah.” He looked down at it coldly and proceeded to walk out the door. He took notice of the sign on the wall that gave the name of the hospital – St. John – and gauged the amount of time it would take to get to his apartment on the other side of town.

“It’s about an hour’s walk from here to my place,” he started, but was immediately met with feminine laughter. He turned and gave Maya a sobered stare, which only seemed to give her more of a rise.

“Oh sweetie,” she began in an almost sympathetic tone, “no. I’m sorry, but you have to understand that after what happened a couple of days ago, I’m a little hesitant to walk the streets of Edgehaven. Here, follow me. We’ll take my car and you can just tell me where to go from there. Besides, I’m a little excited to hear your story.” Aiden rolled his eyes and marched behind her with his arms folded as she escorted him into the parking lot to an obsidian 2016 Lexus that stunned him upon sight. She unlocked the car doors and looked him over as he stood there confused. She admired his strong jawline and dark curly hair. His eyes were common brown, but something in them was uncommonly penetrating, to say the least. He was a strong man, and though not as bulky as a bodybuilder, he proved to be defined enough to stir her innards and steal her breath, which, now that she thought about it, never really happened before. "Well," she began again, "hop in and we'll go for a ride."

Aiden opened the door and descended into the car, and after a moment of consideration, Maya joined him. The intriguing therapist took to the road in a matter of minutes, and as quickly as she did, he began the conversation anew.

"Shouldn't we be in the least bit concerned that I didn't check out of the hospital or get cleared or something?" He asked, but she shook her head.

"I called in a favor with a friend at the front desk. You're all checked out and ready to go. So, you seemed pretty hesitant to speak about your abilities in the hospital. What, are you some superhero and you need to protect your secret identity," she inquired. He shook his head as he reached into his pocket and pulled out a small Bible. He began to search the Scriptures in an attempt to subdue what fatigue remained from his battle with the black-horned demon.

"It's nothing like that. Christ said, 'Beware of practicing your righteousness before other people in order to be seen by them, for then you will have no reward from your Father who is in Heaven.' I don't want anyone to think that these abilities I've been gifted with are for my own merit or self-image." She sat quietly as she pondered his words. He pored over the Scriptures in Isaiah 61, which not only restored his Spirit, but reaffirmed his position. Maya, on the other hand, was fascinated by the whole of who he was, and she became subject to her own raging curiosity.

"So, what exactly are you?" Aiden shot her a threatening glare and immediately she apologized. "I'm so sorry, I just… you're not like anyone else I've ever met." There was a bit of a pause now, as Aiden took her words as naught but cheap flattery. "How are you able to do the things I saw you do in the alley?" He held up the pocket Bible in his right hand, and briefly she shifted a glance at it before she ultimately watched the road like a responsible woman would.

"Everything that I do comes from my faith in Jesus Christ. It's my life and my motivation," he explained. She sighed in slight exasperation as he directed her around a corner.

"That doesn't really explain how you can make bullets explode or melt guns. I'm sorry if I'm intruding, but there's just gotta be more to that than just faith alone." He looked up from the small Bible once again and out the window. He thought back to the darkness that once swallowed him, the mysterious rumble in his ear that pushed him down into the black abyss, and the best friend who would inevitably be lost to it. His heart sped up as the sights and sounds and smells returned with a near crippling potency. Though his skin became cold in an instant his face dripped with sweat and his body began to rattle.

"Are you alright," Maya asked from a place of sincere worry. Aiden, ashamed that she took notice of his unnerved state, closed his eyes and concentrated on the Scripture that he'd previously studied. *The Spirit of the Sovereign Lord is on me, because the Lord has anointed me to proclaim good news to the poor. He has sent me to bind up the brokenhearted, to proclaim freedom for the captives and release from darkness for prisoners...* "Aiden," she called, and broke his concentration.

"Yes," he responded, "I'm alright. About thirteen years ago, I was part of a 12-man joint forces spec ops team assembled to combat terrorists and rogue military personnel. The Air Force dispatched only two of us, while the Army gave four, and the Marines and Navy offered up three each.

We were deployed in Israel and charged with the task of monitoring the prime minister of the time, then believed to be in league with the combined remnants of the al Qaeda and ISIS terrorist organizations. We'd been in Jerusalem for about six months before we discovered he was involved in something much more sinister than simple terrorism." Aiden froze as he inched closer to the memory, to the beginning. Though she watched the road carefully, Maya gently grasped Aiden's hand and stroked the back of it with her thumb.

"It's alright," she told him sympathetically. He exhaled in great relief, as it was clear that blackmail was never her true intention, but rather, it was the satisfaction of her own curiosity that drove her to inquire so much of him. "If you don't want to continue, you don't have to." He shook his head as he squeezed her hand in return.

"No, I can't stop talking about it yet. I think that's been part of the problem. I've had all these things bottled up for years with no chance of relief. This is the first time in more than a decade that I've been able to actively speak with someone about what it was that I was thinking about." Maya looked over to him, her heart aflutter at the heartbreaking statement, only to notice that his eyes, those piercing dark brown orbs that saw through so much of her being were locked firmly on her already. He could feel her pulse accelerate through their joint hands, but before he could finish his tale, the sound of gunfire cracked through the air and a nearby car swerved into the black Lexus.

The airbag in the car failed to go off, and Maya's head bounced off the steering wheel upon collision as the car found itself pressed on either side in a mock blockade that disrupted the natural flow of traffic. Aiden worked to undo her seatbelt, and once she was secure in his arms he kicked her windshield out of place and pulled her into the open. He took her off the road and into an alley while others scrambled for their lives. He could feel the watchful eye of the sniper on them as they moved out of the line of sight, and once firmly under cover, Aiden closed his eyes.

Maya's consciousness returned, and to her dismay she heard the screams of those on the street. She noticed Aiden, whose eyes were closed and whose hands wielded the small pocket Bible.

"Aiden," she spoke, but he placed a finger on his lips to keep her completely silent. Maya, whose panic escalated with every second that passed, grabbed him on the shoulder and shook him to inspire some sort of movement or sense of urgency that he so obviously lacked. "Aiden, we need to go," she urged. He refused to move, but continued to meditate on the Scriptures. "Look, I know you want to pray, or meditate, or whatever it is you do, but now just isn't the time! We have to get out of here before we get—" his hand shot up immediately and cut her off.

"It's *always* time for those things. Scripture commands that we 'pray without ceasing.'" She groaned, but Aiden knew full well that he needed to. It was the only way to restore his Spirit enough to combat the enemy that presented itself. He didn't have the time to tell her though. He was close, he could feel that heavenly warmth that previously enraptured him on Sunday morning return to his body and mind, and any further distractions would only keep him in this state of incompletion. He began to pray the will of his Master done at that hour, and just as before, his typical t-shirt and blue jeans were replaced with the collared minister's shirt and black slacks to match, and right before her very eyes did the hooded robe with flaming shoulders appear to cover him from head to toe.

Maya sat there utterly speechless, and Aiden smiled as the image of a lone masked shooter on the other side of the street flooded into his mind. That smile quickly disappeared, though, when the shooter in the vision stored his gun in its holster and pressed a button on his wrist to detonate the building he must have come from, along with a few cars on street level. Aiden's eyes shot open, glazed over in the same heavenly blue hue as before, and as he began to walk back into the light of day, he told Maya, "Get to somewhere safe." She didn't stay long enough to argue with him, as another explosion sounded just a few yards away.

Aiden emerged from the shadows of the alley and saw the blaze. He lifted up his right hand and carefully surveyed the landscape for the one responsible for this chaos.

"'As the deer pants for streams of water, so my soul pants for you, my God,'" Aiden quoted, and in an instant an overflow of water poured from every underground pipe and exposed fire hydrant in the immediate area onto the flames that steadily raged through the city. After about ten minutes the flames died down, and with the immediate threat neutralized, Aiden was left to locate the perpetrator.

"Your abilities have some very grave limitations, don't they, Aiden," inquired the mechanical voice from above. Aiden looked up to see a slim but muscular man in a red and black flex-armor suit with guns on both sides and an M110 sniper rifle strapped to his back perched on one of the beams left exposed from his earlier offensive. "Look at you. You're shaking, you're wobbling, you're breathing hard. I wonder… what happens if you use too much of your power? Let's find out." Without a moment to spare, the man in the black and red battle suit opened fire as he jumped down from the suspended support. The flames on Aiden's shoulders easily deflected the bullets, but an explosive disk penetrated the cloud of smoke that the disintegrated projectiles left behind. Before impact could be made, Aiden dropped to the ground while the flames on his shoulders rushed after the disk and fully engulfed the bomb in a sphere of holy fire that would ultimately suppress the detonation. The satisfaction Aiden felt in that momentary victory was disrupted by the pain of the masked man's boot in his face. The massive force behind the kick hurled him across the street and into the side of an abandoned gold Jetta.

"Who… are you?" Aiden demanded through clenched teeth as he placed a hand against his temple to stabilize his vision. "How do you know so much about me?" The assailant wagged his finger playfully.

"Don't tell me you've forgotten me. You and I go way back. And after I went through all that trouble trying to keep up with you over the years," he said in a playfully bothered tone. Aiden pushed himself off the ground and stretched out his hand with an exasperated look about his face. "For now, I suppose you can call me Bloodsport. Has a nice ring to it, don't you think?"

"Tell me who you are," he yelled, but in the back of his mind he already knew. Aiden's new adversary lifted a hand to his heart.

"You know *exactly* who I am," he said in all severity, and Aiden could tell that he smiled beneath the mask even though he couldn't see it.

"'Part your heavens, Lord, and come down; touch the mountains so that they smoke. Send forth lightning and scatter the enemy; shoot your arrows and rout them.'" Aiden recited the verse in anger, and in a brilliant flash the lightning of which he spoke shot from the heavens and struck the ground. Bloodsport dashed in a myriad of directions and exhibited great determination as he dodged each of the celestial strikes, but by the time he found himself ready to conclude his little confrontation with Aiden Zane, he'd already gotten away.

"Run while you still can," Bloodsport whispered menacingly. "Time is running out for you, and everything you stand to protect."

Maya ran in her black pumps as though they were sneakers and sought shelter from the villain she imagined followed after her. Out of the corner of her eye she noticed an injured man who kneeled against a building with his shoulder in his hand, but when she went to help him evacuate the area she was stunned to find that it was Aiden.

"What happened to you," she asked in a concerned tone, but he quickly waved her off. He staggered to his feet as his hooded robe and dress attire once again dissipated into the brilliant blue mist from before. He stumbled forward, and she caught him as deep worry shimmered in her eyes.

"We need to get out of here," he stated in as much firmness as he could manage. "I've got no more power left to use right now." Without a word, she lifted his arm over her shoulder and braced him as they walked. "The subway," Aiden urged at the sight of a distant entrance. "Let's pick up the pace." They hastened their stride and descended into the dank and shaded tunnel. Maya slowly lowered him onto a bench and nervously took a seat next to him. She surveyed the terrified crowd of people as they passed by with great expectation of leaving the area, and as the train pulled into the station she hoisted Aiden back to his feet.

He looked into her distressed eyes, and silently kicked himself for her involvement with whatever just happened. *I should have taken greater precautions,* he thought as the inquisitive nature of his facial expression shifted to exhibit the disgust that he suddenly felt with himself. They sat down in the nearest available seats, and Aiden inhaled deeply as the train began to move. Maya stirred a bit at the sudden jolt of the electric monorail and out of paranoia steadily watched her surroundings.

"I'm sorry," Aiden whispered to her. "I didn't mean for any of this to happen. It was never my intention to put you in danger." She instantly met his eyes and smiled shakily.

"You have nothing to be sorry about. I chose to help you out with the ambulance and I chose to stick around afterwards. If that means that I get put in danger every now and then, I'm okay with that," she responded, and tried her best to mask her discomfort.

"But I'm not," he shot back. "If something happens to you then it's my burden to bear, and I will *not* go through that again!" His voice escalated, and the unnerved citizens that populated the train all looked at the two of them with a combined fear and agitation. Maya's eyes softened as she realized how inconsiderate she was. Aiden released a flustered sigh and lightly pinched the bridge of his nose. "Before the attack, I was telling you a little about my history, and about the mission involving the Israeli prime minister. When we're back at my home I'll continue the tale but as for right now I think it would be best if we refrained from further conversation." Maya's eyes widened and she took his hand apologetically.

"Listen, I'm sorry if I offended you in any way," she began, but Aiden raised his hand to silence her once more.

"That man from before…" he started pensively, "he called himself 'Bloodsport.' As it stands now we don't know anything about him other than the fact that he's highly dangerous and is very fond of that mask. It wouldn't be smart to continue to speak out in the open given that he could be right here on this subway with us listening to every word exchanged. So for the time being we should keep our conversation to a minimum." Maya thought to protest, but quickly hushed herself when she realized that he was right. She watched him as he closed his eyes and slipped into what seemed to be a tranquil state of mind, and wondered just how he could be so calm despite the fact that there was someone out there strong enough to weaken him this much. She envied that peace that he had, but what she didn't know was that while she thought him calm and free of any such discomfort, he writhed in pain before her eyes and replayed the incident with Bloodsport in his mind over and over again. He could hear the smugness in the masked man's tone as he taunted him with mystery, and though he just chose to believe that there was no relation between the two of them, Aiden couldn't help but acknowledge the subtle familiarity in his voice. *That's impossible*… he thought, but then again… was it? The car of the train jumped, and he felt as though a thousand knives dug into his skin. The kick from the earlier battle certainly left an impact on him that he'd never felt before.

Aiden painstakingly analyzed every aspect about the man as he felt the subway train pull to a halt. He opened his eyes to get a look at the LED sign that flashed the name of the street. "74th," it read, and with great strain he stood to his feet and motioned for Maya to come assist him on his way out the door. She rushed to him without complaint, and shouldered his weight without a sound as they walked through the oncoming crowd of people who proved fresh to the type of fear that resonated on the monorail.

At Aiden's direction, Maya led him back to his apartment and sat him in one of the ill-supportive lawn chairs. He groaned in pain, but once he was settled in and she took her seat, he prepared to tell her his story.

Chapter Three

"We'd been there six months tracking the Israeli prime minister's movements, and we'd seen for ourselves that he was just as dirty as the rumors led us to believe. One night we'd received word from our commander that it was time to enter the next phase of the mission: assassination. In addition to the prime minister, we were supposed to take out the two men in charge of al Qaeda and ISIS respectively, but something went horribly wrong. The twelve of us spread out throughout the area and waited patiently for the other targets to arrive. Army took to the southward position while Marines took the west and sent the Navy to the east. Hewer and I from the Air Force took up post just slightly north of the building, and once we were all in place we carefully aimed our weapons at the third-floor window and watched for the opportune time to strike," Aiden explained. Maya's eyes remained fixated on him as her interest in his memories grew.

"What exactly went wrong, though?" It was all she could do to mask the eagerness that bubbled inside of her. Aiden flashed a brief smile as faint as water vapor that would dissipate just as fast.

"The terrorist leaders never arrived, and of course we didn't find this out until six hours later. Hewer and I were positioned on the roof of a building just opposite the Kiryat Ben Gurion complex with a clear shot into his office, and in our youthful inexperience and pride we cracked jokes about the target and morbidly mused what his last words would be once the shot was taken. But then the strangest thing happened. The prime minister methodically paced towards the window, and I swear his eyes met mine as a serpentine smile slithered across his lips. He held up a hand with his thumb raised, and to my surprise he pressed the button on the top of a small detonator that at the time I couldn't even see. Explosions from the four different positions rocked the city, and the smoke that rose from the attacks blackened the sky." Aiden twitched as he reflected on the events of that day, but took a deep breath to regulate his thoughts and regain control of himself.

"When the prime minister lowered his thumb, Hewer and I quickly ran away from the edge of the building. We were still launched into the air by the blast, though. We landed roughly on the northernmost edge of the roof and groaned from the boring pain in our bodies. There was a loud ring in my ears and I struggled to regain my sight through the massive cloud of smoke that loomed over us as it ascended into the darkened sky. I slowly picked myself up off the ground, and once stability returned to my legs I slowly walked over to my fallen wingman to help him back to his feet as well. He writhed in agony with his hands tightly clasped against his right side, but before I could even ask what was wrong the tiles of the roof began to shake. The side of the building closest to the government complex began to collapse, and as the roof caved in on itself I lifted Hewer as gently as I could, given the situation." Maya placed a hand on her bicep and slightly squeezed as she attempted to imagine what it was that Aiden felt as he recounted these traumatic memories, and watched the tortured man in the lawn chair across from her. She took note of the dark brown velvet of his eyes that, despite the obvious discomfort that rested in his furrowed brow, emitted the strangest sense of acceptance and calm.

"Together we rushed towards the sturdiest corner of the roof, but Hewer struggled to move. He apologized for slowing me down, but before we could figure out a way to get to the next rooftop and climb down to stable ground, the crack reached the corner and the roof and our only footing gave way. I just barely managed to grab onto the edge of the wall before we fell. Hewer dropped a bit farther, but he managed to grab onto my arm." The images once again flashed before his very eyes. He was taken back to that very moment. "I gripped his hand desperately and held onto the wall as tightly as I could, but he was too heavy to support with just one hand. My arm began to tremble and both of us with it, and when I turned my head to face him I could see the darkness of a massive pit. What was once a floor had turned into a seemingly empty abyss. Hewer shook his head, as if he knew I was about to give out at any minute and begged me not to let go of him, but I…" Aiden's voice trailed off as he swam in a sea of negative emotions, and Maya placed a hand over her mouth as her mind automatically went to the worst possible scenario.

"Please…" she started as she fixed her eyes on him with extreme intensity, "please tell me that you didn't drop him." Aiden shook his head and stood from his lawn chair to pace about the room. Maya watched him and cringed at the tension that emanated from his body. She knew that he only put himself through this torment to satiate her appetite for knowledge, but a conflict of emotions prevented her from releasing him of the burden of his memories.

"I did my best to hold onto him," he started again, wistfully, "but before I could even suggest our next move, my arm gave out and we both fell into that darkness." A breathy sigh followed his words before he remembered the blended screams of Hewer and himself, and though they'd met not long ago, Maya almost couldn't stand to see him like this. "We fell for what seemed like an eternity in the strange dark cavern, and with every foot we dropped I could feel this overwhelming and mysterious power begin to seep into my bones. I frantically looked around for a way to stop myself from falling, but in the black of the hole I couldn't see anything. I called for Hewer, but there was no answer. I heard this ringing sound in the air, like two swords clanging together. Shouts bellowed over the crash of the all-metal collision, as if two strong men did battle at the bottom of the pit below us." Maya's head tilted in confusion.

"How could there have been someone down there? The way you make it sound is as if it was the Bottomless Pit…"

"No," Aiden interrupted with a sternness that sent shockwaves through her body. "It had a bottom, and no sooner than I heard the resonance of blades and the boom of their voices had I met that bottom with a thud. The air was knocked out of me, and a second thud sounded not that far away from where I'd landed. The fighting at the bottom of the pit stopped, and much to my surprise I noticed dim flames attached to the walls of what appeared to be a long corridor. The two figures of incredible height stared at the two of us as our consciousness waned, but quickly refocused on each other. With a resounding shout, the two continued their fight, and I slipped into unconsciousness." He took a moment to walk into the kitchen and grab a piece of coconut pie out of the refrigerator before he sat back in his lawn chair and continued his tale. "When I came to, I was in an unbelievable amount of pain. I remember that I looked around in a panic on a remarkably soft golden canopy bed in a stunningly spacious room with white walls and an ethereal white and gold mold that decorated the top and bottom linings. I stumbled out of the bed even though the pain made me dizzy, and I made a desperate crawl to the golden door when I noticed all of my gear on the chair right next to it." He paused for a moment to take a bite out of the coconut pie, and as he delved in the flavors that danced upon his tongue he found his nerves relaxed enough to enjoy the laxer part of the story. "I picked up my radio and called for Hewer, but there was no answer." Maya shook her head in disappointment, which caught Aiden's attention almost immediately. "Something wrong?" He asked in between bites. She waved it off as nothing but voiced her wishes all the same.

"I just wish I could have seen it for myself," she mused. Aiden walked over to her and placed his hand over her eyes. "What's going on?" she asked immediately, but he didn't respond to her inquiry. He closed his own eyes and braced himself for the pain that was sure to follow, but without another moment to spare, Aiden recited a single line of Scripture that would help her in that matter.

"'The eyes of the blind will be opened, and the ears of the deaf will be unstopped.'" There was a slight glow between her eyes and the palm of his hand, and once the light faded, Aiden dropped to one knee. She observed his shortness of breath, his pained expression, the many beads of sweat that seeped through his pores, and the way he tightly gripped his chest, but with a smile on his face he pointed upward, and much to her surprise she saw a younger, much more battered version of her host hunched over in pain as he spoke into a walkie-talkie.

"What..." Maya whispered to herself in awe. Aiden groaned as he picked himself off the floor and grabbed the small Bible from his pocket again. He flipped it open to the Book of Psalms with a smile on his face.

"That ought to do it. With that Scripture, you'll be able to see and hear the events of that time through the eyes of my mind. Now, let's watch." The Aiden of the past fumbled with the frequency of his radio and tried over and over to signal for help, but it was no use. *This isn't working,* they heard him think. *I'm gonna have to find Hewer and escape the area.*

"That wouldn't be too good of an idea," came a deep and unfamiliar voice from behind him. In a single snap motion, Aiden grabbed the M16 that rested against the armchair and pointed it at his visitor. He observed the bronze skin and curly black hair, the sharp facial features that were almost too defined to be human, and more than anything the staggering height of the armor-clad man in his presence. Aiden charged his weapon and set his sights. "Trust me, Aiden, that would be a much worse idea."

"Oh, really?" Aiden questioned with an air of sarcastic defiance. "And why is that exactly?" The man that stood in front of the door didn't look the least bit intimidated by the weapon that was aimed at his face. "I don't know who you think you are, but I'd really advise you step out of the way and tell me where my wingman is before I have to turn your face into Swiss cheese." The tall muscular man smiled as his eyes widened with anticipation.

"And I would advise you to avoid tempting one such as myself with battle. That would be the worst idea you've had all day. Now, give that to me," said the man as he reached for the gun. Aiden, without hesitation, clicked the weapon into semi-automatic and shot four rounds one after another, but to his amazement the bullets stopped just an inch before the mysterious stranger's face and fell to the floor. The man vanished in a flash, and Aiden all but dropped his gun in surprise as he rematerialized right next to him with his regal, solid gold, gemstone-encrusted sword drawn and pressed against the past Zane's throat ever so lightly. Aiden looked into his golden eyes and saw a surge of lightning spark between the silver dots that lined his irises. That spark, purple and radiant, pulsed through the edge of his blade and caused a drop of blood to slide down the front of his neck and onto the bandages that wrapped his torso. "Let me be clear," said the man, in an almost reptilian hum, "it's not in my best interest to cause you more pain than what you're already experiencing, but if you insist on being this difficult I'd have no other option than to show you just what kind of fight you'd be picking. Now, put down your little toy and let's go. My superiors are waiting for us in the Grand Hall. I would suggest you put on the robes on the back of that chair and find your way to them."

Aiden watched as the man turned his back and walked towards the door. He reached out his arm to grasp the knob but before he could do so Aiden called after him.

"Wait," he shouted with the sincerest sense of worry in his tone. "Who are you? What… what is this place," he inquired as he looked around at the golden floor, white walls, chandelier of pearls, and door of cedar overlaid with gold. The beauty of the room in which he stood was hardly breathtaking enough to distract him from his hugest concern. "Where's my wingman?" The man sighed, but didn't turn to face the younger Aiden.

"You ask a lot of questions. I don't think it's a good idea, since every one of them will be answered in due time. Although I suppose your last one is rather easy to answer. Here," he said as a pair of silver wings lined at the edges with gold feathers manifested in a brilliant radiance on his back. "Does that satisfy you?" Aiden's eyes went wide with frustration.

"I wasn't talking about you! There was another man who crashed with me in that giant pit! Where is he?" Aiden yelled at the top of his lungs, mostly out of concern for his friend but still partly because a man just sprouted wings in front of him.

"Hm…" the angel turned to face him now with eyes full of intrigue. The modern-day Aiden shifted his eyes to Maya, who sat almost literally on the edge of her seat as she anticipated what would happen next. He smiled before he turned his attention back to his former self. "Even though an Archangel reveals himself in your presence you act as if the only thing you're concerned about is your friend. I must say that I'm impressed with your devotion. Normally humans aren't too accustomed to seeing angels in the flesh. You're definitely a different one, aren't you?" He shrugged as he moved towards the door once again. "As I said before, all of your questions will be answered in due time." He left without another word, and Aiden donned the blue and purple robes as quickly as his injured body would allow before he left the room himself. He stepped into a massive golden hall with pillars on either side of him, all engraved with the image of a different Archangel than the last. Every pillar bore a script beneath the image in what looked like ancient Hebrew, so it caught the past Aiden and present Maya off guard when they were able to read it as though they grew up with the language.

Oriphiel, it read. Aiden looked up at the image to see the same strong features of the Archangel that met him in his room, but dressed in the same blue and purple garments that rested on his body. He reluctantly walked further down the hall towards an immense circular lobby with four spiraled golden pillars positioned around the outer rim. The black and gold tiles of the floor had a mesmerizing allure that greatly complimented the white and gold curtains that draped from an invisible frame high above the scene. Aiden slowly advanced, as he was all but hypnotized at the sight of the elaborate and exquisite room, when he heard steady footsteps move in his direction from around the corner. On instinct, he moved behind the last pillar of the lengthy hall that he had not yet left to stay out of the line of sight. *This is no good,* he thought. *I'm in no condition to fight...*

He watched the foyer carefully, and as the footsteps grew louder and louder his heart raced with a beastly rage. He stood there, helpless and without his weapon, but fully prepared to engage in hand to hand combat if need be. There was a chill in the air as the room fell suddenly silent. He peered around the pillar to see a figure in the center of the spacious chamber garbed in red and white colored robes that matched his blue and purple ones. The figure, who had notable blond hair and a milky complexion, registered in Aiden's mind as the wingman that he'd fought and fallen with.

He stepped out from behind the pillar and walked towards the center of the room behind the translucent curtains. The sound of his footsteps startled Eran, who quickly turned to him with fists raised until he realized that the person who walked toward him was the friend he thought he'd lost. Overcome with emotion, they shared a brief hug before they took up their macho mantles once again and surveyed the area in slight embarrassment. To their left, Aiden saw a massive white marble staircase with onyx railings and gold lining on each step. It seemed to climb for an eternity, but neither Aiden nor Eran intended to stay that long. The pair looked the other way, into the direction from which the latter had previously emerged, to see two massive stone doors adorned with the images of two seraphim which faced the center.

"Any idea where we are," Hewer asked as they continued to survey the brilliantly crafted room. Aiden shook his head.

"No clue," he confirmed. "I tried to radio out but there was no signal. If I had to guess I'd say that we're still underground somewhere, and far below the surface at that. It doesn't seem like we're in any danger, though. Well, as long as we don't point a gun at anything we're not." Hewer's eyes locked on him with almost a childlike glow.

"You actually pointed your weapon at one of *them*? Oh man… I'm guessing you didn't get the woman as your attendant." Aiden's eyes went wide.

"You got a woman?" He asked in utter jealousy. "Lucky…"

"Your jealousy is unnecessary," came a feminine voice from the large staircase at the other end of the massive chamber. Aiden and Eran turned around to see the radiant image of a young and vibrant redhead. She had a certain fire in her eyes that both men were instantly attracted to, and yet she still possessed enough heated intensity to keep their advances at bay. They watched her as she strode down the stairs with all the grace of the very thing she was, an angel, and as she elegantly descended from her elevated platform they found themselves all the more taken by her presence. The Air Force duo seemed entranced by her every curve, her every motion, and as she continued to move from step to step they took in the brilliant red and orange skirt with a divide at her right hip, observed the matching flame-colored top, and the golden brown of her bare midriff. Her lush, cherry red lips piqued their curiosity as to what they would taste like when she snapped her fingers. Their attention refocused to her face as she continued to speak. "Angels haven't had much interest in your kind for eons at least."

"She's gorgeous," Maya muttered in an almost envious tone. She watched on as the feminine Archangel reached the center of the room and stood between the younger Aiden and his compatriot. She introduced herself as Uriel and beckoned them to follow her towards the staircase from which she descended. Aiden sat there in awe of her in the present, just as he stood baffled in the past. The two young men followed her up the stairs, and as the past Aiden glared at the body of his guide, she lifted her hand and a ball of fire hot enough to cause the walls to drip formed around her fist.

“You know,” she started, “I really don’t like being treated as though I were some piece of meat.”

“Yes, objectifying her really wouldn’t be a good idea,” Oriphiel chimed in as he manifested behind them in a brilliant flash of lightning. Eran looked at the floor where he appeared and was shocked to see the lack of any scorch marks. “Uriel has a somewhat fiery disposition. Most of the other Archangels are terrified of her.”

“And for good reason,” she quickly added. “There isn’t a man, angel or Archangel alive with enough power to put out my flames. Even Gabriel with his frilly little water spouts doesn’t have what it takes.”

“She’s just that hot,” Oriphiel confirmed. Eran and Aiden smiled as a single shared thought passed through their minds: *In more ways than one…* In a matter of moments, they reached the top of the lofty staircase and Oriphiel walked to the front of the quartet to stand with Uriel. They stood at the very edge of the mystical star-sapphire floor that looked like the night sky and led to a luminous golden set of double doors engraved with the Seven Archangels and encrusted with a myriad of precious stones. Aiden trembled at the very sight of it, as it was the first time he’d ever seen something so spectacular. “Just ahead of you lies the Chamber of the High King. You will tread upon this platform of blue sapphire and proceed to enter into the hall behind those doors.”

“The floor you see before you will determine whether or not you are worthy of entering into the High King’s presence. You’ll receive your answer the very moment you touch the door. If you are approved, you’ll be permitted entry,” Uriel informed.

“What happens if we’re denied,” Eran asked nervously.

"Well that part's simple," Uriel assured him with a smile. She opened her hands at her side and two white flames appeared in her palms. The walls started to drip and the temperature rose to an unbearable height that caused their skin to burn. Oriphiel barely broke a sweat, and Uriel continued to smile as the discomfort they experienced caused the two young men to drop to their knees. Her eyes flashed fire-red and her lengthy hair blasted straight up into the air, but in the next moment the infernal intensity subsided and Aiden exhaled in relief as he briefly enjoyed the cool. "Should you prove unworthy of entry," Uriel continued, "you'll be incinerated on the spot."

"Are you going to…?" Eran inquired with a look of unmistakable concern. Uriel casually walked over to Hewer and placed a warm and gentle hand on the front of his searing-red robes. She leaned in closer and paused with her lips just a warm invigorating breath away from his. Her eyes scanned his tightly muscular body from the ground up until her golden gaze met the icy blue orbs that watched her so longingly.

"Why don't you go and find out?" The sultry tone of her voice caused Eran to shudder with excitement as he readily took his place on the star-sapphire floor. He looked back at Aiden, who could feel the gaze of Oriphiel and Uriel suddenly shift to him. The Aiden of the past stared at the star-sapphire floor that unnerved him so, and pondered over the fate that he would receive. The Aiden and Maya of the present watched on, and as Maya sat at the edge of her seat and rocked with all nervousness, Aiden smiled out of appreciation of her investment in his past. The sensation of that experience was otherworldly, and suddenly he found that he wanted to share more with her. He kept his mouth closed, however, and redirected his attention to the events of his history.

The former Aiden Zane walked upon the night-themed floor, and the numerous white spots that twinkled in the light of the room took up a luster all their own. As the friends drew closer to the doors, they felt a surge of power come over them. They watched as the most painful images of their respective pasts flashed before their eyes and cemented themselves as that moment's reality. Aiden felt the clamminess of little hands pull against his hair, and the disgustingly warm spit of his former "playmates" at the orphanage slap against his face. Hewer relived the painful blows to his belly administered by the neighborhood bully who hurled insults at him and ridiculed him for his lack of a father figure in his life. Both of them stood traumatized, momentarily incapable of movement.

Aiden pressed onward, however, and as he moved forward in the insanity of the past he resolved that he would never go back to that place, of solitude. Eran watched as his best friend powered through, and out of sudden inspiration followed after him. The images that were projected and materialized in the moment, all designed to distract the two of them from their progression persisted, and with each scream of disdain from a past enemy, with every ruthless reenactment of physical and mental abuse, they slowed in their stride but dared not stop. The Archangels watched on with a smile, but Hewer struggled at the sound of his own childish cries. He relived a pain he dared not speak to anyone, wallowed in the disgust and darkness, and he felt primal rage sweep his senses just as it did once upon a time. His pulse quickened and his breath staggered, and as his balled fists began to tremble Maya's eyes began to water.

"What's happening?" She asked as the images flashed in front of her face. She watched a blackness overtake Aiden's dear friend, and looked in horror as he proceeded towards the double doors without him. "Why are you still going towards that door when your friend is suffering?" As the words left her lips, the image that Eran tried to suppress, a severely dark instance from his past took its place before them all. Eran Hewer, no older than four years old, stood with his hands tied to a doorknob. His face was covered in dried tears and blood, and he couldn't help but shriek as his drunken father threw another beer bottle at him. The young boy only narrowly dodged, and as his father laughed at him he only cried the more.

Maya couldn't believe her eyes, and Aiden remembered a horror that he'd thought had long faded. Hewer was frozen in his past, unable to push forward to even the possibility of a brighter future when the Aiden of the age turned around to retrieve him. As he walked back toward his wingman, he staggered into his own memories and fell prey to his own misfortunes, but despite the sudden resurgence of his experiences all he could see was the anguish of the only friend he'd ever had. He walked through every image, doubt, distraction, and heartache great and small that ever afflicted him, and he grasped Eran's hand in such a way that assured him he wasn't alone.

Upon contact, the black cloud and traumatic memory gave way to a brightness and warmth that came with their shared memories of the time they spent in training. Eran opened his eyes and continued alongside Aiden with renewed confidence. Together they remembered everything they'd been through that brought them to that point, and how even though it was hard and they didn't know if they would ever make it out alive, they stood by each other and spurred each other onward. Before the two realized what happened, they stood in front of the doors with smiles on their faces and their hands pressed against the solid structures.

Maya couldn't help but cry out in glee, and the Archangels that stood watching them from the other side clapped as if they'd expected nothing less.

"You ready for this?" Eran asked in between heavy breaths.

"Aren't I always?" Aiden responded with a smile. They pushed the doorway open and walked boldly into a blinding white light.

Chapter Four

After a moment, the Aiden and Eran of years gone by opened their eyes and proceeded into the Grand Hall with a sense of wonder written about their faces. The entire chamber bore the swirled sleekness of marble, and the golden mold along the top of the walls added elegance and flare. Twelve pillars lined the sides of the room and four fountains poured crystal-clear water from the walls into basins that carried it into a downward slope. The central walkway was constructed entirely of onyx in contrasted accent to the white and golden brown of the marble walls, and led to a massive silver throne at the center of the back wall upon which no one sat. Oriphiel and Uriel glided into the room on their great majestic wings and swooped down to kneel before the presumed seat of the High King.

"Master," Oriphiel spoke with his head pointed downward, "the Two have shown themselves worthy and have entered into your chamber triumphantly, having trod upon the darkness of their past."

"In doing so, they have forsaken that darkness and have sought the Light of Salvation," Uriel added with all due reverence. Aiden and Eran slowly approached the throne, and the Archangels that brought them to this magnificent place stood up and turned aside. Another brilliant light flashed, and the elements of light and darkness, earth and wind, fire, water and lightning erupted in unison in the space above the enormous seat. One by one more Archangels, three male and two female, appeared before the throne, each one clothed in a manner that reflected one of the elements that preceded their entry. They watched the two human males with stern intensity as thunder boomed overhead.

Aiden watched in great awe as lightning struck the floor right in front of him. He jumped back in surprise and nearly lost his balance, to which Oriphiel smiled. Hewer chuckled to himself as he watched the bright electrical current dance before his comrade, but the laughter all but halted when a brilliant blaze erupted just centimeters from where he stood. Hewer, captivated by the extremity of the sudden burst, smiled with delight and watched as the flames and flash combined in a bright display of elemental vigor. Aiden regained his legs as well as his composure, and the duo fixed their eyes on the assembly of the Seven Archangels that stood at the foot of the throne.

Trumpets appeared in the hands of each of the Archangels, and as they sounded them another boisterous clap of thunder erupted throughout the atmosphere. A blast of air burst through the double doors that served as the entrance of the Grand Hall and fed into the fusion of flame and plasma that twisted with silent rhythm between the angels and the men.

"Aiden Zane and Eran Hewer," echoed a powerful voice from above. The entire room came to attention for fear of reprimand from the one to whom it belonged, but the voice sounded almost proud of them. The brilliant combination of the elements that shimmered both above the throne and before the young Aiden and Eran drifted toward a space high above the rest of the room, and converged into a single surge of power that left the chamber completely darkened. A small light descended from on high and in a vivid explosion, all color returned to the marvelous environment. A humanoid figure enshrouded in a cloud of light presented itself before the duo. "Welcome," came the powerful masculine voice from before. He spoke at a more comfortable volume with an air of elation. "I trust that my attendants have been nothing short of hospitable."

“You’re the High King,” Aiden asked with a huff of disbelief and watched as the King levitated around the two of them. Aiden’s eyes turned to the Archangels, who knelt in his presence with heads bowed.

“Indeed I am,” the High King responded. “You two suffered quite the fall. You do not understand the utter joy that I feel seeing you stand on your own two feet.”

“Barely,” Eran remarked remorselessly. The heads of every Archangel at the foot of the throne shot up to reveal a universal disgust at Hewer’s insolent tone. The High King paused and held a hand out towards his attendants, who itched for an opportunity to silence the young Airman. The King’s attention refocused on the Two, and with a wave of his hand the wounds from which each suffered were expunged from their bodies.

“There,” said the King. “Does that feel better?”

“Very much,” Aiden responded in surprise. “How did you do that?” The King placed a gentle hand on Aiden’s freshly healed shoulder.

“I can do everything,” he said flatly. “Well, almost everything. The miracles I perform must be explained in Scripture in some form or fashion for my abilities to take effect. Fortunately for the two of you, healing is quite an abundant feature of the Bible.” Hewer stretched out his newly repaired muscles and tossed a few punches with great delight. “Nevertheless,” the King continued, and watched Hewer jump on his hands and walk, “there are limits to what I can do, and the use of these gifts, if used improperly can exact a rather unpleasant toll.”

“Who exactly are you, anyway,” Eran asked nonchalantly as he flipped backwards onto his hands, “and where even are we?” The High King shook his head in embarrassment and motioned for the Archangels to rise.

“Please, forgive me. My memory is a far cry from what it used to be and I have developed somewhat of a bad habit of getting ahead of myself. My name is Elijah the Tishbite, otherwise known as the Flame Prophet,” he enlightened as the brilliant aura that surrounded him gave way to the features of a kind and gentle man of Israeli origin with a great many years of wisdom. The long gray beard did little to mask his smile, and to the bewilderment of the Two, he bore amber eyes that seemed complementary of the gold of the Archangels’, and his robes were a solid golden hue that likewise accented his eyes perfectly. “This place is the Hall of Nabi’im, or rather what would be ‘Prophets’ in your tongue. It has existed since the time of King David’s rule, and has served as the training grounds for the Nabi’im for generations. Since the days I once tread upon the earth, there have always been Two: myself and Elisha, Isaiah and Micah, Jonah and Amos, Jeremiah and Obadiah, and now Aiden and Eran.”

“Whoa, now wait a minute,” Aiden said with his hands upraised, but before he could complete his statement the entire company and the waters that rushed from the walls froze. Aiden alone retained mobility, and in horrified shock he took a step back from the ancient prophet, and his attendants the Archangels. *What... what was that just now?* His mind raced in a desperate search for a logical answer to the question when he saw Elijah smile.

“You will certainly have to be more careful with that,” he said casually. With a wave of his hand the natural time-flow was restored. Eran looked at his comrade with a glimmer of wonder in his eyes, but Aiden remained hesitant to engage in whatever situation this encounter had become.

"Well what do we have here?" Eran asked in a desperate attempt to disguise his copious excitement.

"The Nabi'im are the guardians of this world, my boy. They defend not just the hearts, minds and spirits of humanity, but the very life of God's most precious creation. However, there *have* been instances wherein a Nabi strayed from his path, and due to corruption nearly caused massive ruin to the people he was called to protect. On that note, I feel it only necessary to warn the both of you. Inheriting this limited amount of the Holy Spirit's power comes naturally for those drafted into the ranks of the Nabi'im, but because of the potential you now bear there will be forces that war against you beyond your wildest imagination." The sound of the clashing swords that preceded the fall resonated with renewed ferocity, and for but a moment Aiden recalled the darkened figures that battled at the bottom of the pit.

"That being said," Uriel continued as she stepped forward from Elijah's throne, "you two will follow me. We're going to teach you two how to pray." She spoke in the same no-nonsense tone of voice used by a military training instructor. Eran smiled, even though the comment of prayer confused him, and followed after the Archangel with unbridled enthusiasm. Aiden, on the other hand, refused to move from that spot.

"Now wait," he demanded, to which every head in the massive chamber turned to rest their eyes on him. "I never even agreed to being one of these, these Nabi'im as you put it. What even makes you so certain that you've got the right person?"

"Look," Oriphiel interjected, "questioning the process isn't the best idea. For whatever reason, God Himself selected the two of you to carry out this mission. Seeing as how you're a couple of military men you'd think that following the orders of your assignment wouldn't be much of an issue."

"He is the King of Kings, you know," Elijah chimed in with a comforting smile firmly in place.

"Besides, the moment you agreed to the challenge of entering this room, you agreed to accept your role as a Nabi. There's no backing out now, so just suck it up and come along. You have a lot to learn and a short time to learn it in," Uriel fired, unsurprisingly.

"But –" Aiden began in protest, but with a single enraged glare from Uriel, his mouth instantly closed and he was forced to follow her as she left. Eran took notice of his friend's uneasiness, and playfully slapped him on his shoulder as they walked side by side.

"I know how you feel, Zane," he started with an air of seriousness that contrasted the façade he fed to the angels. "But this is for the best. We failed our mission, our teammates are all dead, and I have a feeling that we'll get caught in the crosshairs of whatever those things were that fought at the bottom of the pit. If what they say is true, then walking out of this place is the same as stepping onto a battlefield. I think it'd be best to be prepared before we do something that radical." Aiden stewed for a moment on Eran's plan to say and learn what Elijah and the Archangels had to teach them. He thought it more rational than his own plan to leave abruptly. They didn't even really know where they were, after all, and on top of that, the prime minister they failed to assassinate would likely have them hunted down and killed should he find them alive. He had to agree with Eran. Staying was for the best.

Uriel led her apparent trainees out of the Grand Hall and into a smaller one completely devoid of any decoration.

“Step inside, kiddies,” she goaded as she walked down the corridor and took a left. They caught up with her and followed Uriel into a badly damaged room colored solely in sleek black. Unlit torches rested upon the walls that added a certain mystique to the otherwise dingy space.

“What is this place,” Aiden inquired aloud. Uriel, frustrated that he asked so many questions, turned sharply so that her eyes locked with his and shut him up once again.

“This is the room where your training will begin. You’ll learn to pray in here. Now, shall we begin?” She asked heatedly. The two nodded, and with that gesture of confirmation, Uriel snapped her fingers. The torches came alive and the door that had been their entry slammed shut on its own. Two pedestals emerged from the floor in the center of the room, and upon them rested Bibles, one red and one blue. “These sacred tomes are your lifeblood from here on out. You will study them, you will carry them at all times, and you will treat them with the utmost respect. Do I make myself clear?”

“Yes, ma’am,” the Two said in unison. Aiden took to the blue one and Eran to the red, and as they placed their hands upon them their bodies surged with radiant power and light. Aiden’s robe transformed into a blue hooded cloak that rested perfectly over the top of his head and shielded his face from easy recognition, and underneath he was shocked to find a black collared ministerial shirt with slacks to match. His feet were adorned with sleek black shoes and a line of blue flames rested atop his shoulders. His body’s shimmer had long since passed, however he could still feel the overwhelming power rage within. The massive Bible that he’d laid his hand on shrunk down to pocket size, and Aiden tucked it away into his royal blue cloak. Aiden, in an odd mix of shock and elation, turned his gaze to his friend and comrade to find that Eran Hewer wore an outfit of identical fashion.

Eran's hooded red cloak rested over a purely white collared shirt with a matching pair of white slacks. His shoes retained the same black gleam as Aiden's, but the flames on his shoulders gave off a red glow that rivaled Uriel's flowing locks. He looked back at Aiden as he stowed his Bible in the pocket in his slacks and smiled, but that smile twisted into a horrified expression when a massive fireball hurdled between the Two. Immediately they turned their attention to the elegant Uriel, whose balled fists were aglow with enraged flames.

"What's the big idea," Eran yelled at her with a nervous crack in his voice. "I thought we were going to learn how to pray!" Uriel smiled as she lifted her hand once again, and a bead of sweat trickled down the side of Aiden's face.

"Oh, trust me," she started as her voice lowered to a sinister yet sultry tone, "you will." She hurled another burst of flames at each of the Airmen, and out of shock Eran froze. Aiden narrowly dodged the explosive projectile that rained down on him and delivered a sharp kick to his wingman. Eran was knocked out of the way of the burning wave and slid across the chipped and uneasy floor of the damaged room. He looked at Aiden with a sense of gratitude rather than anger, and regained his stance as his eyes shifted back to the hostile Archangel.

Uriel expanded her wings, and as she slowly drifted into the air like a hot air balloon, seven fireballs formed in a triangle before her.

"Physical strength won't be enough to get you through this battle, kids," Uriel stated with a sick pleasure in her voice. She pushed one hand forward and the infernal orbs rushed the two men before they had an opportunity to evade, and out of instinct Hewer jumped in front of Aiden with his hands outstretched. Together they watched as the red flames that sat upon his shoulders formed a wall around the both of them, and battled the onslaught of the Fire Queen. Aiden watched in amazement as the challenge seemed to stir something up in the pit of Uriel's soul. She opened her mouth and released a wave of sound that only intensified the flames she put out. Eran held her fire back with his own as best he could, but the force behind her attack proved too much for him to handle and the two young prophets were slammed against the wall near the door.

"How did you…?" Aiden started as he tried to pick himself back up. He hissed out of pain and held his back, but extended his other hand to pick up his wingman.

"I don't even know," Eran responded through gritted teeth, "but now seems like a bad time to get into it."

"The flames on your shoulders come from the power of the Holy Spirit. From here on, He will act as a guide and a guard for you in everything you do. Whether or not you choose to rely on that, however, will determine how strong those flames will become and just what they'll be able to do," Uriel explained. She spread her hands wide, and the room visibly began to melt under the incredible heat that emanated from her. Eran was captivated by this enormous power, by this whole other world that he'd never even seen before, but Aiden was stricken with horror at the sight. His mind raced for any sort of solution to the gigantic problem that was Uriel, but for whatever reason the only thing that came to him was the conversation he'd had with Elijah the Tishbite. *That's it!* Aiden thought back to the marvelous display of power given by Elijah upon his entry. *The miracles I perform must be explained in Scripture in some form or fashion for my abilities to take effect,* Aiden recalled. He pulled the shrunken Bible out of his pocket and opened it to a random page. Uriel's eyes lit with a sadistic hunger for destruction that could only be born of *her* white-hot intensity. She clasped her hands together and pointed them at the Two when Aiden dashed around the edge of the room to stand at the back wall.

He kept his eyes locked on the back of Uriel's head and lifted the Bible into his line of sight as the heat wave she created sparked a sudden flash of bright red fire. It swirled around her and took on the form of a flock of birds before she directed it at Eran. As she compelled her fiery flock to swoop down upon the entranced airman, Aiden's eyes suddenly met the page that rested underneath his thumb.

"'The Lord is my rock, my fortress and my deliverer,'" he read aloud, and as the words left his lips it was as if the flames on his shoulders danced with delight. They grew with expectation and fed on the desperation the young Nabi felt to save his friend, and in the next instant the very floor upon which they stood jumped up to shield Hewer from the blitz in a trio of layers. Aiden's jaw dropped as the multitude of phoenixes assailed the construct of his words but failed to penetrate it, and Uriel turned to face him as an unnerving smile slithered across her lips. She released yet another wail, but the tone of this one varied from her last and the creations born of her insufferable heat merged together into a mighty golem. The stunning red color that the flames once exhibited had suddenly dimmed into a searing blue that matched the tone of Aiden's cloak.

The golem released a deafening roar and charged Aiden with the intent to kill, but as the beast rampaged towards him, Aiden read from the page once again.

"'My God is my rock, in whom I take refuge, my shield and the horn of my salvation.'" As the line of Scripture entered into the atmosphere, the flames on Aiden's shoulders formed a barrier around him, but rather than just fend off the behemoth's advances, the brilliant blue blaze absorbed Uriel's latest pet and dispelled the heat wave she used to keep her trainees sluggish.

"You're starting to figure it out," the archangel mused with a proud smirk about her as she descended to the floor. The stone barrier that surrounded Eran fell to tiles once again, and as it did, so Aiden, too, crashed to the ground. His Nabi garb vanished into a shimmering mist, and once again his body was covered in the same blue and purple robes as before. "Well done."

"Oh crap, Zane!" Hewer frantically pushed past Uriel and knelt at the side of his fallen friend. "What happened to him? What is this?" He spat at her. He spared no ounce of animosity in his tone and gave no rationality to the situation. He knew very well that she could destroy them both without any effort whatsoever, but it didn't matter to him at all with Aiden helpless on the ground.

"The power that you've been given relies on three things. The Holy Spirit is the first. He's the source of all power, so it only makes sense that He'd factor into yours. The second is a combination of prayer and Scripture. You are both prophets, chosen by God. You're His very mouthpieces, His spokesmen. You won't be able to do your job if you don't speak up, or use your power correctly without knowing what the Boss says, right?" Hewer offered no response. Uriel sighed in disappointment and continued. "Anyway, that's the reason you received a Bible when you entered this room. The third thing is the most crucial. It's total dependence on the Holy

Spirit. I said before that He was your guide and guard, but if you act as though you know the way then the guide has no purpose. If you refuse to pick up a shield, it can't defend you from an attack from your enemies." Eran looked down at a now unconscious Aiden, and though anger still boiled hot within him, he managed to keep his cool.

"So, what happened to him," he asked her. Uriel shifted her gaze to the motionless Nabi and shrugged.

"From what I saw, I'd say he could let go just enough to use the power but only for a short time. Because he's still trying to manage it on his own on some not-so-small level, it strips him of the strength in his physical body. He'd still be useful in a fight, but unless he can put his doubts aside and exercise that total dependence, he won't be able to use this gift to the fullest extent." Before she could continue, a loud crash sounded throughout the Hall of Nabi'im. Uriel's wings spread from pure instinct and she looked towards the door as if the very air that surrounded it had changed. For a moment, Eran thought that he could sense something just the same. The door opened to reveal a monster that Eran thought belonged in the nightmares of little children.

It walked on the hind legs of a bear but had the torso of a man. In the place of hands were razor-sharp claws that more closely resembled daggers than any nail Eran had seen on an animal. Its head was like that of a vampire bat, as black as night, and as the beast drew closer to the center of the room, the four clear, fleshy cylinders that pumped a mysterious black sludge into its back became visible. The creature sniffed the air and released a sickened grunt. Its cold white eyes shifted about the room until they locked firmly on the Archangel at its center.

“What is that thing,” Eran asked, clearly unnerved as he pulled an unconscious Aiden up and put his arm around him to brace him. The hideous creature snarled and bared its fangs at the two prophets, and without hesitation it lunged for them with those disgustingly rusty claws extended and hungry for penetration. As the beast flew past her, Uriel nonchalantly extended her arm and expelled an infernal blast from her hand. The creature, while surprisingly not destroyed, was at least catapulted into the far wall on the side of the room. It slowly slid to the floor and for a moment remained completely motionless, but the moment Uriel turned to face the hellish abomination it spurred to life once again.

“Durable, that’s for sure,” Uriel replied with the same battle-crazed look in her eye as before. “Take Aiden and retreat to your room. It would seem that I have some… cleaning up to do.”

“Right,” Eran said without the slightest bit of hesitation. He looked back at the monster as he pulled out the small red Bible that he’d acquired before and opened to the middle. He skimmed the page as quickly but thoroughly as he could, and found a verse that he thought could work well for him. The bat-beast rushed at him with much greater speed than it exhibited upon its entry, but in a single display of purely physical power, Uriel caught it by the throat with one hand, hoisted it up into the air, and drove the monster head first into the hard stone floor.

“I’m sorry,” she quipped, “did that hurt?” The beast looked up at her out of utter disdain, but her attention refocused on the two young humans entrusted to her care. Her eyes lit with a rage that ignited her hair. “What are you waiting for? I thought I told you to get out of here!”

“‘I will hasten and not delay to obey your commands,’” Eran nervously read aloud as he ran for the door, and much to his surprise and relief he ran a lot faster than he thought. He held onto Aiden tightly, and as they bolted through the halls and corridors he watched the development of a battle like none other. Angels and demons, what looked like the Nabi'im of old and creatures of the night warred before his very eyes, and the more destruction they caused with their myriad of attacks, the more it ensnared him. But this was hardly the time for distractions. He knew his mission, and that was to get his unconscious comrade to safety while the Archangels fended off the enemy. He made a dash for the hall he remembered Aiden emerge from, but two massive lupine creatures that, like the bat-beast, walked on two legs labored to demolish it in its entirety. Eran, at his wit's end, pressed for his own hall now, and as the clash of Heaven and Hell that now blasted the floor to oblivion endured around him, Eran did everything he could to push forward and save his wingman.

He turned into his corridor to escape the heat and aggression from both sides, and took a moment to survey the terrain of the battle. All six of the other Archangels took on multiple enemies, and even Elijah took part in the fray with a trio of other Nabi'im. Hewer watched in awe, but when the battle became his primary focus, he heard something from deep within the corridor that unnerved him. Slow and methodic footsteps approached from the other end of the shadowy hall, and Eran leaned Aiden against the wall as he turned to face their mysterious source. A silhouette of a tall man with a wind-blown cape emerged from the pitch black, and as he drew closer to the light of the battleground behind the prophets his features became far more apparent.

His strikingly sharp facial features and muscular physique resembled the other male Archangels to a tee, and his silver-plated armor lustered even in the dark of his surroundings. A black aura surrounded him though, and despite his handsome appearance his red and black eyes sent a message of war and division that chilled whoever met his gaze. Eran withdrew his Bible once more and flipped through pages as the dark being approached him, but the imposter Archangel only laughed at the frantic search of the Scriptures and waved the tome down.

"There is no need for such things," he said in a muscly baritone voice that struck terror into the heart of the young prophet. "I have come for naught a reason than to speak with you." Eran's every hair stood on end, and as the chill trickled down his spine he felt a sudden burn penetrate his chest.

"Yeah, for some reason I highly doubt that what with the demonic eyes and all," Eran shot back, and masked the pain that he felt in that moment. The dark one's eyes widened in recognition as he moved past the prophet.

"Believe what you wish, then. I have only come to tell you that in time, you will assume an incomparable, Eran Hewer. That is why you joined the military, is it not, for power? Soon enough you will have that which you seek. What path you choose to take it, however, is entirely up to you," the mysterious creature said as he walked towards the lobby.

"Wait," Eran shouted behind him. The faux angel turned around and locked eyes with him, which caused the young prophet to freeze before he asked, "Who are you?" The dark being hummed pensively and turned away from him.

"You will find that out soon enough," he replied in deepened voice. He lifted a hand, and after a moment of unmitigated darkness, both he and the monsters that infiltrated the Hall vanished without a trace.

Chapter Five

The images faded, and Aiden took a moment to regain his breath. Maya looked at him with deeper concern in her eyes than anyone he'd ever known, and instantly he felt guilty.

"Please," he begged, "don't look at me like that. I'll be fine, I just need to get some rest." Maya did her best to mask her worry but to no avail. She'd seen how his abilities drained him, and now that she had more of an understanding of just how far he pushed himself and how often he did, she was more inclined to stay with him and tend to him until he returned to health.

"If that's what you need, then I won't keep you for much longer," she said reluctantly as she rose from her seat. She walked toward the door without any further exchange of words, but as her mind raced and her hand touched the doorknob she paused and turned back to him. Aiden sat there, almost motionless, and flipped through the pages of his small blue Bible. "Hey, listen, I was thinking that maybe I could stop by every now and then. You know, to check up on you from time to time and make sure that nothing bad has happened."

Aiden's eyes went wide at her expression of care, but still he remained with his back to her. He let out a deep sigh of joy that she mistook for irritation, and smiled while she couldn't see.

"If that's what you want to do," he responded coolly. She rolled her eyes and shook her head as she opened the door and took her leave. As she walked down the hall towards the stairwell she couldn't help but revisit some of the painful memories of Aiden's childhood. She hated that he was so widely rejected and ridiculed, how he never knew what friendship even was until he met Eran, and how much physical pain he had suffered through. She glanced back at the apartment where she knew he sat, and she realized that the sight of his trials made her much more grateful for the childhood that she had.

She walked through the city and watched as the sun started to set. To her, there was something about the blended reds, oranges and yellows of the twilight hour that made her so comfortable. Perhaps it had something to do with the walks she took with her father through the park in her youth. The extravagant mix of colors inspired her to take one of those nostalgic strolls on her way home, and as she embarked she reminisced about days long gone by. She could hear the sound of her older brother and sister arguing for the thousandth time over who should retain control over the remote control, and she could smell the fresh-baked cookies that her mother prepared in the kitchen.

She walked along the path and smiled when she passed a little girl who held the hands of her mother and father. She let out a thankful sigh, and thought of how fortunate she had been to have had that kind of picture-perfect childhood that most people dreamed of. But as always, Maya couldn't help but think about the people who were less fortunate than her. People like Aiden Zane. She shuddered to think of how much torment he experienced in his youth, how much abuse persisted beyond the visions of his past that he was remarkably open about. Her fists tightened and her heart rate heightened out of pure unmitigated rage.

"How could people treat a child that way?" she asked herself silently. For a moment, she wished that she could have understood the kind of pain he felt, that she could have endured the same sort of maddening isolation that drove him to be so desperate for affection that he'd open up to a total stranger with no qualms of what repercussions may follow. From what she saw in the images of their respective upbringings, it was obvious to her how and why Aiden and Eran became friends. But something still puzzled her about the situation. She saw his memories with her own eyes, but for whatever reason she hadn't noticed anything in them that would be particularly traumatizing.

She strolled across a bridge that stretched over a luminescent stream that ran throughout the park and mulled over the pained expression she recalled upon his face. Was the continuation of his tale really worth physical and emotional torture? She recalled his distressed expression as he recounted the story in the car, and the more she assessed the situation the more she decided it wasn't. She groaned as she resigned from the matter. *I'm sure he'll tell me eventually,* she thought. It was only then that she realized that she never got his phone number to verify if he'd be home or not.

"Excuse me, ma'am," came an assertive masculine voice from behind her. At the mention of the word "ma'am," Maya turned around with her hand upraised to slap the face of the one who dared speak the word, but when she realized that the two people behind her were policemen, she scratched her head with her upraised hand. The officer's eyes narrowed on her as he asked, "Were you about to hit me?"

"Oh no! I'm so sorry, I just haven't had the best week and it's put me a little on edge. I assure you that I would never raise my hand to a police officer on any normal day!" She gave a wry smile but it did little to diffuse the tension of the situation. The cop grabbed her tightly by the arm as his partner, a woman who had suffered too many bruises and cuts at his hands, turned away from the situation. The brutish policeman flashed Maya a quick glare, and pulled her back across the bridge towards the car he'd arrived in. "You're hurting me," she shouted as she attempted to twist away, but the policeman only smiled. "What is this even about?"

"You're that therapist that was rescued by some masked lunatic, right?" He asked with a sick delight in his tone as he tightened his grip. Maya winced from the pain, but she dared not hit the man for fear of immediate arrest and further brutality. *Play it cool, Maya,* she told herself. She cleared her throat and straightened up.

"Yes," she confirmed. "I was saved by someone who called himself the Nabi. I didn't get a good look at his face, but he came around just before the man who attacked me had a chance to rape me. Another man tried to help me by the name of Aiden Zane, but he was knocked out cold almost as soon as he showed up." Recounting the events made her severely uncomfortable, and lying about Aiden's identity distressed her more than mere words could even express, but Maya knew that if she was to break free of this brute's hold, she was going to have to at least pretend to cooperate with him. The mean-spirited policeman led her across the street now to the squad car his partner had already stepped into.

"In any case, we were told to bring you in for further questioning." Maya's eyes widened at the news and she pulled back onto her heels to stop, but because of her lack of substantial mass the officer had no trouble in dragging her along.

"Wait," she begged, "please." The officer reluctantly obliged, but maintained his secure grip on her wrist as he turned to face her.

"What?" He demanded as if he were going to hit her, but despite the size advantage he had on her, she shot him a glare that would freeze the magma in the belly of a volcano. He jerked her wrist and the sound of a loud pop permeated the atmosphere. Heads turned in their direction now, but the vile authority figure didn't concern himself with the attentions of the public. This was the joy that came with the job, and he wouldn't allow anyone to speak ill of it.

"What is wrong with you?" Maya demanded through clenched teeth. The man licked his lips as a smile slithered across his face and pressed her already injured wrist just to watch her squirm. He pulled her closer to him and met her eyes with his.

"This Nabi person had an altercation with a man in a red jumpsuit a few hours ago that nearly destroyed the whole shopping district. We had a few witnesses place you and an injured man not even a block from the scene, so we're thinking you had something to do with what happened." Maya's eyes went wide, but she shook her head. Her heart beat at her chest like an enraged beast against a cage wall, but still she did her best to maintain her composure.

"How does that even make sense?" She demanded in faux disbelief, but the officer's grip got tighter.

"Because when this guy first appeared, you and the man you were seen with were there to witness it. When he blew up one of the most important parts of the city with what seemed like lightning, you two were seen leaving from the same district just moments after the vigilante disappeared. If you don't know where he is, then I don't think we'd be wrong to assume that you're him yourself!" The suspicions of this man were unbearable, and it was impossible from Maya's perspective to tell if he actually attempted to put the case together, or if he simply sought a quick fix to satisfy his abusive nature. She knew that she needed to get away, but she wasn't in any position to force a break, especially with her dislocated wrist.

She took a deep breath, but her heart still raced against her wishes and her head still swirled between a myriad of ideas as to how she could convince this beast of a man to let her go. But there was still the matter of a real escape. She analyzed the body of this particular policeman and noted his Olympian physique, and as she subtly walked her eyes up and down his toned figure she realized that he would probably catch her if she ran.

The lights of the sun began to give way to the shadows of nightfall, and with the decline in temperature she grew more nervous by the minute. *Think, Maya, think*, she screamed at herself. She resolved to try a diplomatic resolution to the problem, but before she could open her mouth there was the loud crack of a gunshot. A mist of blood slapped her in the face, and she felt the man's hand instantly go limp. She looked down slowly, and when she saw the blood empty itself from his veins she reclaimed her hand and screamed as she held it.

The surrounding people cleared out, and the man's partner picked up the radio to call for backup from inside the squad car. It was useless, because before she could complete the order, the same red-masked figure from before swooped down from overhead. He looked back at Maya, who by now stopped screaming and only shook in terror, and with a nod of amusement, he turned back to the mortified and thoroughly enraged cop.

"You really ought to treat the ladies better," he quipped. The cop howled in pain and threw a sloppy punch at the overconfident Bloodsport but was easily evaded. Bloodsport grabbed onto the abusive officer's wrist and forced the man's head and torso downward. Bones popped with the most unceremonious crack. "How would you like it if someone treated you that badly, huh?" The horror-stricken cop shook his head inaudibly, but Bloodsport broke his wrist without any sign of a struggle at all. Maya watched from where she stood, petrified much to her dismay, and before she knew what happened, the red-clad assassin lifted her over his shoulder and darted in the opposite direction. He scaled a fire escape until he reached the roof of a nearby apartment complex and set Maya down gently.

He extended his left arm, the opposite of Aiden, and recited a Scripture with an unbelievable chill in his voice.

"'The first angel sounded his trumpet, and there came hail and fire mixed with blood, and it was hurled down on the earth,'" he said, and just as the Scripture indicated, a fusion of hail, fire and blood rained down upon the spot where the savage cop had been brutalized. Maya reached out her hand as she yelled for Bloodsport to stop, but he released a manic laugh that instilled in her a fear that she had never experienced. She dropped to her knees as the sky lit up again with an intensity that rivaled the day. Bloodsport folded his arms and took great joy as he watched the show.

"So, how did you like the fireworks," he asked in all seriousness. His sudden change of attitude made her tremble, and when he turned to face her, she slowly pulled away from him with her one good hand. "That question wasn't rhetorical," he assured her. Maya stopped and stared at him with disgust.

"How could you do something so horrible in the middle of the public eye?" She barked. He snickered, and carelessly tossed his hands into the air.

"Considering the condition he left you in, you would think that you'd approve of the way I handled the situation," he contended. She spat at his feet and pulled away once again.

“Why would I ever approve of that?” Maya’s eyes burned with more intensity than the ball of flames that rained down on her former captor, something that deeply excited Bloodsport. Nevertheless, his tone was stern and direct when he addressed her next.

“Because you were there to see the scum of this world get what it deserved.” She denied his words with the shake of her head and stood to her feet in terrified boldness.

“That was a *man* you incinerated! He may have been a pig and a brute but his life was still worth something—” she challenged, but with an animalistic roar he cut her off. She fell quiet and almost stumbled over the edge of the roof in her effort to get away from him.

“His life was worth nothing! What, you think there’s something special about these people, that every life has meaning or some childish crap like that?” Bloodsport taunted as he paced towards her. “Humans love to talk about how great they are but they’re the *things* that caused the rift between the angels and their Father! That rift caused dissension in Heaven, and the legions of Hell are mounting up to unite Heaven and Earth under demonic regime…”

“What are you even talking about,” Maya questioned, her voice atremble. Bloodsport released an irritated sigh and clasped his hands together just to make her jump.

“A few billion years ago, before the world you see now, God created the heavens and the earth. In the heavens, He created servants for himself that we all know are called angels, with the highest ranking being the Archangels. They were treated as sons and daughters of their King and served Him without complaint, but it was when the Almighty made the decision to expand his affections and engineer the humans that Lucifer, then the leader of the Eight seceded from the Angelic Order and rebelled against his Father. In order to show the flaws in God's newest and most adored creation, Lucifer appeared to the first humans as a serpent and managed to convince them to betray their creator just as he had, but whereas he was met with expulsion and punishment, they were met ultimately with salvation and love."

"So," Maya began, "you're an acolyte of the Devil?" Bloodsport laughed hysterically at her comment, but in the very next instant he sobered once more.

"So quick to assume. I don't recall telling you anything about myself in all that," he said venomously. "But to answer your question, no, I'm not. I don't think of myself as a servant of anyone or anything. I just do my own thing and wreak chaos wherever I feel the urge to. See, Lucy is planning his own apocalypse, and there's not a whole lot anyone can do to stop him." Maya's eyes went wide with dread. "For Heaven to be united, Earth must fall to pieces, and I might as well enjoy myself while I watch the world bleed out." In the blink of an eye he grazed her shoulder with a bullet from a .50 Desert Eagle. She screamed in pain as she fell to her knees again. He approached her slowly and knelt before her. "Deliver this message to the Nabi: this will end exactly where it all began." Maya breathed heavily as she looked at the flesh-wound on the shoulder of her previously injured arm. Bloodsport held his gun in front of her face and met her eye as he watched the color drain from her face. "I suggest you get moving. The cop in the squad car was still alive, and I bet she called for backup by now. As far as they know, we're partners in crime, so it won't be too safe for you out here for much longer." Without a question, Maya stood to her feet and ran as fast as she could to get away from him. Tears streamed down her face as blood ran down her arm. With every motion of her body her wrist throbbed and the bullet wound stung, but the fear instilled in her by the manic Bloodsport spurred the young woman back down the path from whence she came. The sound of sirens in the night sky drove her mad, but in about ten minutes she'd arrived at Aiden's doorstep.

She furiously rapped against the door, and all the while analyzed the ground as she prayed that no blood trail was left behind. There was no answer. She beat against the solid oak door again and again and yelled at the top of her lungs, but still there was nothing. The police sirens outside the walls of the building grew louder, and as she felt the authorities move closer by the second she began to cry. It was then that the door of the apartment opened. Aiden Zane stood fully prepared to scold whatever heathen disturbed him in his solitude, but to his surprise he was met with a blood-covered Maya who stared at him through streams of tears.

"Please," she begged through her sobs, "please help me!" Aiden analyzed everything that was wrong with her in a matter of moments. Broken wrist, gunshot wound, bruised forearm, but amid all her injuries he felt as if they hardly had anything to do with her tears. He helped her inside and shut the door to his apartment. She winced when he accidentally touched the grazed skin, but still her eyes shimmered with an unspeakable joy that Aiden, in his social ineptitude, completely overlooked. He sat her down in her chair from before and moved frantically throughout his home to close all blinds and curtains. Once he was done he pulled his chair across the room and sat just in front of her.

"'But He was pierced for our transgressions, He was crushed for our iniquities; the punishment that brought us peace was on Him, and by His wounds we are healed.'" As Aiden quoted the Scripture, the injuries that

Maya suffered at the hands of the policeman and Bloodsport started to heal. She watched on in amazement, but when she looked into Aiden's eyes she could see nothing but worry.

"What's the matter," she asked as if she didn't know. He took a handkerchief from his pocket and wiped the trails where her tears had fallen.

"Who did this to you," he asked as he gently moved her dark brown hair out of her eyes. She froze for a moment, and wondered if he even understood how his actions at present made her feel. More than that, she wondered why she felt the way she did. It seemed as if her safety was ensured in his presence, but she was sure that it was mere coincidence. Twice, though, he had saved her, and even now, as the authorities pursued her and sought her incarceration, he provided for her a safety that she knew no other person in Edgehaven would have. "Maya?" His voice was filled with a level of concern that surprised even him, but he knew that now was not the time to fixate on that.

"I was apprehended by the police. They wanted me to go in for questioning about the fight you had with the man in red earlier today. The male cop tried to drag me to his squad car, and when I protested he broke my wrist, but…" she trailed off and nervously looked towards the window to the balcony, as if the psychopathic mercenary would just manifest outside of Aiden's home and blow a hole through his living room wall. It certainly wouldn't have been the first time they'd felt his mania within a 24-hour span.

"But…?" Aiden prodded. She offered no response, and only surveyed the covered window until Aiden gently placed his hand on her cheek and pulled her face back towards him. She blushed when her eyes met his, but she sat frozen under his gaze. "It's alright," he said with an unusual cool, "you can continue. I won't let anything happen to you, weak though I may be." She immediately sat straight up and adjusted her clothing and hair unnecessarily in a desperate attempt to distract herself from the unique way her heart pounded.

"The man from before showed up and rescued me from the cop and whisked me off to a distant rooftop. That's when he called down a giant fireball from the sky and fried the cop like a piece of chicken. He rambled on about some angelic war and how some dude named Lucy wanted to reunite Heaven by causing Earth to fall. Then he told me to tell the Nabi that it will all end exactly where it began." Aiden's eyes went wide and his face drained of color as much as a black man's could. He stood from his seat and paced anxiously around the room. His attention refocused on her and his jaw dropped as a sympathetic look crept across his face. "Aiden," she started as her voice stabilized, "what is it you're not telling me?" He ran his fingers through his curly hair in deep frustration but took his seat again.

"Listen," he told her sternly, "you have to get as far away from me as possible." She immediately shook her head.

"I'm sorry, but there's no way that's happening now," she asserted. Aiden groaned out of sheer irritation as he slammed his fist against the small brown table that sat quite noticeably amid the lawn furniture. The impact of his open palm against the wooden surface was enough to make Maya jump, but it did little to dissuade her decision.

"This is not a game, Maya," Aiden assured her angrily. "Bloodsport, that man in the red suit, is incredibly dangerous and –"

"And *he knows you,* Aiden," she interjected. Aiden grimaced from the remark. "And you know him. I'll ask you again, Mr. Zane, what is it that you're not telling me, and so help me, God, if you dare lie to me I'll end this whole thing before Bloodsport ever gets the chance. Now tell me, what's going on?" He took a moment and desperately searched for a way to get out of that situation, but he inevitably made peace with the fact that there was none and confessed the truth to her.

"Eran and I trained for six more months after the raid on the Hall of Nabi'im. We grew stronger. We were taught to see angels and demons for what they were, and even developed an affinity for certain Scriptures that would become our signatures in training sessions. After our first bout with Uriel, it didn't take long for us to memorize certain parts of the Bible, or for our hearts to truly focus on the source of the words and the power that came with them. We became reliant on our God in all aspects, and our bond had never been stronger. The Archangels took notice of that and at the one-year mark, twelve years ago, we were sent on a mission to Tel Megiddo," Aiden explained.

"What kind of mission?" Maya inquired with an air of curiosity. He looked at her, and inwardly he cried as she grew closer to his world in a way that he'd never wanted.

"In every generation, there are a chosen Two, the Nabi'im, who are to guard the world against demon-kind and prevent the fall of humanity by upholding Biblical truth. With those Two comes the risk that they could be corrupted and facilitate the rise of darkness throughout the world. Adolf Hitler, the most influential man of the 20th Century, proved that he had the Nabi's power to bring about change, but because of his own weak connection to the Holy Spirit, he brought about the abomination of the Holocaust, and a rift between a country and its leadership that will never be forgotten. Division, falsehoods and death are the only things that follow a corrupted Nabi." The word division was enough to send a chill down Maya's spine, but she continued to listen nonetheless. "But there is a third factor that contributes to the cycle. Deep within the bowels of Tel Megiddo, is a cage that must never be opened until the appointed day comes. In order to ensure that," Aiden continued, "the forces of darkness must be kept away from that place at all costs."

"And the reason you were sent there was to stop them from getting into that cage," Maya assumed. Aiden nodded, and the more he thought about the events of that day, the more he envisioned the darkness of that cavern, the more his leg shook with an inconsolable edge.

"There's a pull from that place that affects the people in the area, a dark power that corrupts the unsuspecting, and since Tel Megiddo rests so closely to the Palestinian border, it ensnares people on both sides and only fuels the endless conflicts between the Palestinian and Israeli forces," he told her. The look of wonder in her eyes made him distress all the more, but for the time being he stomached it.

"Where does that dark power come from," she asked him. Aiden turned away from her and wandered towards the covered window. He peered through the blinds to see bright searchlights tear through the city of Edgehaven. The hair on Aiden's arms stood on end and he could feel the air shift around him as he continued to watch the madness without those walls. He took a deep breath and turned back to her.

"The Devil himself," he affirmed ominously, and at the mention of that name their eyes locked once again.

Chapter Six

Maya shot out of her chair in alarm and knocked it over in the process. She hastily strode towards Aiden with a distorted look on her face. Her eyes narrowed on him and her nostrils flared with a combination of anxiety and anger that his deeply saddened eyes had no effect on.

"Aiden," she started, though she had a feeling that she would regret the question she asked next. "What does this have to do with Eran?" He shook his head and placed his hand over her eyes again.

"It would be much easier to show you than to tell you. There are just some things I'd rather not speak of. 'Let your eyes look straight ahead; fix your gaze directly before you.'" The images from Aiden's mind once again filled Maya's vision and in great distress he moved away from her. He refused to watch, or rather, had no ability to do so since the vitality of the moment was ever present with him. Maya stood transfixed by the new vision of her host's past, and even more so by the illustrious beauty that was Uriel.

The lovely Archangel stood with the Nabi'im at the end of a dimly lit hall with monumental pillars on either side. As the path wandered deeper into the earth, all signs of light and life disappeared.

"Your mission," Uriel briefed, "is to quiet a disturbance near the Abussos in Tel Megiddo. If the tension between the people of the area persists, the amount of hostility could weaken the seal to Satan's prison and, for a short while, release the darkest evil ever known upon the world." Eran swallowed nervously as he stood there with a younger Aiden. "The people there are merely pawns, so you'll go unarmed. No one is to fall at that site as a casualty of the battle. Am I understood?"

"Yes, ma'am," the Nabi'im responded in unison. Uriel smiled at how much they'd grown since their very first day, but quickly replaced it with a scowl as she walked in front of them and looked them up and down. Even Maya in the present day noted a change in the young former Airmen, but refused to comment. Her mind worked at a rapid pace in an attempt to uncover the truth, to find out what happened between Aiden and Eran that was so horrible that he dared not mention it.

"Your blood in particular will release the seal entirely, and if you get too close to the Tel, the dark spirits that are affecting the people will sense your presence. That being said, once you get to the halfway point stop and transition to Spirit Mode before you continue. That way when they figure out that you're there, they won't be able to figure out where your physical bodies are. Oriphiel, Michael, and I will assist you in subduing the evil at work since you're not strong enough yet to do that on your own," Uriel reassured them. They both released a sigh of relief, but refused to smile due to lack of proper military bearing.

"Yes, ma'am," they reiterated, and with a wave of her hand they dashed into the darkness of the tunnel. As they drew nearer to the impending site of Armageddon they could hear the screams of the dark souls and demonic spirits that spewed from the mouth of the chief demon's sanctuary. Aiden blocked them out as he ran, and chose to listen to the voice of the God who directed his steps. Eran, on the other hand, looked off to the side with even the slightest whisper of his name.

"What's wrong with him," Maya asked underneath her breath. The Aiden of the present day refused to acknowledge her question or even focus his attention on the events of that day, because the deeper they explored into the mystery of their fall-out, the more it hurt him to his core.

Eran... the spirits taunted with a twisted sense of joy, *Eran*... The young former Airman pressed his hands against his ears to block out the voices, but to his deepest dread they infiltrated every crack and crevasse of his impressionable mind. *ERAN!!!!* The more he tried to shut them out, the more they cried for him as a woman does her lover. It wasn't long before the two prophets stopped to walk, but whereas Aiden stood up straight, Eran all but slammed against the wall of the cave. Aiden heard the thud and turned around to pick fun with his longtime friend, but to his alarm he could see a trio of dark spirits as they closed in on Eran from the shadows. He said a quick prayer and his robes transformed into the ministerial attire covered with the blue cloak that at that point had been known to cause demons to tremble in its wake.

"Aiden," Eran whispered. Aiden's eyes widened as the demons backed off. "Aiden," he repeated. Aiden walked closer to his friend and grabbed him by the shoulders as he slid down the jagged wall of the cave.

"I'm right here, Eran," he said comfortingly. Eran started to laugh uncontrollably and slapped Aiden's hands away.

"Look at how sanctimonious you've become," he said in utter amusement, as if the last year was nothing more than a distant dream with no weight whatsoever. Aiden's eyes narrowed with anger and suspicion.

"What are you talking about, Hewer?" Aiden questioned, and did his best to get his dear friend to look him in the eye.

"We didn't used to act like this before, you know," he whispered as his head descended to the ground. "Don't you miss it?" Aiden briefly looked into the darkness they'd left behind to see three pairs of red eyes that pierced the veil of black. Eran finally looked at Aiden with a sick sense of delight as he started to foam at the mouth. Fresh saliva dripped from his lips as he quivered with an unholy ecstasy and another maniacal guffaw echoed from his gut and into the surrounding shadows. "Don't you miss the thrill of the kill, or the pay that came along with a job well-done?" Aiden slowly stepped away from his friend, whose blackened eyes rested on him with an almost ravenous hunger for pain. The sound of Eran's voice that way made the present day Aiden cringe at the memory, and Maya, who through Aiden's memories felt as if she'd come to know Eran, felt her heart sink as he spoke.

"This isn't you talking, Eran," Aiden propounded in protest of the traits his friend exhibited.

"Oh, but it is! I can't even tell you how much I miss the smell of gunfire, or the taste of alcohol. Hell, I miss the girls I used to fool around with even though I *still* don't know their names! You can't tell me that you don't have a part of you that wishes, if even for a moment, that you could just go back." Aiden extended his hand, and the manic cackle resumed as it had before. His mouth opened, but despite his best efforts no words came out. "What's the matter, Aiden?" Eran moved forward on all fours as if the man he once was had been replaced with some manner of wild beast. His mouth continued to bubble over, and the eyes of the creatures of the shadows squinted in glee. "It's different," he continued, "when you're not just confronted with the weaknesses of your own heart, but the ones of your loved ones as well!" The deranged Eran lunged at his best friend, only to be met with a spinning heel kick to the chest that sent him into the wall once more. Maya clasped her hands around her mouth as her eyes widened in surprise, and though she wanted to look away, she knew more than anything that the answers to all her questions rested in this chapter of Aiden's life.

Eran got back up and uttered a beastly snarl as his blackened eyes turned red.

"Eran, you've got to snap out of this right now! I don't want to hurt you," Aiden whimpered. Tears welled up in his eyes. His abilities wouldn't work and his friend was at the mercy of forces they'd been taught never to involve themselves with. Aiden felt as if his heart was ripped out of his chest. He'd lost all hope, and even Maya clutched her chest from the painful pangs within her.

More of the demons that lurked within the shadows made their move and slowly crept towards him, salivating at the thought of a fresh soul to eat away at. He could feel them enter his mind and invoke the power of his freshly renewed isolation, and for a moment he thought to fight back, but after he looked into Eran's eyes once again he decided that there was no point. It was at that moment, however, that he saw the earth shatter beneath his feet. He watched himself as he reached out and narrowly grabbed onto a ledge just before the ground swallowed him whole, and felt a tight grasp around his other arm. He released a strained scream, and looked down to see his brother Eran dangling by a thread. He saw the smoke in the blood red sky, and heard Eran tell him not to let go, but as much as he wanted to hang on, as much as he resolved to keep his brother alive, he watched in painful horror as Eran slipped into the darkness below. Anger and sorrow welled up within him, and as the vision gave way to the cave in which they sat, Aiden stood up with unprecedented authority. The flames of the Holy Spirit that graced his shoulders intensified enough to give light to the entire cave and fend off that fiendish friend of his for but a moment. Eran shrieked in horror at the sight, but couldn't help but stare into Aiden's eyes as they exhumed a brilliant blue light. Eran's body became clothed in his Nabi attire, and the red flames that danced upon him burst into the atmosphere.

The demons that hid in the shadows howled in agony and were helpless to stop it. The monsters that plagued them both were expelled, and in a single gasp of exhaustion the two Nabi'im fell faced-down in the dirt. Their cloaks reverted to the robes they had worn in the Hall, and as the light in the cave faded, the two brothers looked upon each other with smiles written across their lips. The demons that previously surrounded them had scattered away, and Aiden and Eran felt their consciousness fade with their sinister presence.

"Get up," Oriphiel ordered as he shook Aiden. Aiden stirred for a moment before he remembered the corridor they walked before. He shot up and surveyed the area for any hostile entities and was relieved to find that there were none. Oriphiel moved to Eran, who lay motionless on the ground with his eyes open. Aiden moved with caution to check on him, and was deeply relieved to see that his eyes had regained their icy-blue hue. He began to convulse wildly under Oriphiel's touch, and though Aiden knelt beside him and frantically tried to calm him down, a punch to the gut from the mighty Archangel proved to be the only cure. Eran fell still as the air in his lungs audibly left his body, and for just a second Aiden could have sworn that Oriphiel's fist lit up. Eran shut his eyes with a groggy groan that left Aiden all the more terrified. Maya, baffled and enraged, threw her hands up as she watched the insanity of the moment.

"What was that for?" She almost screamed it. She looked over to her host to find that he too watched the traumas that he lived, and at the sight of the single tear that slid down his face, her anger washed away and she quieted down.

“Eran,” the past Aiden uttered in a panic, but Eran slipped further away from him. Oriphiel lifted to his feet, but the distraught Aiden shook his friend to snap him out of whatever daze their “rescuer” put him in.

“Shaking him isn’t a very good idea,” Oriphiel said with his signature catchphrase. Aiden’s head snapped around, his face distorted with anger, and in less than a second the enraged Nabi stood in front of the powerful Archangel.

“What did you do to him,” Aiden demanded. Their eyes were locked, Aiden’s fierce, Oriphiel’s passive, and without a word, Aiden’s former guide walked away from the pair. “Where do you think you’re going?! What just happened to him?”

Oriphiel stopped and turned towards the Two. His gold and silver eyes were steeled with irritation at first, but softened when he realized just what Eran Hewer meant to him.

“Lord Eran was attacked by the Insecurities and the Imaginations. This tunnel is filled to the brink with the little vermin, and they seek out impressionable minds to latch onto and feed from. The blow you saw me deliver to your friend was absolutely necessary. The only way to deal with the Imaginations is to demolish them, which is a lot easier for me to do when they’ve already wiggled their way in. As for the Insecurities, they must be taken captive, which is why I extracted them from Lord Eran and placed a seal on him to prevent any more attacks like that until the mission is complete. That being said, he’ll be out of it for a while. It would be a good idea if you waited here by his side.” Oriphiel disappeared after he explained the situation, and Aiden turned back to the now fully unconscious Hewer.

Aiden kept watch over him in silence for over an hour and wondered if his wingman would ever wake up. Oriphiel's attitude from before made Aiden question the reliability of what he said, and because of that, he prepared himself for the worst possible outcome.

"What a crap-fest this has been, huh, buddy?" Aiden whispered. He checked for a moment to see if any of the oddly named creatures returned, but the entire cave was still and quiet. He could tell, though, that the parasitic monsters watched them as closely as a dog watches steak, but despite that fact he had no intentions of resting his guard for the duration of this mission. "I feel like you keep getting the worst end of the stick," he continued. Eran groaned, and Aiden smiled. "But that's okay, because it makes you like me. I don't think I ever told you this, but I've never really had a friend before. Heh, when I was a kid it was like I had one of those faces that you just wanted to hit. Lots of people did, actually." Aiden paused and checked on him once again. He walked over to Eran and sat down next to him. Eran groaned and his face twisted into an unsightly grimace, and Aiden's eyes shimmered with tears as he begged God for something more to do for Eran. He wiped away the drops of water that spilled down his cheeks and he continued to speak to him. "And I left," he picked up again. "I joined the Air Force and for the first time ever I felt like I was a part of something. It was the first time anyone ever wanted me on their team. Somehow, though, it still got pretty lonely. During mail calls when you and the others would get letters from your families, I was always reminded that I was alone in the world. But then, we got closer and before I knew what happened it was like I had a family too." Maya struggled to hold back an emotional outcry as she listened to his story. The Aiden of the past kept his eyes firmly locked on his unconscious friend now, and as streams of water ran down his face he wiped the tears away with the sleeve of his robe and did what he could to stave off audible sobs. "That's why," he pressed on with a tremble in his voice. He was no longer a Nabi, no longer a member of the joint forces team, no longer even an airman or a man. He was the lonely child in the orphanage again, and the idea of reverting to that reality proved too painful to even stomach. Aiden cried for the first time in a long while, but still he continued. "That's why I can't lose you, Eran. You have to get back up," he demanded as he slammed a fist against the rocky floor of the subterranean grotto. His fist throbbed from the impact but he didn't care enough to even attempt to sooth his own pain. He was frozen there, helpless and angry. He waited with sincerest hope that Eran would speak or move or show some sign of life, but there was nothing.

Maya's eyes went wide with despair as she watched her frequent protector powerless at the side of his spiritually beaten comrade. She thought about the kind of pain this moment must have had on him, the pain that she now felt as she lived it through his memory. She looked over to the Aiden that protected her, the one who shielded her from the police at his own risk, who soothed her so gently and brushed the hair out of her face, and saw his face twisted in sorrow. She knew from the beginning that this day, these moments tormented him, but still she pressed him to share them with her. She subjected him to this pain, and the moment had long since passed where an apology would bear any weight.

She redirected her attention to the visions of the past and of Aiden in unquestionably broken form. The only sound that penetrated the quiet of the crypt was the cry of a terrified man. No angels came to his aid, and the only person he'd ever known to reassure him that things would turn out alright lay before him just as broken and immobile. It almost proved too much to watch. A wind tore through the cave, and to Maya's surprise, the supine Hewer latched onto Aiden's arm. Aiden slowly looked at his friend, whose eyes remained closed for a moment. They opened slowly as he turned his head towards his guard and smiled.

"You know you really shouldn't go punching stone like that when we've been given instructions not to bleed," Eran joked as he slowly sat up. "What are you trying to do, doom the whole world?" Aiden chuckled and hastily wiped the tears from his eyes before Eran could even notice them. He hated crying in front of his wingman, but he never fully understood that Eran didn't care as long as he was going to be alright. Eran stood up and dusted himself off, but as he moved he felt a sharp pain in his chest. "Aiden," he asked.

"Yeah?" his brother responded. Eran looked at Aiden with a renewed focus and intensity.

"It's time to go to work," he said with a half-cocked grin, and without warning the young prophet darted into the distant darkness. Aiden smiled widely as he shook his head, and without another moment to spare he pursued. "The center of the cave shouldn't be too far from here," Eran shouted back at him. Aiden quickly caught up, and within the span of five minutes they caught sight of Michael and screeched to a halt.

"This is the point," affirmed the Archangel. Aiden and Eran quickly took their places on the ground and Michael vanished in a brilliantly metallic flash of light.

"You ready to do this?" Aiden asked him out of more concern than anything. Eran met his gaze and nodded in all seriousness, and without any further exchange the two pressed their hands together and began to silently pray in the Spirit of the Living God. Before they knew, their bodies stood up with eyes glazed over and watched the calm of the cave in anticipation of the arrival of some fierce otherworldly force, while their Spirit Mode counterparts continued on ahead.

Their speed and strength amplified by a thousand, and when they came to the furthest wall of the tunnel they pushed through it with no difficulty. What they saw when greeted with the light of day were thousands of the same aberrant beasts from before. They were attached to the humans that fought and cursed in the valley and spurred them on with twisted smiles in place as others marched their hosts up the sloped side of the Tel. A hypnotic scarlet glare erupted from the summit of the great hill, and the sky adopted the ominous hue before the beam of light disappeared. Eran pushed forward and quoted Scripture after Scripture as the Archangels Uriel, Michael, and Oriphiel poured out waves of lightning, steel, and fire from the skies above. The mob of Palestinians and Israelis that warred with one another in the lower valley separated from their demons one by one, and with the departure of the perfidious spirits went the bulk of their hostility as well. Still an enormous congregation of monsters persisted and more swarmed in by the droves, and Aiden knew that they would not be defeated in time unless he joined the fray, but the red light that he saw upon his entry to the battle reminded him all too much of the blood-red sky of the vision from the cave.

Is this… is this that moment, the past Aiden and the present Maya considered simultaneously.

"Lord Aiden," Oriphiel shouted from the skies, "we'll never stop them at this rate if you don't join the battle!" Though the Archangel beckoned for him, he remained stationary, petrified by the events he was sure would come. Eran, on the other hand, gradually pushed through demons in an effort to reach the Tel. The wind pushed against the grass of the field and lightning flashed in the heavens. Rain poured down upon the people, who only seemed to grow stronger in their renewed rage.

The lips of every demon present at the skirmish curled into a smile as a Palestinian man possessed by not one, but seven of the maleficent spirits rushed to a truck parked on the side of the road that ran through the terrain and pulled out an Uzi. He fired round after round into the crowd, indiscriminate in regard to those he shot, and as the blood splattered against the grass and flowers of the field the ground pulsed. The air started to burn hot despite the cool rain that fell, and the Archangels bolted through the atmosphere in frenzy. Aiden watched as Eran pressed towards the top of Tel Megiddo, and as he grew closer to the unfortunate souls bound by the enemy and forced into the depths of the pit of Satan's prison, he shook with fury at the monsters and at himself.

"Move," Aiden heard a strong voice whisper into his ear. His eyes widened and his legs started to press forward through the storm and the bloodshed after his wingman and brother. The more they moved, the faster he got until he ran at full speed after Eran. Eran made his way into the ruins of an ancient city positioned at the top of the Tel and wandered over toward an old well that ran deep into the earth.

Eran, came a voice from the depths below. Eran grabbed his temple and hissed from a sharp pain that penetrated his skull. He looked at the black mouth of the well for a moment before he donned his flame-shouldered cloak with the intention of running towards it and jumping down into the darkness.

"Eran," Aiden yelled from the edge of the abandoned city with a troubled shake in his voice. Eran ceased his advance and turned to him, and with a horrifying smile listened as the commotion in the valley below fell deafeningly silent. Aiden turned out of curiosity, and was mortified to see the sea of hellish beasts and the hosts that they tormented create a path that led to the base of Tel Megiddo. Two figures ran at top speed and dashed through the split in the crowd. For a moment their identities were unbeknownst to the younger Aiden Zane, but as they drew nearer with each passing second, he saw that it was none other than their physical bodies who now scaled the ancient mound. Aiden's body ran through his Spirit Mode form and the two were united once more. He looked at his hands, which were now physically tangible, in shock and disgust.

Eran, who had also been restored to his physicality, stood with his back to his brother and released the same twisted cackle as he had in the cave.

"Eran," Aiden started with a deeply worried air to his voice, "Eran, you have to get out of here. In the cave, I –"

"Had a vision," Eran completed. He smiled as his cloak manifested in the earthly reality. He slowly made his way to the well and gave a dark smile as he strode. "I had one as well, Aiden. I was a hero in the eyes of all the inhabitants of Heaven. They praised me and adored me because of my ability to do what no other Nabi – no, what no other *human* – has been able to do since the dawn of mankind." The sound of Eran's voice sent a chill down the past Aiden's spine and made the hairs on Maya's body stand on end. The present-day Aiden furrowed his brow in a mix of anger and sorrow as he watched the past version of himself suffer.

"What are you talking about," the younger Zane inquired. His heart pumped with deadly ferocity as Eran Hewer, his friend, his wingman, his brother, turned to face him with a deranged gleam in his eye.

“Today I take the first step, Aiden,” he growled with an unsettling delight, “in uniting Heaven itself.” He opened the palm of his hand over the pitch-black pit, and the flames on his shoulders spiked with foreboding enthusiasm. “‘Therefore surely as I live, declares the Sovereign Lord, I will give you over to bloodshed and it will pursue you,’” he quoted, and as the words left his mouth, the skin that ran on either side of his nose split open and poured out his blood on the ground. The winds grew stronger and the rain intensified, but Aiden strode forward in an attempt to stop his brother from taking this dark path. Another pulse emanated from the sky above as the bright red light from before reemerged and now surrounded the ancient ruins, and Eran in utter satisfaction continued. “Since you did not hate bloodshed,” Eran spoke with a gasp of ecstasy as the palm of his hand split open just as his face had before. The winds pushed Aiden back, and though he desperately tried to root himself in the ground, it proved to do no good whatsoever. “Bloodshed will pursue you,” Eran finished. The blood that rained from his face slithered around his outstretched arm and joined that which dripped from the open gash in his palm. The world instantly fell silent, and the storm that persisted ceased. All that remained was the sinister cackle of Aiden’s maddened brother… and then the earth would swallow him up.

Chapter Seven

A blast of black shadows rose from the abyss, and a laugh more sinister and maniacal than any that Eran could produce resounded in the atmosphere. The Crimson Nabi'im watched with the greatest air of pleasure about his countenance, and clutched the fabric above his heart as he felt something truly dark begin to fester… and he embraced it. The demons in the valley below left their hosts, and drifted aimlessly towards the dark pillar that stretched from the depths of the earth. The winds blustered and rain descended from heaven with unrelenting force. Oriphiel landed beside Aiden, his eyes widened in shock and disgust, and as Eran turned to show him the bloodied wounds on his face, Aiden lunged for him.

"Lord Aiden," Oriphiel exclaimed. Aiden paid him no mind whatsoever, and fiercely grabbed Eran's collar with both hands and hoisted him into the air. Aiden, overcome with emotion, desperately searched those deranged eyes for some trace of his wingman's humanity, but all he could see was the same darkness that emanated from the hole behind him. He pulled his best friend closer and looked on him with disgust and fear as the ground beneath their feet rumbled.

"Do you have *any* idea what you've done?" Aiden's voice trembled as the horror of the vision from the cave materialized in increments before his very eyes. Eran lit up with a sadistic euphoria, and as the evil in his heart dispersed throughout his being, it seemed as though a voice familiar only to him called out to it. His head turned to the pit, and the conflicted Nabi'im watched as a figure shrouded in shadows emerged. Eran immediately recognized his dark aura, his chiseled body, his silver-plated armor, and those unmistakable red and black eyes.

Oriphiel trembled where he stood and watched the demon look around with inexplicable joy as he relished in his newfound freedom. Aiden released Eran out of sheer awe of the otherworldly force in his presence that he knew his training had not prepared him for. The second his treacherous friend's feet touched the ground, Evil caught sight of them all.

"Ah," the beast began as his eyes widened with horrific glee, "what a glorious day this is indeed. Hm…" he paused for a moment as the red in his eyes began to glow. "I sense no trace of demonic influence within you. But those cuts… yes, no doubt about it. You were the one who broke the seal, weren't you, Eran?" Eran nodded eagerly in response and panted after the malevolent being, which made the Shade's mouth curl into a smile. "Then that must mean that the Seed I sent was planted successfully and sealed in place… This is an interesting development indeed. Now we shall create an apocalypse so fit for a Devil that all of creation shall unite under my splendor!" His eyes shifted to Aiden, who stood frozen in terror at the creature's awesome power.

"What are you?" Aiden asked shakily as his eyes scanned the powerful frame of the dark figure. The demon flashed his pointed teeth in excitement at the question.

"I am known by many names: The Devil, Enemy, Dark One, Traitor, Deceiver, Hungry Lion, Strong Man, the Prince of Worms, and the Shaitan or Satan depending on your predilection of Hebrew or Arabic. But *my* name, the name that was given to me by my Father is—"

"Lucifer…" Oriphiel completed. Lucifer, upon the sound of his own name in his ear, looked upon his brother the Archangel with a deep-seated disdain.

“Oriphiel,” he all but hissed, and Oriphiel drew his massive gem-encrusted sword.

“Are you ready to finish what began outside of the Hall of Nabi’im?” he barked over a sudden howl of the wind. Lucifer flashed an amused grin as he withdrew dual black blades from his back.

“Oh, I am more prepared than you could possibly imagine, little brother. But you should know that I am much more formidable than the shadow you fought before.” Lucifer licked his lips in excitement, but Oriphiel’s face remained steeled. His eyes briefly shifted to the two young men in his charge, but when he looked back at his older brother he found that his attention now focused on the two.

“This is bad,” Aiden muttered to himself. Eran’s attention refocused on him, and the twisted smile that was in place upon Lucifer’s arrival to this realm gave way to a terrifying scowl that Aiden had never seen before.

“No,” Eran challenged. He spread his arms and looked up at the scarlet sky. “*This* is the beginning of my own rise to power!”

“Eran… How can you be so blind to what’s happening around you? If you don’t help us cage him back up then millions of innocent people will die because of it,” Aiden persisted. Eran delivered a sharp punch to his former brother’s jaw that spiraled him through the air. He landed awkwardly on his shoulder, and gasped in pain as he struggled to regain his legs.

“Tell me, Aiden, how many people are actually innocent? War, slavery, racism, abuse, deceit, infidelity, rape and murder… these convey innocence to you?” Eran’s fists balled out of his increasing indignation. “There is no innocence, just the strong screwing with the weak. The whole reason I joined the military was so I could stop sympathizing with the latter.

I worked alongside people like you to eliminate terrorists left and right, but I did that to prove that I'll never be made anyone's victim ever again. Forget innocence, Zane. The only thing that determines survival now is power." Aiden dusted himself off as his brother spoke. "As for me, I'll take that power for myself at any cost." A fully recovered Aiden charged at his best friend now as the Archangel and the Demon Prince watched on. He launched a kick at the side of Eran's head but was easily evaded with a basic duck. Much to Eran's displeasure, Aiden had enough foresight to follow up with a low knee to the face. The blow connected, and Eran Hewer slid on his back across the jagged earth upon which they fought.

Aiden walked closer to him and kicked him in the midsection to keep him from moving away, and as the air left his compatriot's body he rested his foot in his chest to force him to listen. Anger ran hot through their veins, and suddenly the threat of Lucifer seemed irrelevant. His friend, his only friend, sought not only to abandon him but to destroy him, and Aiden was desperate to keep that from happening.

"Do you even understand the gravity of what it is you're talking about, Eran," he interrogated. "You would create mass genocide, global panic and more just because you're on some childish power trip? What would your mother say if she were here to see you like this? Do you think she'd be proud? Do you think she would jump with joy to see her son prepared to end millions of lives for a futile dream that will *never* come to pass?"

"Don't you *dare* bring her into this! My mother did everything in her power to stop my dad from beating me, from *raping* me, Aiden, but it wasn't enough! She wasn't strong enough and neither was I! And I'll never go back to that place! Not for you, or for anybody else!" Eran spat as grabbed Aiden's foot and pushed in an effort to free himself of the hold, but Aiden ground his heel into Eran's ribs as his face twisted all the more.

"No, you don't get to go," Aiden barked. "Not while you're acting like this…"

"I would have to disagree with you," Lucifer asserted, and with the slightest twitch of his left eyebrow, Aiden was flung into the air.

"Lord Aiden!" Oriphiel turned to run to the airborne Zane, but to his alarm he was met with an underhanded elbow to the face when he did. Lucifer's expression was less than jovial now, and as he stepped over his brother with swords lifted into the darkened sky, the ground beneath them trembled with a might that rattled the foundation of all the mortals in the valley below. "Lord Aiden! Get out of here as quickly as you can manage!" Aiden struggled to pick himself up again, and as he did so he looked into Eran's eyes as he moved closer. Aiden refused to leave, though now he bled through his hands and his shoulder. He felt the physical sting of Lucifer's overpowering hatred, and though he had been abandoned by the only person he'd ever had a connection with, he was determined to fight to reclaim that bond, even at the cost of his own life.

"Listen to yourself," Lucifer grumbled with an air of embarrassment and hatred. "You, Oriphiel of the Thunderbolt, born of a higher class than even the angels in Heaven, debase yourself by bowing down to an inferior race. Tell me, brother, what do you stand to gain from that kind of degradation?" Oriphiel looked into his eyes with a smile and spat at him.

"A relationship with our Father that extends beyond a cage in a pit," replied the spiteful Archangel. The red in the eyes of the liberated Lucifer glowed with fresh rage as he thrust his swords downward. Oriphiel blocked with the blade in his hand, and the clang of metal on metal caused the earth to shudder once again.

"How dare you?!" Lucifer exclaimed as he pushed both blades towards his brother's throat. Oriphiel smiled and kicked him hard enough in the gut to force a break.

"Very gladly," he retorted as he bounded back to his feet and lunged at the master demon with sword upraised. The metal clashed and sent another unbelievable tremor through the earth, but Eran stood over Aiden as if no problem existed.

"You should join me, Aiden," said the darkened Nabi. Aiden's heart sent a shockwave through his bloodstream as the words were uttered. "It'll be just like the old days, but much better. We would be the engineers of a brand-new world, one where we're so strong we could do whatever we wanted." Aiden pounded the dirt and braced himself as he stood up once more. He considered it for a moment —no, wrestled with it — and the longer he stewed on the possibility, the sweeter it sounded to him. *What would even be the point of fighting on,* he thought as he closed his eyes. *Am I willing to sacrifice my brother for what could possibly be a lost cause?*

"Eran…" he started sympathetically. "You know that normally I'd support you in anything that you do…" The very utterance of the words made Lucifer's ears tingle and Oriphiel's heart sink. The Devil applauded from a distance with his gaze firmly fixed on his brother the Archangel.

"What a splendid turn of events," Lucifer began. "I will admit that Eran was on my list of… acquisitions from the very beginning, but to turn Aiden to my side as well—"

"I'm not on your side," Aiden quickly corrected. Lucifer's head turned around in a rather owlish manner and a victorious grin slithered across Oriphiel's lips. Aiden leapt into the air and delivered a crushing knee to the face. Eran was instantly knocked on his back, and could only stare up at his brother as a light from Heaven above broke through the dark clouds in the crimson sky. "Eran," he said as he redirected his attention from the beast that watched him, "I've always considered you my brother, but you ask far too much of me. I was given the task of serving my God and His people, and I will continue to do that… even if it means that I lose you." There was a deep sense of anguish in his voice that momentarily shook Eran's core, but he quickly regained his composure and sat up.

"'Serve God's people,'" he repeated with a chuckle. "They're the worst of all! They preach love and peace, redemption for all, but they perpetuate hatred and animosity and judgment in their place. Tell me, Aiden, how much love was at the heart of the Crusades, during which thousands of people died because of a lack of faith in God and imperial ambition? How many black people were bought and bartered, traded and abused because they were believed to have been created inferior? How many so-called believers in this God of ours have protested the funerals of brave servicemen and women who died in the line of duty? Please, tell me exactly how these people you intend to serve represent the example of Christ, who died for humanity!"

"I agree with you, that over the course of history our kind has forgotten and even forsaken what it truly means to strive after Christ. You're right in that we don't represent the example, but our imperfection is the reason why the example *is*, and the fact that we are the way we are only makes the sacrifice of Christ stand out even more, because no matter how you look at it, we're not worth that much effort," Aiden explained. Eran shot to his feet and grabbed Aiden by his collar in a rage.

"Then why, Aiden," Eran begged, "why subject yourself to the threat of destruction? Why burden yourself with thankless service to a people who don't care whether you live or die?" Aiden slapped his hands away and pushed him back a couple of feet.

"Because 'God demonstrates His love for us in this: While we were still sinners, Christ died for us.' The very foundation of the call on our lives, what we were intended to do here, was to introduce a new standard to the people of this world. We're supposed to be the salt, the flavor that raises the quality and catches the eye. The light that shows them the way to the One who transformed us from the lowly beasts that we used to be. The solution, then, is not to destroy the people but teach them. Those of us who know better and put their standards into practice are the only ones capable of doing just that, and after this last year of training I'm convinced that you know better, Eran." Lucifer screamed at the top of his lungs and lightning blasted from heaven. The border around the ancient town went up in flames, and the rain that poured from the skies above did little to quell the heat. His whole body faced the Nabi now, and his eyes showed no trace of color; only darkness remained.

Oriphiel unfurled his great silver wings and dashed towards the monster of all monsters with abounding urgency, but with a pulse of his dark aura the Archangel was propelled into a tree in the opposite direction. Lucifer gave a low growl as his jet-black wings expanded and pointed at Aiden.

"I've heard… enough of this," he breathed. "The entire *world* must be made to tremble before me! The final fall of humanity has come! I will be restored to grace and my legions along with me!" He lifted his hands above his head and violently thrust them downward towards the ground.

The earth began to split, just as it had in the vision from before. Smoke rose to the blood-red skies and the screams of the people below the Tel echoed through the night. As the foundation of Tel Megiddo crumbled beneath his feet, Lucifer bounded into the air with a single beat of his awe-inspiring wings and vanished into the distance. Oriphiel remained motionless on the ground and Uriel, who at one point hovered above the terrain and did battle with the lethal spirits below, now found herself fully preoccupied with her efforts to save as many people as she possibly could before the abyss could devour them whole. Michael then took to the air, and with a barrage of blades held back the remaining monsters that preyed on the weak.

The split in the ground beneath the Nabi'im jerked open to swallow them, and just as he had seen hours before this point, Aiden reached out and grabbed onto the edge of the earth with one hand. Eran grabbed onto him, and in a small moment of hope his darkened eyes regained their icy blue tint. The sharp pain in his shoulder caused Aiden to scream into the night sky, and much to his horror he saw Eran dangling just barely by Aiden's arm. Aiden's eyes welled up with tears and Eran's followed suit as he reached upward. The combination of sweat and rain weakened the hold the two had on each other, and in that moment Aiden knew that it would be impossible to save them both.

"Oriphiel!" The two of them called the name of their guide and defender repeatedly, but their cries fell on unconscious ears. Eran began to slip, and in the face of imminent doom, the hardened prophet cried as he gazed upon his comrade Aiden.

"Don't let me go…" Eran begged as he slipped even more. "Please." Aiden did his best to lift his friend, to rely on his faith to hoist him up but the fear that the moment caused, the fear of losing him and worse, the fear inspired by Lucifer's words proved too immense to stave off. Aiden was helpless to help the only person he'd ever known as "friend," and within seconds he watched as Eran Hewer slipped from his grip and descended into the deep dark of Tel Megiddo.

The image faded, but the grief that Aiden felt had been brought to the surface. He stood for a moment, but ultimately dropped to his knees. He was physically drained and emotionally disturbed, and the experience of revisiting the most traumatic event of his life, his biggest failure, made him cry as if the wounds were fresh. Maya moved her dark brown hair out of her face again as she walked across the room to the lonely prophet. Without a word, she pulled him into a warm embrace and stroked the back of his head comfortingly as the tears poured down his face.

"It's alright," she whispered. "I'm right here." Maya consoled him until he stopped crying and helped him to his chair. She handed him the small blue Bible that rested on the brown table and sat silently as she observed him read. *Just how much*, she wondered, *is this man willing to do for us? How much will he put himself through just to ensure our safety?*

"It's him," Aiden whispered. "Eran, it's Eran, he's alive." His speech pattern became progressively more frantic, but he shook it off and stood again. A strange mix of excitement, sorrow and regret overtook him, but he knew that this wasn't the time to think about it. He glanced over to Maya, who sat there with her sapphire blue eyes locked on him, and thought of what he could do to keep her safe while he left the city to confront Bloodsport. Of course, his own departure from Edgehaven would be a challenge given that the police thought him to work in tandem with his old partner, but still, he had to figure something out. He turned to face her fully now and noticed the globs of blood that dotted the living room floor.

"Maya, why don't you go into the back and change into some pajamas? If the police arrive and question me as to your whereabouts it'd be best they not see you. I'll clean up the blood and run out to get you something fresh to wear."

"Alright," she hesitated. She wasn't very fond of leaving him alone, but the fire in his eyes told her that there was little she could do to console him now. He watched her walk out of the room and quickly strode into the kitchen to fetch a bucket and a sponge. He turned on the faucet and added soap to the bucket before he placed it in the sink. He leaned against the counter and contemplated his next move.

"Involving this girl in this conflict is a poor idea," Oriphiel spoke as his body materialized. Aiden sighed and massaged his temple.

"It's a little late for that now, Oriphiel," Aiden replied in a hushed tone so that Maya's suspicions wouldn't be raised. "She's been involved in this from the very beginning. All humans have." The bucket slowly filled to the top, and Aiden turned the faucet off and carried the bucket from the sink to the living room. He dipped the sponge in the soapy water and began to scrub the tiles until the bloodstains started to give way.

"That isn't what I meant. This is different than before. Lucifer walks freely through the earth for the first time since Christ shed his blood at the place of the skull, and even more severe is the fact that he actually intends to pursue this futile dream of reuniting Heaven through man's destruction. And then there is the matter of Eran… I understand the nature of the Seed of Flesh, and I know that it can be removed under normal circumstances, but…" Oriphiel trailed off as an image of his older brother's devilish red and black eyes crept into his mind. Aiden briefly turned to look at his new guest before he ultimately returned to his work.

“Believe me, I understand that these are not normal circumstances,” Aiden responded. He dug into the cracks between the tiles with the edge of the sponge as he wrestled with the persistent dark red stains. Oriphiel shook his head in protest.

“No, you don’t understand a thing. The longer Lucifer remains in this realm, the more he feeds on your kind. He delights in their misery and their confusion and draws staggering amounts of power from it. Your old friend, with his selfish ideology and murderous shows of his own strength, is the primary source of Satan’s power as well as his most prominent agent of destruction whether he wants to be or not. You’ve seen that in your encounters with him today. You’ve seen that through Maya and her injuries. How much will it take before you stop mourning him and start to fight him seriously?” Aiden slapped down the sponge in a fit of rage and stood back to his feet. He had in his heart to yell and to fight but the woman in the other room provoked in him a more civilized behavior.

“You know as well as I do that I will never hurt my brother. Even if he hurts me.” Oriphiel punched a hole in the nearby wall, but the noise of a crash was so common in this area of town that it did nothing to warrant Maya’s attention.

“You may not have much of a choice in the matter,” Oriphiel challenged through gritted teeth. “It’s already been twelve years since that day, and I can tell you now that whenever my brother takes his time it generally isn’t good.” Aiden paced the room anxiously and slid his hands over his forehead into his curly black hair. It wasn’t easy for him to admit, but Oriphiel was right. Something had to be done about Eran, especially given the key role he played in Lucifer’s apocalyptic scheme. The fact that he toyed with the lives of Edgehaven’s people and targeted Maya to get at

Aiden only offered more of a reason to bring him down. The Nabi grunted in dissatisfaction, but conceded nonetheless.

"Can you find him," he asked Oriphiel as he returned to his sponge work. Oriphiel paused out of shock but crossed the room to kneel beside his prophet.

"Yes," the Archangel said as he placed a hand on Aiden's shoulder. Aiden ignored the gesture and continued to scrub with a fury like none other.

"Then I need you to go to him. Tell him to meet me at the top of Edgehaven Tower. We have a lot to discuss." Oriphiel nodded at the order and did his best to withhold the smile that pressed its way across his face, but he found the task impossible. As he turned away from the Nabi, Aiden stood up and placed a hand on his shoulder. "Oriphiel," he called, and the angel met his gaze. "I feel as though our little parley might warrant some… mediation. Would you—"

"I'd be more than happy to oblige," the Archangel said, and in a grand cloud of purple mist he vanished without a trace. *Eran*, Aiden stewed as he returned to his work, *this will end here.*

"That was incredibly refreshing," Maya said as she came back into the room. She paused for a moment when she saw the massive hole in the wall. "What happened here?" Aiden continued to scrub with his eyes focused on the floor.

"Nothing, I just slipped carrying the bucket from the sink," he assured her. He lifted himself to his feet and grabbed his Bible from the table. "I'm going to get you something new to wear. Stay inside, and under no circumstances are you to open the door for anyone."

"I'm not a child, Aiden," Maya said as she folded her arms and wandered over to her designated lawn chair. "Besides, I'm dressed in a pair of men's sweatpants and a baggy t-shirt. With the bob I've got going on someone would easily mistake me for a hip-hop loving emo kid and that's just not something I want to cap off my day with. I'll gladly accept anything you can bring me."

"Good. If you get hungry, there's food in the kitchen. I'm off," he informed her, and before she had the chance to tell him to be careful he was already out the door. He descended the steps and left his apartment building with haste. The heat of the day and the vibrant color of the sky were gone, and all that remained was a strikingly familiar combination of cold and dark. He hurried down the street and into an alley as a police car circled the block. Luckily for him he had no visual signatures to pick up on besides his face, so as long as he kept a low profile he could cross the city undetected. Still, he climbed the nearest fire escape as a precaution and moved towards the tower by the rooftops. The site of the meeting was only a half-mile from his home, and Aiden knew that the time was upon him to do what he hadn't been willing to so many years before.

The sirens of the cop cars below blared through the city while helicopters patrolled the skies. *This might be more challenging than I thought,* Aiden mused. He ducked behind the billboard of the next building and peeked around the corner to count the choppers within the span of his present position. *Five of them,* he thought. *This should make for a nice warm up.* Without warning he dashed across the rooftop, and just a second before the searchlight hit him, he jumped to the next one. Aiden avoided stops in order to escape the possibility of being caught, and with a few leaps more he broke the halfway point. A loud crack of thunder sounded overhead, no doubt Oriphiel's signal that Bloodsport received the message, and as he moved ever closer to the mark, his mind went wild in imagination.

He imagined what Eran's eyes would look like once their natural color wiped the black out for good, whether or not Eran would embrace him as a brother or despise him for tricking him, and more than that he imagined the look on Lucifer's face when he realized that his main power supply had been cut off. *How will Eran feel to once again be free?* Aiden knew there was only one way to find out.

"Eran," Aiden growled with a Uriel-esque excitement, "I'm on my way." He mouthed a quick prayer under his breath, and in a subtle flash, the blue hooded cloak returned. The flames of the Holy Spirit that rested on his shoulders flickered about with an excitement that mirrored the beat of his heart, and without a second to spare he dashed faster into the night.

Chapter Eight

Bloodsport mulled over the events of the day as they played back in his mind. It had been twelve years, so why couldn't he get the image of Aiden's devastated expression out of his head? His heart ached day after day with no sign of an end. The images flashed like lightning in the depths of his mind, and his comrade's screams of anguish penetrated the silence of the still world around him. *So what*, he forced himself to think as the sights, sounds and smells of the incident recreated themselves in horrid lucidity. He watched his own actions, actions he was proud of play back, and for the life of him he, in his ambitious rationalization of the situation, couldn't understand why his brother hadn't joined him. A grin of disbelief slinked across his face even now. It was almost as if Aiden, who all but literally walked through fire with Eran, didn't want to see him come into the power that he was destined to take. No doubt this little meeting was an ill-planned attempt at swaying him from his goal, but he knew that it was already too late. He had taken all the power that he had ever wanted, and before Lucifer destroyed the world, Eran was intent on exercising every ounce of his new strength. Still though, something spoke to him out of the darkness that he embraced so readily. He closed his eyes in an effort to extinguish that voice, but instead heard the brother he so willingly abandoned scream his name as he watched Eran fall into the black abyss below Tel Megiddo.

He must be destroyed, called the Seed of Flesh. *Start with his heart!*

Shut up, Eran snapped inwardly. *I know what I'm doing... don't I?* Even now he had his doubts about his darkened path, and even now he wrestled with the nature of the Seed despite his own drive for a heroic life. The Scriptures that were drilled into his mind warred with the life that for twelve long years rooted itself in his selfish ambitions, his fits of rage and his hatred, and while the sliver of his true self, the Nabi that was buried in the mire of such a sinful nature as this sought liberation, he found himself overwhelmed by the weight of the black that rained upon him.

He opened his eyes to the present pain that persisted through the twelve years since that day. The sound of thunder roared up above as lightning flashed through the dark clouds veiled by the all-encompassing shadow of the night sky. His eyes narrowed in unparalleled ferocity. Bloodsport, the product of the Seed's growth that overshadowed what was once Eran, watched Edgehaven Tower in eager anticipation from the Marianne Luxury Hotel across the street. He longed for Aiden to appear upon the structure, as did the sliver of soul that still resided in that body, for the appearance of his former friend would either mean his deliverance from the Seed's controlling power, or a small victory for the man Eran had become.

Everything was in place for this encounter. The projectile disk he'd prepared with a video message had found its place in the side of the tower's helipad. The gift that he'd prepared for his brother had been delivered to his apartment building. All that there was to do now was wait.

I look forward to destroying him, came the hateful and sadistic voice of the Seed. It ate at him more and more as the days went by, and the fact that he maintained any glimmer of Eran Hewer at all was an act of God alone. Eran did his best to block out the voice of his maddening desires, to regain control of his body and mind, and prayed endlessly for some kind of release from his bondage. He begged God Almighty for the chance to show Aiden that he was still in there, just as he had done moments before his fall. Bloodsport, incredibly annoyed by the thoughts that continually filtered into his mind, closed his eyes yet again, and this time decided it best to confront his weaker half outright. It wouldn't have been the first time that he needed to take control, and he expected that it would likely not be the last, either.

"Why do you still hold onto that pathetic little prayer," Bloodsport asked. Eran, who within his own body hung from a fleshy cross with six bright red eyes, spat at his feet. He knew that it was the Seed's attempt to convince him to concede full control, but after twelve years, how could he do that? "You don't regret embracing me, do you?" Eran, who was too exhausted to speak aloud only continued to pray out of the deepest sense of desperation. He received the power of his Nabi form, only to have it siphoned away by the adulterated symbol of hope from which he dangled. The Seed of Flesh, Bloodsport, laughed at his attempt to break free. "Even now you're convinced you'll break free just because you pray about it. You realize that every time you take that form you just feed me your power, don't you? Give it up. It's been twelve years, and you're not going anywhere," it said as it drifted closer to Eran and placed a taunting finger on his forehead. "Not unless I say you are, that is." Eran spat in his eye this time and hoped that his defiant act would provoke Bloodsport to kill him, and though its temper did flare, the Seed of Flesh knew that in order to accomplish the Master's goal to do away with the Nabi and the world after him, Eran must be kept alive. Bloodsport turned his back to his prisoner. "You've only got your little Archangel friend to thank for this mess, you know," he said calmly as he wiped the saliva out of his eye. "The seal that keeps the demons out is what keeps me in, and since the Master planted me during the night of the raid on your precious Hall, all it took was a little Insecurity attack to ensure my immunity from your friends. By the time you stood at Tel Megiddo, all I had to do was give you a little push and the rest was easy. I think the funniest thing about it is that you actually thought that Aiden would join you." Eran, wide-eyed, looked up at the icy blue stare that matched his own. His face crumpled with a deep-seated sorrow and hatred that proved enough to halt his prayer. That hatred which burned deep within the pit of his belly poured into the cross and drained him all the more, much to the Seed's delight. "Oh, don't look at me like that," Bloodsport mused as he cupped his hand around his chin. "Aiden's a fighter. He's overcome every obstacle put in his path, beaten every challenge, and steeled his will beyond compare. All this time you assumed that you were chosen because you were destined for strength, when in actuality you were just weaker than the one we really wanted. I mean you had to know that to us you're nothing but a meat sack to be used for our entertainment. Once we're finished with you, you'll go the same way as those you've crushed in the past, just as weak, just as pathetic, just as alone." Eran hung from the cross in silence, completely defeated by the revelation of what was, and the Seed, Bloodsport, continued to watch the rooftops for any signs of life.

He'd calculated it perfectly, and as the clock ticked closer to the start of the most epic game he'd ever played, he relished in the silence. Aiden would arrive in about five minutes more. Eran watched from within, and grieved the actions he'd taken that led to this moment. His mind flashed back to the darkness of Tel Megiddo's pit. A mysterious force from within him caused his arm to reach for an unseen crevice in the wall of earth at his side. The momentum of his body proved too much for his joints and caused his shoulder to dislocate, but to his astonishment the same mysterious force that ultimately broke him repaired him just the same. Eran looked into the blackness and gulped at his brush with death.

That was a little close, wouldn't you say, came the eerily childlike voice of the Seed of Flesh from within him. Eran looked around in search of the source of the voice, but found nothing but unsettling black. *You can't create a new world if you die upon this rock.*

"Who are you," Eran called into the nothingness. The snicker of the Seed churned his stomach, and despite his hunger for a better civilization he knew that something was off when the voice assured him, "I'm the one who will save your life."

Eran refocused on Edgehaven Tower just the same as Bloodsport. Another crack of thunder sounded, and it was in a brilliant flash of light that they knew that Oriphiel was near. His heart beat faster now as his salvation was almost assured. Bloodsport closed his eyes as he breathed deeply, and calmly listened to the pitter-patter of raindrops against the concrete tiles of the rooftop. Though he felt the soft thud of water droplets against his body, his black and red flex-armor body suit prevented the water from soaking in. Four minutes remained, and the two realized that their closest friend and fiercest enemy, the most egregious of transgressors and magnificent of rescuers would soon wander into the location of his choosing. Eran reached behind him into one of his cargo pockets. His fingers lightly brushed against the edge of the chipped Airman's coin he'd received upon his graduation from basic training with Aiden at his side. A sense of accomplishment washed over him as he vividly remembered that day. For a moment, he could see the luster of the sun in his eyes and feel its warmth kiss his skin as he stood at attention and waited for the MTI to move his way.

The blow of the wind cooled the spots that the sun warmed, and with the shift of the trees he could also feel Aiden's eyes watch him with pride from the line behind him. Somehow he knew, even then, that the two would be connected for the remainder of their lives, and as the Technical Sergeant placed the coin in his hand, he knew that they were brothers with a purpose. He allowed the nostalgia behind the item, and even more so behind the moment to intensify as the hour drew near. Bloodsport furiously retracted his hand from the pocket and wondered why Eran was able to move his limbs of his own accord.

Three minutes remained, and with little hesitation he fixed his sights on the darkened rooftop. He could feel the air begin to chill as his racing heart slowed and his focus intensified. Bloodsport knew that Aiden and his Archangel friends were the only ones capable of breaking his hold on Eran besides, of course, the hostage himself. *They must be destroyed,* he repeated to himself, and more importantly to Eran. The Seed pulled the M110 from his back and aimed it at the space just in front of the disk. Two minutes. His body became loose as this tremendous weight lifted little by little from his shoulders. His eyes widened with a bloodlust he'd never even experienced, which surprised him given that he was the very *source* of bloodlust. He fantasized about the destruction of his foe, the pleasant scream of anguish that would erupt from his throat and the pool of blood that would form on the ground. He thought about how sweet it would be to watch as the light left his eyes, and how much sweeter it would be to hear Eran's screams as the one tether to his humanity vanished before his very eyes.

One minute. The thunder resounded overhead, and the image of the last time he saw Aiden smile crawled into the forefront of his mind. A tear slid down his cheek as his blood boiled to the point of eruption. To his horror, Eran could feel his hand tightly brace the handgrip of his weapon with his non-firing hand, and in the blink of an eye the blue flames of the Nabi's cloak shone in the darkness across the way. Bloodsport and Eran watched as the 35-year-old Aiden walked briskly to the helipad at the center of the roof. He looked around in the dark for his friend, but when he found that he was alone his eye caught the shine of the screen on the disk in the side of the landing. Bloodsport pressed a button on the side of his flex-armor mask, and the empty shine of the projectile's screen switched to an image of Eran's deranged smiling face. Eran felt his heart stop as Aiden froze in horror at the prerecorded video that he'd been forced to shoot earlier that day.

"Aiden…" he said teasingly. "Hi Aiden. I got your message loud and clear. Do you happen to know what your name means? I figured you might, since you were so fond of that kind of thing, but let's say that you didn't and I was revealing this information to you for the first time. It's an Irish name and it means 'little fire.' Well… you certainly lived up to that meaning didn't you? You were always the kind of person to just rush in guns hot, never taking the time to actually figure out a strategy. You thought you could just get me to show up to your little meeting and why? So you could trap me with Oriphiel and extract me from your little friend?" As he spoke, Eran jerked at the bonds of flesh that tied him to the cross. *Don't you talk to him,* he demanded. "I have news for you, Little Fire. Eran's mine now, body and soul, and there's nothing you can do about it." His tone became more menacing on the screen, and in reality he lay only a few meters away. *Aiden…* Eran, the real Eran, called his name over and over inside his own mind, still with the hope that his past connection would be able to reach him now. Bloodsport licked his lips, and as the video progressed, his finger slowly moved from the magazine well to the trigger. "Let me just teach you why that won't work. You see, my name means 'watchful one.' I see all, and I will always find a way to dash your hopes and crush your soul, in this life or the next. To put it simply, Aiden, you can't escape these eyes," he told him. "Now, Little Fire… burn away." The screen went black, and without another second of hesitation he pulled the trigger. The loud crack of the gun was masked by the thunderous boom of the heavens, but by the time the bullet left the muzzle, Eran regained control for only a moment and screamed to his wingman in despair.

"Aiden!" At the sound of that familiar voice, the flames on Aiden's shoulders engulfed the bullet and pointed back in the direction of its travel. Aiden, now aware that the Seed was not merely an influence but a separate entity entirely, caught sight of his comrade's body as it hunched over in pain. Eran grasped his head and staggered towards the edge of the roof, but Aiden waited silently where he stood. Bloodsport screamed in agony as the red cloak manifested on his shoulders over the flex-armor suit. The blaze of the scarlet flames burned his shoulders with an intensity that the falling rain failed to compete with, but in the next second it vanished. Eran fell from the ledge and plummeted toward the pavement below, but before contact could be made, Bloodsport grabbed onto the nearest window ledge. He looked down for a moment as his heart raced, and as he dangled there by a single arm, he groaned when the brilliant shine of a helicopter searchlight hit him.

"Hold on," said the pilot over the megaphone. "We're going to help you down." Bloodsport grabbed the Desert Eagle from his waist and pointed it at the windshield. The pilot opened his mouth to speak when the Seed fired without a thought and within seconds, the bullet that was launched forward penetrated the pilot's heart.

Blood splattered against the remainder of the glass and the man from whence it came fell onto the controls instantly. As the copilot found that his partner covered the radio with his body and there was no way for her to signal for help, she made the decision to jump from the now out of control aircraft and onto the roof of a nearby building. The assassin inhaled deeply as he pointed his gun at her, and savored the smell of the gun smoke before he fired once again. Much to his pleasure, the sound of her scream filled the night air and she fell like hunted game to the ground below. Eran's heart sank at the sound of the splat against the street, but the unfazed Bloodsport quickly pushed himself back to the top of the building where his signature rifle lay. He stowed it on his back and relished in the lack of resistance from his host.

"Was that really necessary," Aiden shouted from across the way as his anger boiled over. Bloodsport looked at him with those demonic black eyes of his as a vulpine smile crept into place.

"Not as necessary as this," he admitted as he pressed a button on his right cuff. A blast exploded from a few blocks behind Aiden which drew his attention for a moment. Bloodsport smiled, but before he slipped away into the now stormy night Aiden refocused his attention on his nemesis.
"Understand this, Aiden," Bloodsport cautioned as he pointed back, "I'm never gonna give up your little friend, I'm never gonna stop hunting you, and I'm never gonna stop destroying the things you love most." Aiden froze as the twisted Seed darted for the distant edge of the roof and jumped downward into an alley. He smashed his fist in aggravation against the side of the helipad, and broke the disk that contained the video message. He rushed back the way he came and jumped again from rooftop to rooftop. The blaze that lingered in the distance proved large enough to make the night shine like the day, and as he neared the origin point the heat began to escalate and take its toll. He wiped his brow and pressed on, and as the fire

spread, the flames of the Holy Spirit cloaked his entire body in a protective blaze that issued no warmth of its own.

Aiden watched as the fire took over and moved from building to building until walls of fire divided that section of the city, and while the sirens blared below and people ran for their lives, he dove to the street only to see that amid the raging inferno was none other than his own apartment building.

"Maya," he gasped in horror as he watched the windows explode and the glass pour onto the sidewalk. He immediately picked up speed and headed for the back of the complex, and though he hesitated, Aiden hurled himself into the blaze. The heat was unbearable, even with the protection of his cloak, but he couldn't stop. He had to find Maya and get her to safety. He made it up the stairs to his apartment, and walked through the doorway to find the unconscious therapist on the floor in the middle of the small space between his kitchen and his living room. He ran to her and immediately checked her pulse.

It was weak, but present, and the Nabi scooped the woman into his arms and carried her hastily outside. Fire trucks started to roll in, and Aiden ran as fast as he could while he carried the unconscious young woman.

"Oriphiel," he huffed as he ran. The Archangel who hovered in the skies above swooped down and grabbed him under his arms. He carried them into the air, and Aiden couldn't help but watch as the only place he had to rest his head went up in smoke. "We need to land somewhere."

"I agree. The time has come to properly assess the situation." Oriphiel descended to a dark alley out of the way of the choppers and squad cars that circulated through the main points of the city. Aiden gently leaned Maya against the wall and was careful to keep her out of immediate sight.

He turned his attention to the Archangel for but a moment before he considered it best to monitor her condition. "So, what do you intend to do now? Your plan so far has been disastrous at best and it wouldn't be a good idea to involve this one further," he said with a nod to Aiden's unauthorized companion. Aiden kept his eyes focused on her, and did his best to stabilize his heart as he placed his hand gently on her ribcage.

"'But He was pierced for our transgressions,'" Aiden started as her breathing got weaker. His resolve was shaken in the moment and his attentions divided between three separate issues. A faint light gleamed beneath his hand, but quickly faded. No change occurred in Maya's condition.

"She needs a hospital," Oriphiel suggested. "It would be a good idea for me to take her to one. You will need all your strength for your battle with Lord Eran. Bloodsport has no intention of giving him back, and with time as short as it is, it would be unwise for you to waste energy healing this single girl when the entire world hangs in the balance." Aiden perked up in indignation and turned to face his guardian and advisor.

"You have to take her to the Hall of Nabi'im," he pressed as he stood to his feet. Oriphiel's eyes flared in surprise at the obviously asinine request, and though he sought some kind of confirmation that this was a joke, Aiden offered none.

"That is impossible," Oriphiel responded when he realized that Aiden was serious. "The Hall is only accessible to the Archangels, the Nabi'im, and of course, the Lord Himself. No outsider has ever breeched those walls—"

"Except Lucifer's shadow and the demonic forces he led," Aiden shot back as the flames on his shoulders flared in his anger. "Now's not the time to argue about this, Oriphiel." He looked over to the young woman that he'd saved so many times within the span of four days, and prayed for her out of the desperation of the situation. "Having her taken to any hospital in the city is out of the question. The police have been after her since we escaped the skirmish with Bloodsport earlier and considering the fact that three policemen and women have died in pursuit of her, the situation won't look too promising should she awaken. And the way things look right now…" Aiden paused and bent down again to check to see if she still drew breath. She did, shallow though they were, but the fact that she was still alive was more than enough to ease his rocky nerves.

"She could die at any minute," Oriphiel interjected. "For that I am deeply sorry, Lord Aiden, but there are greater things at stake than the life of one girl! Surely you must understand that if you waste any more time, the chance for salvation could be lost permanently! Armageddon is upon us, and you want to sit here and coddle the pretty blonde!" Aiden lost his temper and immediately delivered a punch to Oriphiel's jaw. It didn't faze him, but still the angelic host struggled to hold himself back.

"Allow me to enlighten you on the situation, Oriphiel. Maya is a person, just as I am. In case the concept went over your head, that means that her life is just as significant as any other out there, and *that* means that she deserves the opportunity to enjoy the salvation you want me to bring about. That's exactly why Christ died on the cross at Golgotha, isn't it? So that all would have the opportunity to enjoy the benefit of salvation at His expense?" Oriphiel remained silent, as he very well couldn't formulate an argument that would stand against the logic Aiden presented. "Take her to the Hall. Immediately," he commanded before his guardian had the opportunity to protest. "Have Elijah tend to her. I'll be there as soon as I finish up in Edgehaven." Oriphiel walked over to Maya, and with an aggravated huff scooped her up again and held her in his massive arms. He walked out of the alley, and in a literal flash of lightning the two vanished from Edgehaven entirely.

I'm never gonna stop destroying the things you love most, he heard Bloodsport repeat in his head over and over again. Aiden slammed his fist hard against the brick wall that Maya once rested against, and the foundation of the building itself seemed to rattle.

"You planned this," Aiden barked through the falling rain. He ran to the nearby fire escape and ascended to the rooftops as the thoughts circled in his mind. The only reason Bloodsport agreed to the meeting he didn't actually attend was so he could lure Aiden away. He attempted to assassinate him, but in the event that it didn't work the contingency plan was always to blow up his apartment building with Maya in it. *So,* he thought as his anger started to take control, *you've been watching me all along?* The fury of the rain escalated and the winds grew more ferocious. Lightning flashed overhead and thunder roared as a wild beast does in the thick of the jungle. The city was blanketed in what was a mirror of Aiden's rage. None of this would have happened if he'd been able to rely on his God rather than himself, if he'd let go of the past and focused on the future.

Aiden howled in frustration and watched as the helicopters retreated, but he refused to seek shelter. Where did he have to go? No, he realized in that moment as the image of Maya's unconscious body flashed before his eyes that it was time for him to abandon his misery and seek the righteous power that enabled him to shine with light in the darkness. He breathed in deeply for but a moment, but with the next flash of lightning he made his descent and ran for the location where he'd last seen his old war-buddy and the thing that held him captive.

"'I do believe; help me overcome my unbelief!'" Aiden shouted the words of Scripture into the night sky as he moved for Edgehaven Tower, and as the final expression crossed his lips the flames flared with an intensity that forced a stop. Aiden felt a wave of heat rush over his body and the cloak that covered his length glowed radiantly enough to dwarf the shine of the lightning that flashed overhead. "What… what's happening to me," he barely had the strength to ask aloud. His veins pumped with an ineffable power, and the sound of his voice was almost alien to him. He fell to his knees and his eyes met his reflection in the ripples of a puddle, and he saw the Hebrew inscription for "Nabi" written in pure light along the front of his hood.

He stood straight up and charged into the darkness as images of Bloodsport's path filtered into his vision. A street sign that read "Marlon Road" appeared to him, and without missing a beat, Aiden Zane dashed across the street and through a series of alleyways. He saw an abandoned gas station next that looked as though it was positioned between a small inn and a convenience store, and as his vision focused on it he knew beyond a shadow of a doubt that his brother was holed up at that location.

Aiden could hardly contain himself as righteous anger took over, and with a voice that echoed the ferocity of the thunder, he yelled into the chaos of the storm, "Eran!"

Chapter Nine

Oriphiel materialized in the dark tunnel just outside the Hall of Nabi'im with the injured Maya in his arms. He glanced over his shoulder at the spot where he once did battle with Lucifer's shadow over the Two, and where Aiden and Eran had descended from the world above. He remembered the shock he felt as he peered upon their faces for the first time and he knew, not out of some vision given to him by God, but by their sheer determination to live despite their injuries that those two men would be a force to change this world of theirs. The Archangel contemplated that feeling, and wondered if he was wrong to assume that the two of them were capable of such a feat. One had been corrupted by his own selfish ambition of achieving ultimate power, while the other became so enthralled with the protection of each individual that he seemingly overlooked the world as a whole.

He looked down on the sleeping girl. Her fair skin reminded him distinctly of Eran, though it was much paler than his due to her growing lack of oxygen, and he pushed her mussed brown hair out of her soft-featured face.

"I don't understand what he sees in you that he would forsake his calling," he started as he walked closer to the ancient stone doors of the Hall. *Her life is just as significant as any other out there and that means that she deserves the opportunity to enjoy the salvation you want me to bring about.* Aiden's words echoed in his mind as if to answer the question. He shook his head with a smile on his face, as no other Nabi before him was so intent on the preservation of every single human life, but his heart for the people couldn't have come at a worse time.

Oriphiel marched for the doors, and when they opened on their own they revealed the black and gold patterns and spirals that decorated the Hall's lobby. The other Archangels descended from above at the sudden change in the atmosphere and surrounded Oriphiel.

"Why have you brought this woman here," Michael, the eldest of the hosts demanded with an irate shimmer in his gold and silver eyes as he trained them on the girl. He was stronger than Oriphiel, and perhaps the strongest of all the Archangels. His silver armor bore sharp edges that set it apart from Lucifer's and signified his position as the undisputed leader of the pack, no matter how much fear Uriel instilled in him. "This place isn't for her, Oriphiel. You know this."

"Of course I do, Michael," Oriphiel sighed in reply. "I would never bring her here of my own free will. You of all the angels in Heaven should know that."

"Then why would you bring her?" Uriel questioned from his left.

"Lord Aiden demanded that I do so. She's dying, and her injuries are beyond his ability to heal." The congregation of angelic warriors all widened their eyes in utter shock. "I've been instructed to take her to the High King so her life can be spared."

"Oriphiel, do you even have any idea how many laws you're breaking with this one act? Regardless of if someone else ordered you to do it, this is wrong and you know that full well," Gabriel of the Tidal Wave spoke from behind him as he brushed his blond hair out of his marble-toned face and meticulously straightened out his ocean-blue robe.

"Now, now," came the understanding voice of the High King, Elijah the Flame Prophet, as he descended to the center of the room from the Grand Hall. His long silver hair drooped around his head like an umbrella and his soft amber eyes came alive with joy at the presence of another human. He walked over to her and gently placed a wrinkly hand upon her forehead, and as a small light emanated from his palm the girl jerked to life for but a moment. Her breathing returned to normal, and the angels in the room stood amazed at the feat. "Whether or not you can see it, Aiden was right to bring this woman here. The poor thing has been thrust into a world she knew nothing of, and involved in a war in which she has no business. It is only natural that we shield her from any more harm, rather than allow her to perish in the crossfire. After all, it is our duty to protect all life on earth, and by that standard we would break all the laws by turning away those we thought unworthy of our service." The crowd of generals in the Lord's army dared not argue with a King. Elijah turned from them and headed for the hall at the upper right of the room that lay opposite of the one Aiden once called his home. "Come along," he beckoned, "we do not have these vacant rooms so they can collect dust." Oriphiel marched along after him until they came to a large emerald door. Elijah smiled as he opened it, and ushered in his servant and their impromptu guest.

The interior of the room was an extravagant emerald design lined with ivory accents, and the comforter on the bed was the perfect shade of brown to give the room the impression of an immaculately kept garden. It was by far Elijah's favorite room in the entire Hall, as it not only possessed the solitude he sometimes needed, but reminded him of what his earthly life was like before his ascent into Heaven. Because of that semblance of life, he could think of no better place in all the world to facilitate her healing.

Oriphiel placed her gently on the bed and left to tend to his brothers and sisters, but Elijah stayed by her side. It intrigued him that Aiden would have a connection to a woman at all, let alone have her teleported to the

Hall of Nabi'im for protection. Ever since he and Eran first wandered into this life, Aiden always seemed to be a man for the job and nothing more, and Elijah was left to wonder if this entanglement with the lovely brunette would blossom into something more.

He desperately wished it would, because he never had the opportunity to find love for himself, and as the days flew by he was alarmed to see so much of himself in the young Nabi. Still, it was exactly that similarity that told Elijah that Aiden would most likely never seek out a wife.

"Times have changed, I suppose," he muttered to himself upon the reflection of his mother's voice, how she at one point so many centuries ago urged him to take a wife. He looked down on the young woman and smiled to mask the tinge of sadness that she couldn't have seen. "Hopefully," he spoke to her with an infinitesimal air of cheeriness in his voice, "your condition changes as well." He maintained his watch over her in the tranquility of the emerald room and basked in his memories for a while. He spent so much time in expectation of the future that he found his relief in the events of the past.

The Kerith Ravine was perhaps his favorite place to go. He remembered the way the water of the Jordan sparkled at the time, and how the sand on the riverbank would shimmer in the light of the setting sun. He walked over to the green and white chair that rested by the door and sat down to rest his old bones. Even now, some 2900 years after his first encounter with the beauty of that place, he could feel the sun against his skin and the stillness of the area in his very soul. He leaned back in the armchair and rested against the comfortable headrest, and as he basked in his memories he gently drifted off to sleep.

As he snored, Maya's heartbeat quickened and her brow began to sweat. Images of deformed beasts and panicked people flashed in her mind. Fire and lightning surged on opposite sides of a majestic green field, and while the former swept over the people the latter took down the monsters until the forces of nature met at a slab of earth in the center. A pair of giant black and red eyes that she knew to be Lucifer's opened in the scarlet sky, and the lush green color of the plants on the terrain was drained until naught but black remained. The elements wrestled with each other in the center of the field as the eyes fed off the light and the life of everything around them. The view expanded, and while the tornado of elemental bursts was still visible, the entire planet came into focus, and little by little, the radiant mixture of green and blue and white all vanished to leave only darkness in its place. She gasped in awe, and in the next instant numerous lines of red spread over the globe like veins through the body, and like pus-filled cysts, the mountains and the hills of the earth erupted with molten lava.

"What is this," Maya asked in terrified astonishment as the red slowly mingled with the black, and at the sound of her voice the delighted red eyes that watched the world at a distance turned their attention on her.

"You," came the menacing baritone that was Lucifer, "you will die here." A gargantuan armored hand appeared in the vast darkness and slowly moved for her.

"No," she screamed as she tried to outrun it, but her efforts proved fruitless as the lengthy fingers of the silver-clad hand slowly closed around her.

"I am destined to rule this world," Lucifer asserted. "I cannot allow you the opportunity to change that." As his sentence came to a close, so did his fist, and what little light rested in her line of sight vanished entirely.

She twitched in her bed, but her breath remained steady and her heart still beat. *Excellent,* she thought, *I'm still alive.* A bright light flashed in her consciousness, and to her surprise she stood upon a golden platform that floated high above the heavens and the decayed earth below. The pulse of lightning and the blast of fire still did battle below, unaware of what their environment had become, and as they reached their final altercation, a cataclysmic blast shattered the world like glass.

"It doesn't look very good this way, does it, Maya," she heard a strong but soothing voice whisper from the background. She looked around into the nothingness and saw a faint shimmer of light off in the distance that stood out among the stars. She stared for a moment, but yelped as the platform itself readily sped off to meet that striking illumination.

"What on earth is going on," Maya screamed as the speed continually picked up. The voice from the background chuckled.

"I have brought you here to show you what will happen if Lucifer is allowed to remain outside his cage. My Nabi'im will become so distracted by their own personal warfare that my wayward son Lucifer will be able to initiate an Apocalypse all his own. He will reign in darkness upon the earth until the entire world is corrupted to the point of irrevocable death," explained the voice. Maya stood confused on her suspended disk.

"What does that have to do with me?" she asked as she continued to flash forward on the golden stand.

"Since the very beginning I made you special, Maya. Ever since you were a little girl wrapped in a blanket in your mother's arms, I've known that you would come here." Maya felt a slow chill ease its way down her spine as the mysterious voice spoke.

“Who are you,” she demanded. The voice chortled again as the mobile base slid into a stop at the massive doorway that surrounded the previously distant light.

“I apologize for my rudeness. You see,” he continued to explain, “there was once a time where I would speak and people would recognize my voice automatically. Over time, however, I have been cast aside little by little and my Enemy of a son worshiped ever the more. It doesn’t strike me as odd that even my chosen don’t know my voice when I call, nor does it upset me. In fact, I relish in the opportunity to grasp their attention and remove all doubt as to who I am.” Maya stepped into the light, and once her eyes adjusted to the luminescence, she noted a mountainous throne with an emerald ring around its legs at the center of a long onyx-tiled floor, and from the seat itself emanated the familiar glow of blue flames. The voice spoke again, but more passionately than before, “I am the one known as Elohim, Jehovah, Yahweh, the King of Kings and Lord of Lords! I am the Alpha and the Omega, the beginning and the end, the Christ, the Messiah, the Savior.” As His words echoed throughout the universe its foundations rattled and Maya, insignificant as she was in that moment, fell absolutely still. “You have no reason to be afraid, my dear child. Very few ever get the chance to step into my presence, and when they do it isn’t because I want them dead.”

“Then if I may ask,” started the girl with a tremble in both her voice and her body, “why have you brought me here? What do you mean, I’m special?”

“You are familiar with the Two, yes?” He asked as a small ball of flame detached from the massive inferno that rested above the throne and met her across the room as its hue changed from blue to red. She nodded in confirmation. "Since the day Lucifer was contained in the Bottomless Pit at Tel Megiddo, I knew very well that he would do everything in his power to break free of the bonds placed on him upon my death at Golgotha, all in some less-than-grand attempt at throwing off my plans. That's why the Two endure to this day. Their purpose is and always has been to protect the world from demon-kind and to restore balance to nature, both spiritual and carnal."

"And now they're stuck in an endless cycle of bloodshed and battle with each other," Maya said as she looked away, and imagined the cold betrayal on the day of the release twelve years prior. She began to shake in fury and sorrow, and as her eyes filled with water she turned back to the floating ball of fire. "Please, you have to do something to snap them out of it."

"I can't," He said flatly, which threw the poor girl, a mere child in His eyes, into a state of unmistakable confusion.

"What do you mean you can't?" She begged desperately. "You created the entire universe from nothing, engineered biology and physics and chemistry, provided the foundation for all that we know and keep the secrets of all we don't and you say that two little boys throwing temper tantrums are somehow beyond your power?"

"There was a time around the middle of my ministry on the earth where after I finished my travels for a short while, I returned to Nazareth, my hometown. I taught in the synagogue to any who were willing to learn of the Kingdom of God and the salvation that I brought. I performed very few miracles in that place, however, and do you know why?" Maya shook her head, and the blazing orb continued. "The reason why I was unable to do much is because I can't change the conditions of people who don't trust me completely. In the beginning, I gave you the choice to come to me of your own volition. A standard that I keep and have kept over the millennia is that I will not override your choices under any circumstance."

"Then this is bad," she all but yelled. She began to pace the floor, horrified that the possibility of that dream of hers would inevitably become the reality of the world.

"No, it isn't," He said, which stopped the frantic woman in her tracks. She turned back to face Him with her hand raised slightly below her chin and a hopeful expression on her face.

"What do you mean?"

"Tell me, Maya, why exactly did you take such an interest in Aiden's life in the first place?" The question caught her off guard. She hadn't really thought about the motivation for her fascination, but she had always felt drawn to him, or rather, to something inside of him ever since she first accidentally ran into him on the sidewalk. But then it wasn't just him. Even when she learned of his past and became distantly acquainted with Eran, she knew that she had a connection with not just one, but both of them. It was as if they'd always been familiar to her. That's why she sat with Aiden for three days while he slept soundly in a hospital bed. That's why she asked him—no, begged him—to share more of his story than what he felt was comfortable with. She didn't know it at the time, but she had always been connected to them. "Are you wondering why they pull you in?" She nodded in discomfort at having her mind read so easily. *I always figured myself much more complex than that,* she mused. "Nothing is complex in my eyes," said the Lord. "There has always been something inside of you for such a time as this that would only come out once you got in contact with the right people. The state of things may look grim to you, but I've always had an answer to this problem: you."

"I don't understand," Maya quickly protested. The Lord hummed in curiosity.

"What is there to understand? I've already equipped you to change the situation. You have that power, and I was careful to place people and even my Archangels in your life to help you refine it for the effective rebuilding of my Kingdom on Earth. All you have to do now is trust that what I've given you will be enough." The color of the ball of flames changed again, only this time to the same emerald hue as the ring beneath the throne. The orb encircled her slowly before it touched her lips gently and parted them. The ball of fire entered her mouth, and as she closed her lips again she felt a rush of power surge within her.

"What just happened," she asked aloud as she looked down at her hands.

"I have put my words in your mouth. See, today I appoint you over nations and kingdoms to uproot and tear down, to destroy and overthrow, to build and to plant. Return now, Maya, and walk in the power that you've been given." In an instant, the heavenly realm vanished and she was pulled sharply downward as the great flame watched. She picked up speed and screamed as she plummeted to the world below, and in the next moment all was dark.

She heard the sound of an old man's snores fill her ears, and in a panic she jolted awake in the emerald room. She held her head as she watched the world around her spin in a hopeless attempt to make it stop. She let out a soft groan as she contemplated the wild dream she must have had and slid her hand down her face. Her lips burned upon contact, and for just a moment she was under the impression that the dream was in fact much more than that, but soon remembered that she had previously been in a fire at Aiden's apartment.

Where am I... she questioned as she looked around at the stunning green and ivory. She slowly picked herself up from the bed and wandered over to the wall to run her hand along the side. Something about the color scheme just clicked with her. *There has always been something inside of you for such a time as this...* she heard the voice of the Lord echo from the back of her mind. Still her sense of reality was warped. She walked along the edge of the room silently so as not to disturb the sleeping man who, for one reason or another, seemed strikingly familiar to her.

She watched him as she moved beyond the bed, and out of the corner of her eye she noticed a robe of green and ivory adorned with embroidered leaves that sat on a black chest at the foot. It all but called to her, and as she moved closer to the garment and fell deeper under its spell, she failed to notice the opening eyes of the man who guarded her. She lightly brushed her fingertips along the length of the robe. It was soft and warm, and most unusual to her, she could feel a manifestation of life within the threads. It was as if these clothes had a heartbeat of their own. Elijah watched her in silence and smiled, because though she remained clueless, he knew exactly what was happening.

"You seem to have taken a liking to that robe," he commented as he watched the way her hand lingered over it, even as she jumped in surprise. She looked into his old amber eyes and realized exactly who this man was.

"Wait a minute," she began, "you're..."

"Not to worry, I will allow you to get changed. You should come to meet me in the Grand Hall later." He stood up from the chair and straightened out his clothes before he opened the emerald door and departed from her. She found it frustrating that he hadn't bothered to stay and answer her questions, but then realized the terrible condition of her now smoke-scented clothes and figured that a change of wardrobe was probably the best course of action for that moment. She stripped off the blood-soaked, smoked out, ripped and dirty dress that at one point had been so elegant and clothed herself in the pure and vibrant robe laid out for her.

She took a moment to truly feel the warmth of it against her skin and admired herself in the mirror. She felt as if every outfit she owned was a mockery of the one that graced her body here and now, and the illustrious designs and big names that filled her closet were nothing in comparison. Still, the immediacy of her curiosity prompted her to return to her present circumstance and glide gracefully away from the mirror and towards the door. As she approached, she could hear the familiar voice of Oriphiel argue with several others. She slowly opened the door and moved into the lengthy and dimly lit hall. She silently crept toward the open space that was the lobby and noted the images of the Archangels on the pillars. She stopped behind the one closest to the foyer and leaned against it to keep out of the line of sight. She looked up to see a name printed in the same ancient text as before, and to her shock she could read it through her own eyes as if it were her first language. It read "Michael," and the image above it depicted a strong masculine Archangel in a solid silver robe with powerful features and terrifying gold and silver eyes. They matched those of his siblings, however she felt that they were somehow much more forceful.

"Look," Oriphiel begged in exhaustion, "it no longer matters what the reason is for her being here, the fact is that it isn't safe for her to return.

Why is this discussion going on when the High King already approved of her refuge here?"

"It isn't the verdict, Oriphiel," came the voice of the silver clad Archangel who stood at the far rim of the circular floor, "It's the principle. You violated the laws that we are appointed to uphold."

"The fact that we obey the King of Kings is what sets us apart from Lucifer and his kind. Are you really so eager to throw your hat in with the likes of *them*?" Uriel questioned. Oriphiel's attention shifted to her, and though inwardly he fumed with rage, he did his best to contain himself.

"If it were so pertinent to keep her away from this place as you so repetitively point out to me," Oriphiel snapped, "then why would the High King insist that we house her? What grounds do you have to doubt the will of the one who hears from Elohim when even we do not? Besides, if she was truly meant to be kept from entering this place, the doors would never have opened to her regardless of the company that brought her here." The Archangels fell silent for a moment as they stewed upon his words. Maya watched on from her position behind the pillar and rubbed the space above her heart. She, who had always been taught that she was something special, suddenly felt as if her presence were nothing more than a bother. "I'm waiting," Oriphiel insisted. "Please, give me your response. Let me know exactly what I did wrong in bringing someone here who was obviously meant to be involved in this!" His brothers and sisters remained silent. "Then if that will be all, I suppose I should go tend to the girl and see how she's doing. If you'll excuse me…" he trailed off as he turned away from them and walked in her direction.

As if on cue, she walked out into the open from behind the pillar to the surprise of all that stood in the room. She approached Oriphiel cautiously and instantly locked eyes with Uriel as she expected a fireball at any moment. As she drew nearer to the Archangel of her immediate choice, she caught a glimpse of Michael, and felt a shockwave pulse through her body. She looked back at Oriphiel, who stared down at her in curiosity, but quickly pressed onward to the elder of the two. Michael watched in aggressive confusion as she approached.

"Pardon me," she started, and the cluster of angelic generals gawked at her in awe. She immediately grew self-conscious, but decided to express her question regardless. "I was told to visit Elijah in the Grand Hall. Would you, by any chance, be willing to take me?" Every pair of eyes in the room fell on Michael, but his were locked on the small girl who stood before him. His heart beat at a rate he was unfamiliar with, and suddenly a cool washed over him, as if this was meant to happen.

"How can you speak in this tongue…?" he asked her. The room was silent as each entity eagerly awaited an answer.

"That's ridiculous. I've always spoken Eng—" Maya started. Before she could finish her thought, however, she heard a language other than the one she started to confess spill from her lips. "I-I don't know…" Michael met Oriphiel's gaze, and to his discomfort his younger brother brandished an overly confident grin. He turned his attention back to Maya as Oriphiel walked towards the colossal white marble staircase. He scratched his head for a moment, and then tensed his body entirely.

"Yes," he answered sternly. "I will take you to the chamber of the High King." With a glimmer of hope in her eye, she followed him as he started for the stairs and clasped her hands together in fear as she remembered the trial that would surely come.

Chapter Ten

Lucifer watched Aiden remotely from a portal in the shadows as the faith-filled Nabi chased Eran through the city. Aiden continually screamed the name of his best friend, fed up with the chase and eager for its end, and the Seed that controlled Eran's body grew exceedingly determined to drag it on just a little while longer. The Devil smiled as he turned away and walked along the grotesque spider-like growth that filled the massive crack through the remnant of Tel Megiddo. He sought the well, that wretched hole in the ground that for so long had been his prison.

A horde of feral demons covered the base and slopes of the Tel with their eyes locked on their master as he moved. The snarls they breathed were but music to his ears, and as he strode he realized how much he missed it. He took a dagger that matched his eyes from its sheath on his belt and slit open his open palm. A black slime emerged in the place of blood, and as he approached the hole in the earth, his eyes glimmered with a sadistic glee as the feeling of unencumbered victory settled in.

"Finally," he spoke to himself with a shiver, "a world created in *my* image!" Lucifer basked in the glory that his demonic minions offered him, and fed on the numerous displays of sin around the globe. His darkness had become much stronger now than it had been twelve years prior, and the time was almost right to unleash his ultimate chaos upon the unsuspecting world around him. Still, he would be a fool to overlook the obvious power of Aiden Zane. Lucifer reached the well and turned his back to it. He opened his blackened palm and thrust his hand into the sky.

The clouds emptied of their light and swirled together to form the eye of a massive storm. Lightning struck his palm, and the feeling that rippled through his arm satiated him with pleasure. In that moment, he could feel the darkest of his servants stir from within. The opening had already been made; the life force had been given. All Lucifer needed to do now was watch and wait. The screeching snarls of the beasts that surrounded him drew louder now, and heightened his sense of euphoria. The black sludge that rested in his palm now spilled over onto the ground. Two puddles formed, and as the slime started to stir, Lucifer's eyes glowed brightest red and darkest black.

"They're coming," he howled into the dark clouds above. "Arise, Legion the Multitude! Come forth, Moloch the Incinerator! Take your rightful places at my side and rid me of my enemies! Seek out the one known as the Nabi; destroy him that is known as Aiden Zane… and then the world shall be ours!" The dark aura that rested on him slowly encased the puddles of ooze that lay to his right and to his left. They pulsed and expanded, and the Dark Master watched on as two shadowy figures emerged from their depths.

The first solidified, and as the rather slim figure opened his eyes he erupted in a blood-chilling screech that caused uproarious snarls throughout the dark army below the Tel. Nothing but pure darkness covered his naked body, and with a maniacal laugh he kneeled before Satan. The Devil looked upon the many scars that marked his sharp-featured face, and as he placed his right hand upon his pitch-black hair, the evil manifestation he'd called from the depths donned the same sinister red and black eyes of his master.

"Whatever you command, my lord, we will carry it out to the letter," spoke the monster. Lucifer's smirk grew all the wider at a sound most pleasant to his ears.

"Legion," the Author of Confusion spoke with what sounded like affection. "It has been quite some time since we worked together on anything. Tell me, how would you feel about getting your feet wet in a fight against a Nabi?" Legion's demonic eyes lit with a bloodlust unique to him, and the serpentine grin that slithered across his lips chilled the Devil himself. "Very well, then. Now, we should be expecting company at any moment." Their eyes shifted from each other to the other pool of black sludge as a much larger beast emerged. He appeared at the base of the well fully clothed in black silk that accentuated his muscles, much unlike the shadow-clad creature conjured ahead of him. The horns of a bull protruded from either side of his bright red scalp, and the air began to sting from the heat that emanated from his body. He bellowed from the pit of his gut as he slammed his fists against the ground. His eyes opened and immediately locked with Lucifer's. His facial expression twisted in displeasure, and Lucifer knew immediately that this particular summon would be problematic.

"Why have you summoned me here," demanded the great beast. Lucifer's eyes lit with a vampiric bloodlust as he balled his fist at his side. "I am a god. It does not bode well for me to do business with the likes of devils."

"The mouth on this one," Legion giggled from the background. Moloch's already crimson eyes locked on him with a sort of hungry disposition. "We don't like it… Shall we rectify it for you, my lord?" The dark aura that surrounded Legion flared with excitement, but Lucifer paid him no mind.

"You were once a man, and are a god in regard only," spake the Demon Prince. "Your followers have long since faded into the growing distance that is the past, and so what godly influence you once held is now diminished." Lucifer marched over to Moloch and stared him down with those monstrous eyes and whispered, "Do not forget that it is because of *me* that you retain any power at all." Moloch growled and pushed Lucifer to the ground, and the pack of ravenous beasts that guarded the slopes of Tel Megiddo exploded in irate howls and snarls. Lucifer held up his hand as he picked himself up, and though the monsters couldn't see it, all fell silent at his command. Legion made no effort to withhold laughter as he watched the fiery power leave Moloch's massive body and enshroud Beelzebub. The pagan god dropped to his knees and trembled uncontrollably.

"What did you do to me," he questioned as he spat at Satan's feet in disgust. Lucifer, who tended to take great pleasure in the helpless confusion of others, scowled at his defiant servant as he passively lifted a single finger into the air. To his horror, Moloch was swiftly hoisted above the ground and suspended, and Lucifer watched him in disturbing severity.

"Allow me to make something unmistakably clear to you, Moloch. You will obey me," he said as he twitched his finger and caused the meaty oaf to fall to the earth, "or you will witness first-hand my destructive capabilities." He returned power to Moloch, and the revitalized minion bowed begrudgingly before his new master.

"Very well," he started in a reptilian growl, "but perhaps you can help me to understand something." Lucifer smashed a fist against the ground, and a spiky black throne erupted from out of the earth. He sat upon it and motioned for his slave to speak. "I can understand why you would bring me here. But why would you pair me with this *thing* when you know full well that I can handle any challenge set before me on my own?"

“Because the challenge we face is a Nabi by the name of Aiden Zane,” Lucifer clarified with calm irritation. He watched Moloch twitch with anger at the mere mention of the word “Nabi,” and the sting in the air intensified. The horns on his head lined themselves with flames and the beasts that walked the valley below vociferated in agony. “Watch yourself, Moloch. You have been without sacrifices for quite some time. I would assume that you would be more conservative, lest you permanently revert to your human form.” Moloch, deeply angered though he was, knew that that was the cost of his power. He looked over at Legion, envious that he was born a demon and had no limitations to his strength, and the more he analyzed the monster beside him the more he realized that no matter how much of a god he thought himself to be, he would always be nothing more than a pitifully disgusting man. The sting in the air ceased, and the beasts below groaned in relief as they dropped to the ground to bathe in the coolness of the dirt.

“The temper on this one,” Legion cried humorously. He bounced around the terrain and toyed with Moloch’s cheeks. “We might have to be careful playing around with you.” Before Moloch could speak a word, Lucifer raised his hand and the demon wannabe closed his mouth.

“That is more than enough, Legion. There is much to discuss.” The jovial Legion returned to his spot on the left side of the well and faced his master Lucifer. “The time is upon us to stake claim to this world with me as its new ruler, and I have selected the two of you to aid me in that endeavor. As it stands, I am in control of one of the Nabi’im and have successfully tempted him from beyond the walls of my prison with his own dark desires, but the other, this aforementioned Aiden Zane, is not so easily swayed to abandon the side of light. It is not important that I go so far as to explain the details. All you need to know is that he stands in my way. So, destroy him, and when you lay his broken body at my feet I will bestow upon you gifts the likes of which you have never imagined."

Legion jumped with joy at the mere mention of destruction, but Moloch remained as stern as when he appeared. There was but one thing that he wanted, one thing that eluded him since his time as the first king of Ammon: absolute power. Without protest, the freshly determined bull demon bowed his head before Lucifer.

"As you command, my master," he said to the surprise of the Devil and his Legion. *I will not go back... I cannot be made a human again.* Lucifer stood from his seat and placed his hand atop the bald head of Ammon's King, and like Legion before him he accepted the black and red irises that connected him to the others.

"Excellent," Lucifer hummed. He turned to return to his throne as the two minions watched him. "I trust you know that failure is not an option. You may leave me." Legion and Moloch exchanged a disgusted look and quickly refocused on their leader. Lucifer rolled his eyes and twirled his hand in the air as he painstakingly asked, "What is it?"

"Forgive me, Lord Lucifer," Legion answered, "but you haven't appointed a head for this operation—"

"And I would sooner be damned than take any orders from this *thing*," Moloch interrupted callously. Lucifer's eyes widened in a combination of humor and rage in response to Moloch's continued insolence.

"You will follow the command of a braindead chimpanzee if I decide it appropriate, *mortal* King of Ammon," the demon prince shouted. Moloch cringed at the title that reeked of his past more than he did the undeniable fury of the one who controlled him. The sweet scent of fear and torture that radiated from his body made Lucifer smile. "Besides," he continued with a more jovial disposition, "I conjured you from the depths of Hell itself. Your damnation is already cemented." Legion fell on his back and opened his mouth in an amused manner, but the screams of tortured souls erupted from his belly where laughter should have been. Lucifer and Moloch both stared at him in disturbed awe, as neither one had been prepared for that outburst.

"What?" Legion asked as if the entire situation was nothing more than a game. Lucifer shook his head and returned his attention to the object of his humor.

"The reason I selected you two was that you have a remarkable knack for getting things done on your own. How much greater will the chances of success be if both of you fight by my side? Hm… Given your ability to figure it out, why not decide between yourselves which of you will inherit the responsibilities of leading this particular task?" Moloch gulped and Legion clapped with a gleeful expression plastered across his deranged face.

"Ooh, by what manner do you mean, Master? How should we make such an important decision," asked the Many with unparalleled excitement. A cunning grin swept Lucifer's face as he tapped against his forehead from the comfort of his throne.

"In the many millennia since my imprisonment I have found a stark lack of entertainment. Therefore, the two of you will engage in a battle until my amusement reaches its peak, and whoever is left standing will become the authority between you." The false god and the multiple personalities stared each other down with unparalleled joy at the possibility, and with a single wave of his hand, Lucifer spoke once more. "Begin." In no time at all, the two demons slid backwards and away from each other. The shadows that surrounded Legion began to take on forms of their own, and in an instant Moloch found himself surrounded by monsters of many faces.

He counted them slowly, and considered every possible motion before he jumped backwards into the air to crush the demon to his rear under his girth. He quickly rolled away from the spot and the circle of nineteen other monstrous entities. He smiled, as the victim of his natural body left nothing more than a cloud of smoke behind.

"Please, tell me," Moloch taunted with an unimpressed smirk, "that you have more than these feeble little clouds of dust and ash. I am Moloch the Incinerator! I create the smoke you worship!" Lucifer smiled in delight as the cloud that was left behind morphed into two more demons more fearsome than the first. Moloch took them in, their broad shoulders with spikes as long as elephant tusks and those fiendish red eyes that cooled even his blood. The new creatures charged him as the others watched, but as they struck at the false god they were easily deflected into each other. Moloch once again emerged the victor.

Just as before, the monsters of Legion's creation evaporated in clouds of smoke that regenerated into four much more fearsome creatures. Moloch smiled with excitement as Legion laughed in the background.

"Fool! I am Legion, for we are Many!" His voice was almost as sinister as Lucifer's as he hissed his signature phrase, and with a twitch of his eyebrow the four new beasts opened their mouths and swallowed air in a fearsome fashion. They gagged, and like a rocket launcher they spewed vomit towards the Ammonite King. With an expression of pure disgust, he jumped into the air and over the monsters. The vomit that landed upon the stone ruins of Tel Megiddo dissolved the rock like ice in hot water, which piqued Moloch's intrigue. He clapped his hands together, and the thunderous force that was born from the collision created waves of sound that swept through the twenty-five nightmares and shattered the ground upon which they all stood. The waves reached Lucifer, who sat upon his throne unfazed and even offered up his approval. "My, this is getting interesting," came Legion's voice from the pall of tar-black smoke that loomed over the battlefield.

"How amusing," Moloch responded as he clasped his hands together and watched the giant cloud condense into a massive blue beast with long jagged horns that curled backwards around its ears. It had the face of a bull but the naked body of a man covered only by the smoke that it exuded. The beast snarled at the now irate Moloch as he continued his thought, "I was just thinking the same thing."

He smashed against the ground as the slothful behemoth approached, and black flames raged towards him from the four corners of the desolate ruins. They swarmed around him and consumed his body, and as the flames merged with the black aura that he'd inherited from his master Lucifer, his form began to shift and grow. The sound he made was as fearsome as a jaguar, and only his black and red eyes could be seen from the inferno. Moloch flexed, and when the blaze dissipated he was revealed to have the head and torso of a bull with the arms and legs of a man. His black silk robe stretched to fit, and his horns flared with the same black flame that once encircled him. Lucifer sat at the edge of his seat as the blue and the black ran at each other.

Legion threw a punch at Moloch, only to be sidestepped by the fiery Minotaur and subsequently flipped. The Multitude managed to land on his hands, though, and happened to springboard backwards into his aggressor to connect with an elbow. Moloch was taken to the ground but rolled through while Legion kipped up to his feet. The two battling demons stared each other down with eyes that glistened with intense enjoyment.

"What trouble you cause us," Legion spoke, though his mouth didn't move. The stillness of the air only amplified the tortured voices that lived inside of him as they echoed his thoughts. "We do not take this form very often. We offer you the utmost respect, King of Ammon." The beastly bull that was Moloch smiled at him with a fury that rivaled the Devil's as he charged forth.

"I am no mere king," Moloch protested as he grappled with Legion once again. He delivered a sharp knee to the Many's gut, to which the latter laughed like a child, and knocked him to his back with a mighty elbow to the face. Moloch stamped his feet against the shattered ground beneath him and bellowed at the Multitude, "I am a god!" Upon the conclusion of the phrase, a copious amount of black flames blasted from Moloch's mouth and covered a hopelessly satisfied Legion. Moloch finished, and momentarily gazed upon the motionless body that was his opponent. He marched his way over the broken battlefield and back to his master, fully prepared to accept the role that sparked this mockery of a battle. In Moloch's mind it proved no challenge at all, even though the creature with which he warred coaxed his most devastating of forms out of him.

Lucifer smiled as he pointed to the space behind the ancient Ammonite king. Moloch turned and saw that Legion had returned to his feet, and blades that dripped with a slick oily substance had extended from his palms. Legion, still in his massive and deformed state, licked his lips from the thrill of this fight.

“This… this is so much fun!” He charged Moloch with extraordinary speed and thrust the blades in his palms directly at the Ammonite’s face. Moloch ducked the blow just enough to where the flaming horns on his head clashed with the slicked metal. The collision of flame and oil caused an explosion that knocked Legion off his feet, but before he could fall to the ground, his opponent the king wrapped his claw-like finger tips around the demon’s throat and hoisted him up into the air.

“I agree,” he responded, and threw his captive down at the foot of the spiked throne of their master. “I believe that I will be the one to take charge on this little excursion.” Lucifer applauded as the black flames consumed Moloch and ate away at the beast until only the horned man remained.

“I agree. Legion,” he called with a snap of his fingers, “get up. The hour of my apocalypse swiftly approaches. Go, the both of you, seek out this Nabi and his little friend Eran. Feel free to toy with them as you see fit, so long as you eradicate them both.” Legion stirred himself into a bow before the dark lord and quickly rose to stand alongside the battle’s victor. “Oh, and Legion?” He turned around with a twisted but nervous smile as he responded to his name. “Should you fail me, expect treatment much worse than what the Ammonite gave you. That will be all. Both of you, begone.” Without any further deliberation, the two monsters marched away from their hellish prince and dove into the depths of the pit. Lucifer waved his hand passively, and the shadow portal through which he spied manifested before him.

“Eran!” Aiden, almost hoarse now, continued to scream for his lost friend as he felt the sudden change in the atmosphere, as if something unbelievably horrible was about to happen. He ran the streets of the city until he reached the gas station on Marlon Road, but slammed his head against the wall when he found nothing. The rain continued to pour down from overhead as he ran back into the thick of the storm and resumed his search for his best friend.

Lucifer sat in the comfort of his throne and twiddled his fingers as he took delight in the prophet's desperation.

"Run, run, little fool," he whispered to himself as the beasts in the valley below barked at the fading sun. "It will do little to save you. I was destined to rule over this world, and nothing shall stand in my way."

Legion and Moloch erupted from the black of the gas station mere moments before Aiden pressed on and watched him quietly from the shadows. Moloch's mind rushed in search of the proper course of action. Ever since his days as king when he would battle against the champions of Aram Damascus and Moab, it always occurred to him to prepare a strategy before going to war. Legion, on the other hand, was little more than a salivating dog who desired to chew the bone that had been placed before him.

Legion was never a man, and therefore it never occurred to him to try and think like one. He preyed upon the weak of spirit, those people with so little a soul that it would be easy to not just remove their essence, but absorb it into his darkness until they became as twisted and demonic as himself. Despite his predilection for those helpless spirits, he trembled with excitement when he thought of what it would taste like to devour the soul of one of the Two. Or both, even. He began to move out of the station and into the open street, as the scent of his adversary's soul proved too tantalizing to resist. Moloch, clearly the wiser of the two, extended an arm to hold him back.

“Not quite yet,” he whispered to the manic Multitude as they watched their prey slip away before their very eyes. “I am not strong enough to endure a battle with the Nabi just yet.” Legion stared at him coldly.

“What does that have to do with us?” He asked bluntly. Moloch grabbed Legion by the throat and slammed him against the wall. The entire building shook, and the Many cried out in pain under the grip of their king.

“Understand this, you filthy mongrel,” Moloch snarled as he tightened his grip and relished in the dog’s helpless whimpers, “you will not address a god king so carelessly, do you understand?” Legion nodded with a truly hurt look in his eye. “I am in need of sacrifices. That is the price of my power. Unfortunately, I am not permitted to carry out the deed myself. The offerings must be provided by another.”

“So that is why you keep us waiting!” Legion gasped. Moloch smiled.

“And here I thought you were nothing more than a deranged mutt. Go into the city and gather as many children as you can. We will convene here in an hour, and I promise you that if you touch a soul before I give you clearance, I will end you. Even in this state I am more than capable of dismantling you. Now, get to work.” Moloch released his hold on the timid monster, and he watched it hastily slip into the darkness on behalf of the Ammonite monarch.

Bloodsport rested on the roof of the gas station and watched as the creature slipped into the depths of the city. *Great, now I have to share my living space,* he thought sarcastically when a rumble came from beneath him. Moloch hammered his massive fists against the floor of the station and with every moment that passed, a stone figure pushed itself through the pavement. Eran took a moment to ponder the conversation he'd so happily eavesdropped on, and when he and the Seed realized just what monster struck the earth beneath them, they dashed across the rooftops and into the night. Bloodsport knew from his millennia of snaring men with their own vices that Moloch the Ammonite King, a man who slaughtered his own brothers for sovereign reign over his ancient tribe, the primal founder of the Kingdom of Ammon, was nothing to mess around with. How he could ever forget that distinct scent of ruthless treachery confounded him. Eran had only heard stories from the Archangels of all his terror, and how through a deal with Satan he managed to acquire the power of a demon at the cost of all the children in his kingdom. The cost for his ensured future was the destruction of a family's.

"This is bad," they said in unison as they continued to dart through the rain. "We need to find Aiden." Bloodsport cringed, but even he had to admit that in the face of the king, he was severely outmatched on his own.

Chapter Eleven

The rain splashed towards his body from heaven above, but the flames of the Holy Spirit that rested on his shoulders proved hot enough to evaporate whatever water dare touch him. Aiden Zane outwardly shined through the darkness, but as he endlessly sprinted through the streets of Edgehaven in search of his wingman he couldn't shake the feeling of impending darkness. His lungs burned, and sweat dripped down his face only to be instantly licked up by the fire. He stopped for a moment and leaned against the nearest brick wall as he stared into the blackened sky. *How much of this is just smoke,* he wondered as he reflected upon the earlier explosion that caused his separation from Maya and Oriphiel both.

He glanced back over the path he'd traced with the hope that Eran would fall under his gaze, but what he saw instead was a bright red light and a cloud of smoke on the rise over the city. Immediately he ran back in that direction, but in the next instance a chaotic burst of fire shot into the night sky. *The gas station...* he thought as he recalled the vision. *So, there was business there after all.* The people who lived in the area were jolted awake, and the screams of horrified parents filled the night air as one by one each family in the vicinity realized that their children had gone missing. Aiden powered through the pain on sheer whim, and groaned with frustration as it meant that he would once again have to table his inevitable confrontation with Eran.

He closed in on Marlon Road, and the putrid smell of burnt flesh filled his nostrils. He gagged at the scent and his eyes watered from the tainted smoke that drifted into the air. He continued onward through the streets past all the shops and apartments until he could see the space off in the distance where the station once stood. Aiden noticed the monumental image of a bull's head on a man's body erected in its place, and the middle of the idol was hollowed out to display flames as they roared over what looked like a mountain of small human bodies.

"Horrible, isn't it," came a familiar voice from the height of a nearby rooftop. Lightning flashed, and there upon the roof Aiden could easily make out the unmasked face of his best friend and greatest rival.

"Eran," Aiden started in shock. The former Nabi held up his hand to halt him from speaking further.

"There isn't any time for that right now. We need to get out of the area and lay low for a while." The rain poured even more now, and as Eran spoke Aiden could only see the great rift that had grown between them over the years. On some level, as if the spirits of the two young prophets were intertwined, Aiden always knew that Eran survived that fall, and everywhere Aiden lived since that day he moved to because he always felt that a familiar presence pulled him that way. But despite that depth of connection, logic dictated that after the fall Eran would have most certainly been dead, which always led him to question just what it was that tugged at him all those years. Now here they stood, face to face, brothers in arms once again, but their proximity could do nothing to bridge the gap between their adversarial personalities.

"You know what's going on with that," Aiden questioned in an attempt at seriousness, but the pain in his throat made it more laughable than anything. Eran, who had his own conflicted emotions to process in the moment, merely nodded as the water from his rain-soaked blond hair ran like a waterfall over his face. Hewer jumped down from the rooftop and landed sternly on his feet. He casually strolled over to his former wingman with his arms up to signify peaceful intentions.

"That would be the work of Moloch the Incinerator. He was the first king of Ammon, but towards the end of his reign he sold his soul to Lucifer in order to acquire the power of a demon. His people heralded him as a god, and because of the many tribes that waged war on the kingdom, they did what was necessary to maintain that power for him," Eran explained with a look of utter disgust on his face.

"They sacrificed their own children to him in fire," Aiden finished when he recalled the story. His eyes went wide with horror as he looked back at the flames that flickered within the belly of the idol, and a darker anger than he'd ever felt crept into his heart. "But what business does he have here?" His voice was much more forceful now which stunned them both, but Eran answered nonetheless.

"Well, from what I overheard, he seems to have a bone to pick with you," he stated with a slight smile on his face. Aiden tensed, as it became apparent that the person who stood before him was not his brother, but the thing that held him hostage. "No need to be so uptight, Aiden. I'm on your side, for now."

"And why is that," Aiden questioned as his eyes narrowed and his brow furrowed.

"I'm your biggest weakness," Bloodsport stated outright. Aiden was caught off guard, though when he realized there was no cause for surprise, he quickly adjusted himself. "Moloch isn't like other demons. He was known for being a callous and calculating strategist in his day. That being said, if he was sent here after you then there's a chance he'd come after me first since he's probably learned all there is to know about us. With you out here screaming my name at the top of your lungs, you've managed to reinforce his intel and establish it as fact." The creature that controlled Eran's body licked his lips in satisfaction at the idea of the destruction of his enemy, which made Aiden quake with fury.

"So the only reason you're not trying to kill me right now is that you need my help to keep yourself alive. Is that it?" Eran clapped with a smile on his face.

"Bingo," he said, and gestured for Aiden to follow him. "We've wasted enough time here. It's time to go." Aiden opened his mouth to protest, but before any words could spill out of him a deafening roar shook the entire city. The air began to sting and the rain evaporated before it even hit the ground. Aiden took one last look at the great stone statue and watched as it started to crack before he and Eran ran through the silent streets side by side.

"Where are we going," Aiden demanded as they darted around the corner of Marlon Road and Austin Avenue. The ground shook with a violent force that reminded them both of that dark day twelve years ago, and prompted an immediate response from Bloodsport.

"Shut up and follow me," he barked. The flames at Aiden's shoulders surged with his rage, but Eran couldn't have cared less. "Legion lurks in the shadows so whatever important information we have should be kept to ourselves. There's no telling how many eyes he's got on us right now." Another pulse in the earth shook the city, and the Two made a sharp left towards the end of Austin into an alley illuminated by a misplaced streetlight. They came upon the side door of a small funeral home, and after Eran picked the lock they slipped inside unnoticed. "Get away from the window," Eran ordered when he caught Aiden checking to see if they'd been followed to their present hideout. “It’s like you don’t remember anything you were taught. We won’t be aboveground for much longer. Moloch will start ripping through the city soon and Legion is undoubtedly on the lookout for easy pickings to scarf down.” Eran pulled him away and directed him towards a narrow flight of stairs that descended into the basement.

Aiden, at this point sick of the orders that his friend-turned-enemy barked, led the way despite a lack of knowledge as to where to go. Bloodsport allowed him to pass, and as he followed his nemesis through the open doorway he felt the Desert Eagle to ensure that it was easily accessible. Aiden looked around the dank basement and hoped to discover something useful to the strange bedfellows, but to his disappointment the subterranean room appeared empty. He turned to Bloodsport with a hardened look on his face.

“Where do we go from here,” Aiden asked, to which Bloodsport rolled his eyes and tread across the room to the back wall near the corner. He placed his left palm on the wall, and after a small light flashed, a door opened up to reveal a dimly lit tunnel. He stepped out of the way and extended his arm toward the underpass.

“Right this way, Aiden,” he responded spitefully. *It’ll all be over for you soon enough.* Aiden watched him as he passed into the dark hallway. The sense of nostalgia battled endlessly with the deepest feeling of distrust, but still Aiden advanced ahead of his old friend. “You know it’s a shame that things had to end up the way they did,” Bloodsport spoke as he followed the Nabi into the dim light. The door behind them slammed shut, and just like that it was as if they’d never set foot in the old funeral home.

“Yeah? And why’s that, Eran?” Aiden inquired with a somewhat threatening tone. Eran lightly placed his hand back on the handgrip of his Desert Eagle as they continued to walk. Aiden felt a shift in the cool air of the tunnel, and braced himself for the possible confrontation that would ensue in mere moments.

“Well, somebody’s got an attitude this evening,” Bloodsport chimed from behind him. His face was alight with joy at Aiden’s paranoia. After all, this kind of victim was the most fun for him. He preyed on the weak and the fearful, and the longer he dragged it out, the more he could truly enjoy Aiden’s squirming. “I just can’t help but think about what it would have been like if you’d have joined me that day.” His eyes narrowed with an almost demonic flare. “It isn’t too late, you know. We could run the world, you and I. All we’d need to do is let the demons bring about Armageddon and take advantage of the confusion.” Aiden’s rage boiled over, and the flames on his shoulders burst to the ceiling of the shaft.

“Eran!” Aiden all but roared the name as he spun around to confront the thing that lived in his body. To his shock, however, Bloodsport stood there with the .50 Desert Eagle drawn and pointed at his old rival.

“Eran isn’t here right now,” he said with a dark smirk as he slowly moved his finger from the shaft of the weapon to its trigger. “You know, I had a feeling that you’d react like that. You were always so blind to the bigger picture, Aiden, and you never knew when you were outmatched. This is your opportunity to be strong for a change! Side with me, just like the old days, and nobody will ever cross you again.” Aiden balled his fists at his sides and felt his entire body stiffen.

“So that’s your plan, huh? To usher in chaos and watch the world burn for kicks before you overthrow the demons and reign supreme,” Aiden demanded, and the Seed of Flesh laughed for a moment. "So this entire time it's been about you."

"But of course," he confirmed with a dismissive shrug. "I'm selfishness personified! I thrive on the chaos and manipulation, and I'll do whatever it takes to get what I want. What I want now…" he paused and firmly grasped the gun, "is my freedom." Bloodsport prepared to fire the weapon, but just before he could pull the trigger, Aiden quickly ducked underneath the firing hand and pushed his enemy's hand into the air.

"'No weapon formed against me shall prosper,'" Aiden quoted, and the weapons on Eran's person began to melt away. Aiden delivered a knee to Bloodsport's chin that sent him across the gravel-covered tunnel ground. The fire at Aiden's shoulders pulsed with life as he strode across the terrain to his supine adversary. "You don't have any of your little toys left," he taunted. Bloodsport grew nervous at the sight and sprang back to his feet from his downed position. He spat out a little blood against the wall, but smiled. The assassin couldn't remember the last time he actually had to dirty his hands with a fight. He dashed at Aiden with lightning speed and attempted a punch to the stomach, but to his surprise the Nabi with whom he warred deflected the attack and followed up with a sharp elbow to the ribs.

Bloodsport stumbled back for a moment with his arm over his ribcage and sized up his opponent. His icy blue eyes lit with excitement, and he charged again. Aiden sidestepped him and brought him down to the ground with a leg sweep. The collision of bone against the sturdy tunnel floor momentarily knocked the air out of him. Aiden walked over to him and stomped in his damaged ribcage. He leaned over the now immobile Eran and stared into those blue eyes that he thought he knew so well.

“Don’t toy with me, Seed.” The Seed of Flesh glared at him with more intensity than Moloch’s flames as he pushed Aiden off of him. He scrambled to his feet once again and his face twisted into a demented grin.

“As you command, Lord Aiden,” he mocked. The two ran at each other and punched simultaneously. The collision of their fists sent a wave of sound through the channel in which they battled. Aiden went for a knee to the face, but Bloodsport jumped backwards on his hands to deliver a kick of his own. His foot connected with the bottom of Aiden’s jaw, and the enraged Nabi staggered backwards. Eran, who had landed in a crouched position, ran at his former best friend and tackled him into the wall. He pinned Aiden there, but as he ground Aiden’s back into the façade he was surprised to feel the Nabi’s arms wrap around his midsection. Aiden lifted him off the ground, and with Eran’s head pointed downward, dropped down in a seated position.

Bloodsport’s head was driven into the dirt with relentless force, and as a gasp of air exited his lungs Aiden kicked him away and stood back to his feet. Bloodsport picked himself up as before as Aiden paced the ground like a lion on the prowl.

“You’ve gotten stronger,” Bloodsport was forced to admit. Aiden smiled. “But you’re still not stronger than I am.” He charged again, and as Aiden extended a foot towards his enemy’s chest, Eran used it as leverage and vaulted over his adversary. He landed on his hands and thrust his legs into Aiden’s back. Aiden released an agonized scream that filled the tunnel from one end to another, but rolled his body downward and attempted to kick at Eran’s face. The calloused mercenary rolled out of the way, and both men stood to their feet again. Eran lifted a hand and motioned for his rival to bring it.

Aiden attacked with a punch that Eran easily pushed to the side, but to his bewilderment, Aiden wrapped his arm around the back of Eran's neck and pulled his head into the dirt. He rolled on top of him and unleashed with a flurry of punches to the man with the striking blues. Anger boiled within him, because Aiden knew that this thing beneath him was not the airman he'd walked beside for so long. It was a monster, pure unmitigated selfishness, evil at its very core, which meant that it was Aiden's job to rid the world of it before it could cause any more damage.

Bloodsport kicked Aiden at the back of his head to knock him off balance, and in the next instant he reversed the position. Eran wrapped his fingers around the throat of his friend and began to squeeze, but the flames at his shoulders spiraled around his arms and burned him. He screamed in agony as blood fell from the wounds, and Aiden used the wall behind him to slowly pick himself up.

"You'll regret that," Bloodsport spat, and the red hooded cloak manifested in a dark flash over his body. No flames spawned on his shoulders, but black lightning surged around his body as a dark aura encircled him. "I'm going to erase you… just like I erased your home, your hope, and your little girlfriend! Witness the power of my ambition! 'Keep me as the apple of your eye; Hide me in the shadow of your wings!'" As he quoted the Scripture a wave of shadows washed over his body, and in the next instant he was gone. His maniacal laughter echoed from the darkness as the lights in the tunnel flickered off one by one. Aiden's eyes shifted back and forth in the tunnel as he watched for his enemy.

All fell silent, and Aiden calmly listened to the air around him. Bloodsport struck him from behind in the darkness, but when Aiden turned around he saw nothing but the unnerving black that surrounded him. Eran laughed like a madman from the shadows, and struck Aiden from behind once more.

"So that's the game you want to play," Aiden whispered as his adversary cackled in the background. "So be it. 'The light shines in the darkness, and the darkness has not overcome it.'" Aiden's body began to glow and the flames on his shoulders grew all the brighter until the darkness in the tunnel was dispelled. Eran's boot came down upon the ground and without warning Aiden spun to knee him in the chest. Bloodsport narrowly put up his hands in time enough to block, but was still shoved back and away from the Nabi. His frost-blue eyes and sickened scowl reeked of surprise. Eran stood there in a standstill with Aiden as they took in the bright light birthed by the flames. Bloodsport smirked as he opened his mouth once again.

"'I will stand there before you by the rock at Horeb. Strike the rock, and water will come out of it for the people to drink.'" Aiden's eyes went wide as Eran spoke and then struck the rocky ground upon which they stood. A burst of fresh water erupted from beneath them and slithered through the tunnel as a snake. Aiden ran from the waters that hungered for his flames and pressed his hands together as he sought for Scriptures to pray in return. His eyes widened as one crashed into the forefront of his mind, and once he'd built enough distance from the torrent and its master he began to speak.

"'Reach down your hand from on high; deliver me and rescue me from the mighty waters,'" he recited, and the ceiling of the tunnel began to twist and pulsate. He continued through the Psalm in the presence of his enemy, "'from the hands of foreigners whose mouths are full of lies, whose right hands are deceitful.'" A slab of earth shot from the roof of the tunnel and blocked the flow of the water before Aiden could be affected by it. It transformed into a hand-like platform that lifted the Nabi from the ground and turned so that Eran came into his view. He smiled at the irate monster that clasped his burnt and bloody hands at the other end of the tunnel. "You'll have to do better than that if you intend to win here, Eran."

"'The earth is broken up, the earth is split asunder, the earth is violently shaken!'" Eran breathed the verse out of a mix of frustration and desperation, and the clay construction broke in half. Aiden bounded forward and rolled along the ground of the tunnel before the giant manifestation of the Scripture crashed down on him, and extended a hand toward his old teammate. The Hebrew symbols on the front of his hood glowed even brighter in this darkness.

"I've had about enough of this," he asserted, which only made the fruit of Eran's Flesh laugh in hysteria. "'Now those who belong to Christ Jesus have crucified the Flesh with its passions and desires.'" The ground behind Bloodsport split, and from the depths of the opening came a cross made out of pink and brown flesh that bore seven blood-red eyes on all its sides. Eran's eyes locked on it, and the manic laugh was almost immediately replaced with the sound of vomit. Nothing came out of his mouth at first, but he continued to gag as he fell to his knees. Eran's body began to shake, and he lifted up those burnt hands defiantly against the cross before he slammed them against the turf. A vile orange liquid slowly trickled from his mouth, and as the gagging continued it became more and more strained, as if a person had been lodged in his esophagus. He held himself and tilted his head downward, and Aiden just watched on in humored disgust.

Eran heaved all the more, and as he did Aiden was able to witness the expulsion of sickly orange veins. The thing seemed to move more smoothly now, and the veins that were previously ejected were followed by what appeared to be a foot. Eran's mouth expanded almost unnaturally as a small, orange, child-like body slowly began to emerge. Veins covered the grotesque creature from head to toe, and a single black and red eye rested in the center of its belly. The eyes on the cross of flesh began to glow, and the Seed's tiny arms were forced to extend on either side of its body. It turned around now and faced Aiden as Eran slowly slid to the ground, unconscious.

The Seed levitated before him, and instantly found itself slammed against the front of the fleshy structure. Strips of skin and bleeding muscle formed bonds around the creature's arms that restrained it no matter how hard it tried to break free.

"Isn't this fitting," Aiden said as he methodically paced towards the grotesque tree. His eyes briefly shifted from his incapacitated comrade and then back to the beast that was extracted from his body. "You spent the last twelve years holding a man against his will, and now you find yourself a slave in your own right." Bloodsport continued to squirm frantically, but resolved to beg for his life when he found the task to be fruitless.

"Please," he whined, and the high-pitched tone of his voice sickened Aiden to his stomach. "Have mercy on me!" Aiden's ears itched with irritation at the word.

"'Part your heavens, Lord, and come down; touch the mountains so that they smoke,'" Aiden spoke, and the skin of the Seed of Flesh began to smolder. He screamed in agony, and Aiden, in a sadistic display of joy, closed his eyes to savor the sweetest sound of torture. "You have the nerve to speak of mercy to me when you walk the streets killing without a second thought?"

"Please," the Seed cried, "I don't deserve this!" Aiden's eyes grew wide with fury as he charged the cross and quoted Scripture.

"'Send forth lightning and scatter the enemy; shoot your arrows and rout them!'" His fist charged with a strong electrical current, and in barbarous fashion Aiden jammed it into the only eye of the little imp. "Don't you dare tell me what you do and don't deserve! Do you think that those officers deserved to be executed for doing their job, or that Maya deserved to be shot? What about Eran? Did Eran deserve to become your slave for more than a decade of his life?" The Seed opened his eye barely, and when Aiden noticed it, he drove his electrified fist into it once more. "You should have given him up a long time ago, but you were blinded by your selfish ambitions and your pathetic need for chaos and power. Is this chaotic enough for you now?" Aiden yelled at him as he kicked the sightless head of the creature. It dared not speak now, and softly whimpered from the pain. Aiden's usually brown eyes glowed with a blue hue that rivaled the intensity of his flames. He placed his hand on the head of the Seed and leaned in closer to whisper into its ear. "What was that verse that you made Eran speak when you first took control?" The creature stammered as he struggled to recall the words, but questioned his decision to even open his mouth at this point. Aiden cupped his free hand around his chin and thought about that wretched day over and over again, about how he watched as the only friend he'd ever known unleashed the most abominable evil that has ever existed. He remembered the way his heart sank and shattered. He reflected on the separation caused by Eran's presumed death and the bittersweet emotion behind his return. Just as much, he remembered the way that thing carelessly endangered hundreds of people just to make a statement, and how he killed policemen without batting an eye. An image of Maya's unconscious body on the floor of his burning apartment filtered into his mind, and he almost lost it. Aiden's grip tightened around the feeble head of the creature and he remembered the verse. "Ah, yes," he said with a sinister smile all his own, "'Therefore surely as I live, declares the Sovereign Lord, I will give you over to bloodshed and it will pursue you.'"

The Seed erupted with cries of agony as the blood within its body began to spew from its pores. It splashed the walls to either side of the cross, but the flames of the Holy Spirit that guarded Aiden so closely singed the liquid before it could make contact with him. The creature continued to scream as it hazily watched its very life pour out of its body, and the repetitive vociferations of pain and fear caused Eran to stir.

"A-Aiden…" he groaned with an unsteady voice. Aiden turned around as the last of the blood spilled from his victim, and saw the tearful eyes of the friend he'd thought he'd lost. He moved away from the cross as it absorbed the Seed's lifeless corpse, and as he knelt down the brothers watched it recede into the earth. Eran, with a sigh of relief, soon returned to an unconscious state with a smile on his face while Aiden continued to watch the opening and relished in the fact that Bloodsport was no more.

Chapter Twelve

It had been twelve excruciatingly long years since Aiden was able to use that much power at once, and it had been just as long since he sat this close to the person who caused him so much pain. They rested against the wall of the dark tunnel now as Aiden's cloak evaporated in a cloud of brilliant blue mist, and Eran was still out like a light. The tears he'd shed once the battle with the Seed was over had long since dried, and once he'd finished healing the burns on Eran's arms he began to fade.

"My brother," he said softly as his consciousness faded. "I've missed you." His eyes closed, and the stillness of the path soothed him into a deep sleep.

"You handled that well," came a strange and yet somehow familiar voice. Aiden's eyes snapped open and before him stood the figure of a man cloaked in blinding light.

"Who are you," Aiden asked. The figure of light drifted closer to the seated prophet and placed his translucent hand upon the man's head. A distant image of the past came to the forefront of his memory. Aiden saw this figure in physical form as he tread across the desert for forty days with neither food nor water to satiate his appetite. He watched him interact with Lucifer, with the two of them quoting Scripture at one another just as he had done with the Seed mere hours ago. He watched this seemingly natural entity perform the miracles of Heaven and teach multitudes of people, challenge authority and bestow power. He watched him take a beating for the sake of those he loved, even though he did no wrong, and heard the sickening tears of his flesh as it was ripped from his body. Aiden stood there at the Place of the Skull, and saw from the foot of a rugged cross where this man, no, this God hung His head and breathed His last. His eyes widened, and he humbly dropped his hands and face to the dirt when He retracted His hand.

"You're…" Aiden was at a loss for words, and an overwhelming sense of unworthiness swept over him.

"Yes, I am," He confirmed warmly. "Come, walk with me." A bead of sweat dropped from Aiden's forehead to the ground.

"But—" Aiden started from his prostrate position and squinted his eyes in earnest.

"It's alright," interrupted the God in his company. He walked over to the downed prophet and helped him back to his feet. "It's been a long time since we've had the chance to visit with one another." Aiden's eyes shot to the ground as he recalled his catatonic state after Eran's fall. He'd been a broken shell of his former self, defiant to the Archangels and the High King that watched over him. All he could think about was losing the only semblance of family he'd ever had. He remembered the day that Uriel blasted the door to his room down and pulled him by his curly hair into the Grand Hall.

"Kneel," She commanded as Elijah the Tishbite appeared upon his throne. She turned her attention to him. "What is your command, my king?"

"Take him into the Holy of Holies," he issued with a wave of his hand. "The King wants to see him." Aiden resisted with everything he had at the time, but the firm grip of Uriel's hand on his arm proved more than enough to keep him under her control. She marched him into the furthest chamber to the back of the Grand Hall and shoved him through a doorway. She closed it and, to his dissatisfaction, locked it from the outside. It was when the door closed that he noted the unusual and yet somehow recognizable light that gleamed from behind him and absorbed his shadow entirely. He turned around and witnessed the same figure that came to see him there in the tunnel.

Aiden refocused on his Master, who for reasons unknown to the Nabi, walked side by side with him as they moved deeper into the tunnel. Aiden couldn't help but glance over his shoulder out of concern for Eran, which caused his King to gently place His hand upon his shoulder.

"You really are something else," He told him. Aiden looked at Him in confusion. "That last battle of yours reminded me why I chose you two in the first place. You two have a special bond that transcends your ties to the military, and even the relationship you've fostered beyond those ranks." Aiden refocused on the path before them.

"I'm not entirely sure I understand, my King." The Lord chuckled.

"I expected as much. It isn't apparent from your angle, or at least it isn't when you first think about it, but the two of you possess qualities in your personalities that both compliment and contradict each other," He explained as they further paced the dark path. Aiden glanced back over his shoulder again, then refocused on the light of the King of Kings.

"What do you mean?" It had been so long, and Aiden wasn't even sure if he remembered everything about Eran's personality. He wondered if he would be the same as he was before, or if the Seed had changed him into someone completely different.

"Your friend is a tangible kind of person," the King explained. "He acts based on what he can see, what he can touch, and the more he learns about his environment the more he relies on that knowledge. You, on the other hand, seek understanding in all aspects of life because since your youth, people have misunderstood you. But knowledge is the foundation of understanding, and understanding is the ability to replicate and apply that knowledge. Think about the connection between your mind and your heart. They influence each other and can be of great compliment to the person as a whole. However, if there is no balance between the two, whichever one is the dominant in that person will take control and blind the individual to the benefits of the other."

Aiden considered the demonic attack on the road to Tel Megiddo those twelve years ago. His eyes narrowed on the path.

"So because of Eran's lack of understanding it was easier for him to be attacked. That's why the Seed latched onto him, and how the Insecurities got into his body between the Hall and the Tel," he proposed. The King nodded.

"Yes, that's exactly it. Eran has struggled with faith all his life, because the harshness of his childhood, being molested and abused by his father, taught him that the only thing he could rely on was what he could see. He experienced great difficulty during his time as a Nabi, and was easily corrupted by his own ambition to become the most powerful in the world and rid it of all he saw as scum. However," He continued, which attracted Aiden's gaze, "your understanding of the situation misled you into believing that you could handle it on your own, even though you knew that your trust was better invested in me than in you. The reason why I called you both was so you could reinforce one another, but I always knew that at some point the two of you would clash."

"I see…" Aiden felt a tinge of pain in his heart as he reflected upon the truth of what the King said. He turned his attention back to the path and kicked a rock further down the tunnel.

"Not to worry," the King continued. "I always had faith that you would be able to pick yourselves up again. You just needed to push beyond your limitations and admit that you needed help. No doubt you noticed that peace that swept over your body and mind after your battle with Bloodsport." Aiden nodded and kicked the rock again.

"I did," he confirmed. "I can't remember the last time I felt that."

"Twelve years ago," the King pointed out. Aiden looked at Him as He placed His hand gently against his upper back as a father does his son. "What do you think changed? Why did you come back to me today and not at any point in the last twelve years?" Aiden thought about it as they started their way back towards Eran. He knew that the King already knew the answer, but tested him in this way so that the lesson behind his suffering would resonate.

"The people around me were in danger. My home was taken from me. I was on the verge of death for most of the day, and even though someone needed to stop the chaos that Eran… that Bloodsport perpetuated, I was helpless to do so. I called on you because I needed you, and because the lives of those people in the city needed balance," Aiden explained. The King clapped His hands as they walked and chuckled with a great sense of pride and approval.

"Excellent," He praised excitedly, "but now that you know to rely on me in times of crisis, remember that that crisis never truly ends. Life on this earth is a continual battle against Lucifer and his servants, and if you choose to handle it on your own, you will almost certainly be destroyed. Bear in mind that I am always with you, and that at this point in your life you are only alone if you choose to be so." Tears ran down Aiden's cheeks as the words of the King reached his heart. The King opened His arms and took Aiden into them as though he were a small child, and immediately the young Nabi felt an ethereal warmth and comfort that soothed his very soul.

The King dried Aiden's eyes and walked with him until they once again came to the unconscious Eran. Aiden stared at him for a moment as his body tensed.

"Will he be alright," he asked the King. The Alpha moved over to Eran and lightly pressed a hand against his forehead. For a moment, it seemed as if reality itself pulsed under His touch, and the red hooded cloak flashed into place with red flames at double their intensity upon his shoulders.

"Aiden," Eran whispered. A single tear trailed his cheek and he smiled in his sleep. The King turned back to His Nabi.

"By the looks of things, he'll be just fine. Now, up ahead, just a few yards beyond where we turned around, there is a fork in the path with two separate roads. They both lead to the same place, however it would be best for the two of you to move together on a decided path. You never know what traps might await you, and in Eran's fragile state it wouldn't be wise to separate so soon." The King turned towards the tunnel and walked away from the Two.

"Wait," Aiden called after Him. "Are you sure that we can handle that thing out there?" The King stopped and paused for a moment. He laughed at the question and started to walk again.

"My boy, I wouldn't have chosen you if I had any reason to doubt," He told the Nabi, and as he paced into the shadows of the tunnel, that otherworldly light that enshrouded his body vanished.

Aiden awoke next to Eran as if he'd never moved. He scanned the area for any sign of the King, but was slightly disheartened to find that the

Two were alone in the shaft once again. The ground beneath the Two trembled slightly, and chips of earth fell from the ceiling to the ground. *Moloch must be on the move,* Aiden thought. He nudged Eran with his foot in an effort to wake him, but the second Nabi only snored as he fell over to his side. Aiden rolled his eyes and couldn't help but smile. He understood that the world aboveground was in turmoil. He knew that Maya was in critical condition. He knew that he and the apparent log next to him were the prey that the false god and the Multitude sought. All this resonated with him at his core, but still he smiled.

"Eran," Aiden whispered in caution of what creatures might still lurk in the darkness. Eran snored on without a care in the world. "Eran," he repeated at a more moderate volume. Eran stirred and rolled over to make himself more comfortable when a massive quake rattled the burrow. Eran jolted awake from the tremor and locked eyes with Aiden. Aiden, who was forced to one knee as the result of the quake, smiled at his old friend. "Nice of you to join us. Sleep well, princess?" Eran rolled his eyes as he pushed himself upward against the wall.

"Shut up," he said as his lips curled against his will. Aiden helped him to his feet, and started hastily down the path.

"Smile later," he commanded, "we need to get out of here before the tunnel caves in and figure out a strategy to take down Moloch and Legion." Eran followed his wingman down the tunnel with a bewildered expression on his face.

"What do you mean Moloch *and* Legion?" Aiden stopped for a moment at the question and caught sight of the scars left behind from the burns that he'd inflicted.

"Now's not the time to get into detail but the short version has the Devil taking a hit out on the both of us. We need to get to a secure location and work out a strategy as soon as possible. I mean, Legion is pretty easy to take, but it's Moloch I'm worried about." Aiden took off down the shaft once again, and as the roof started to cave in as predicted, Eran let out a huff and followed suit. Aiden analyzed the pathway in the hopes that the dream he'd had before was more than just that. He quickly found his hopes realized as two separate paths came into view.

"Which way do we go?" Eran shouted over the noise of crumbling rock in the background. Aiden opened his mouth with every intention to suggest they split up when he remembered the warning of the Most High.

"Let's go right," Aiden called back to him. Eran pushed himself until they ran at the same pace, and instantaneously they were taken back to Lackland Air Force Base. They could feel the chilled morning breeze brush against their skin, and see the overlapping colors of the break of dawn as they ran laps around the PT track. It seemed so distant to them now, and yet so recent. Eran looked at his brother with a smirk on his face and nostalgia in his eyes.

"I'll race ya," he challenged. Aiden looked at him in disbelief.

"Our lives are in danger and *you* want to race?" He asked as an even bigger smile took its place between his cheeks. He shook his head as he laughed into the cave. "Fine, you're on." As the burrow around them crumbled, the Nabi'im prayed silently and donned their hooded cloaks, and flashes of red and blue bolted through the darkness. Aiden took the lead for a while, and purposefully moved in the way of his best friend to prevent passage as they banked down the right side of the fork.

“Oh, so that’s how you want to play this game?” Eran called to him from behind. “Fine. ‘Do you not know that in a race all the runners run, but only one gets the prize? Run in such a way as to get the prize.’” His feet took on the red flames that flared upon his shoulders, and with a smile on his face he drifted towards and then onto the walls until he successfully passed his brother.

“That’s so cheap,” Aiden yelled, and Eran laughed. *A twelve-year rift,* he thought, *gone in a flash.* Aiden pushed his hand forward and smirked as a Scripture came to mind. “‘I press on toward the goal to win the prize for which God has called me heavenward in Christ Jesus.’” Just as with Eran, Aiden’s blue flames engulfed his feet, and he attempted the same maneuver along the wall. Eran took note of this, though, and ran along the other wall. The two Nabi’im spiraled through the course until they realized that their surroundings proved sturdy enough to pause. Eran unexpectedly pulled to a stop, which prompted Aiden to reduce his speed as well. “What’s the matter?”

“Look,” Eran responded as he pointed up ahead. The path sloped upward and light shone from a presumed end. Aiden gave a sigh of relief as he moved towards the bright gleam, but something about it deeply disturbed Eran. “Wait,” he cautioned before Aiden moved too far out of the tunnel. He walked in front of his wingman and focused his attention on the mysterious light. “Who’s there?” The sick laughter of Legion erupted from the other side of the light, and in the blink of an eye the shine disappeared altogether.

“Oh, what a tragedy,” spoke the many voices of the Multitude as a set of glowing red eyes stepped from the slope into the last stretch of the tunnel. “We had sincerely hoped that at least one of you would fall into our little trap.”

“Yeah, well perhaps we would have if you were smart enough to set one properly,” Eran quipped. Aiden snickered, and the demon roared.

“You are Eran Hewer right? You seem to have a lot more personality than we would have guessed. Here we thought you were nothing more than Bloodsport’s puppet. Hm… Something tells us that we would have preferred it that way,” Legion teased as he inched closer and tilted his head to the side in a disturbingly childish manner.

“That’s far enough, demon,” Aiden said as the flames on his shoulders lunged forth. Legion jumped backwards and wagged his finger through the air.

“Spitting fire? Now, now, little Aiden, where are your manners,” spake the monster in their midst. Aiden crossed his arms as his scowl intensified.

“Well forgive me if I feel as though my courtesies would be lost on a vicious hell-beast like you,” Aiden snapped back. Legion’s demonic red and black eyes narrowed on the Nabi’im.

“Spitting fire indeed,” he commented as the shadows that surrounded him slowly manifested pair after pair of the same Satanic dichromatic eyes. “We really hoped that we would not have to fight you both at once, but it does not look like we should be that lucky today.”

“Well I wouldn’t say that,” Eran responded before Aiden had any opportunity to confirm Legion’s doubt as fact. Aiden moved in front of Eran and stared at him inquisitively.

“What do you think you’re doing,” he demanded, and crossed his arms. Eran held up his hands and moved his comrade out of the way.

“Look, I’ve got this,” he assured him with a cocky grin and quickly locked eyes with Legion and his many shadow beasts. “Why don’t you just sit back and enjoy the show?” Aiden stared at him for a moment longer out of concern, but when he noticed the fire in Eran’s eyes he realized there was very little he could do to dissuade him.

“Fine,” he finally consented as he walked over to what remained of the tunnel wall and leaned casually against it. “Try not to take too long, though. We have another problem to take care of on the surface and I’m sure it’ll take a little more effort to put that one down.” Legion roared again, irate that these humans, so lowly and despicable in his eyes, would dare speak of him as if he weren’t as big a threat as Moloch.

“We… we hate it…” he panted in a rage. Eran raised his eyebrows in amusement.

“Oh?” The crimson Nabi stood by in anticipation, and watched the red-eyed shadows multiply all around him and grunt out of hunger for a fresh human soul. They numbered a hundred easy, and the way they looked at Eran as if he were some sort of delicacy made Aiden’s stomach turn and blood boil.

“We hate being made fun of!” The voices of children left his lips, and Aiden and Eran both glared at their adversary. The shadow creatures slinked around the terrain until Eran was completely surrounded, and as they charged the scarlet-clad Nabi he lifted his left hand.

“‘By day the Lord went ahead of them in a pillar of cloud to guide them on their way,’” he quoted in unbothered calm. A blast of wind encircled him to push back his aggressors, and fueled the flames of Legion’s anger in the process. The demon screamed as he struggled to hold his ground, but nevertheless Eran continued. “‘And by night in a pillar of fire to give them light, so that they could travel by night.'" A spiral of flames broke through the ground and fed on the wall of air until all the shadows in the vicinity were consumed in a captivating flash of light. Clouds of smoke blotted out the luster of the bright red flames, and Legion beat against the stone-covered ground as Eran stood at the center of a dual layered tornado with his arms crossed smugly. "You'll have to try a little harder than that if you want to get through my defenses. C'mon, I'm looking for a little bit of fun here. What are you waiting for? Entertain me." Legion's mind flashed back to that accursed command that ushered in a crushing defeat at a weakened Moloch. His temper burst at the seams, and the two Nabi'im watched in surprise as he absorbed the shadows into his own body before they had the opportunity to reform and multiply. His appearance changed from the human figure it once held. The bones of that body cracked and shifted, his chest and legs enlarged, his arms bulged with incredible muscle mass, and the face that rested around those heinous eyes became all the more distorted. His nose and mouth condensed into the snout of a wolf, and the skin on his face was slowly overtaken with fur.

The beast snarled at Eran, who now dispelled the blaze tornado and locked eyes with the creature.

"We will devour you both! Just like we did with all the children!" Legion barked at Eran. The flames on the prophet's shoulders hit the ceiling of the tunnel and made the darkness shine like the day. The beastly Legion began to convulse wildly until he split into fifty of the colossal wolf-men. They stalked the Crimson One in a circle, but Eran stood his ground and extended his arm once again. Before he had the chance to speak Scripture into existence, five of the massive clones charged him at once. In a brilliant flash of red he leaped into the air to deliver a revolving kick that connected with all their jaws. The next wave of the assault came, but found themselves blasted back by the flames on his shoulders.

"What do you mean, 'just like all the children?'" Eran snarled. The Legion clones smirked with a devilish delight at the memory as the few that lay on the ground took to their legs once again. He held himself and cackled maniacally as he savored the distant sounds of their tortured screams. Aiden's eyes went wide as he recalled the mountain of burning bodies that rested beneath Moloch's shrine, and in a rage he pounded his fist against the wall and sent a crashing sound throughout the tunnel. Eran glanced back at him, but quickly refocused on the mutant pack of wolves that hungered for his soul. "Moloch," he said as he reached the same revelation. His fire, both inward and outward, burned hotter and brighter than before. He stared at the monsters in trembling hatred as he remembered Legion's MO. He seeks the spiritually weak and the impressionable, and then eats them alive from the inside until they become a permanent part of his multitude. *To target children...* Eran thought as the Hebrew inscription for "Nabi" appeared on the hood of his robe in holy light as it had for his wingman, *is unforgivable.*

"But you will die worse than they did," taunted the abhorrent creature, "we will see to that personally!" Legion's voice deepened as he charged, but Eran held his position without falter. He extended a hand to Heaven, and reopened his eyes. There was a glow of red in them that the beasts were unfamiliar with, and a sense of overwhelming fear swept them to the point where they froze. The words of the prophet Elijah seeped into Eran's head like water, and consumed his heart like the fire did his shoulders.

"'If I am a man of God, may fire come down from heaven and consume you and your men,'" Eran screamed. All eyes drifted toward the roof of the tunnel, and the immediate silence of the moment filled the demons with a false sense of security. As they inched for their prey, the ceiling burst into flames and fire engulfed the demonic hoard. They screamed in agony, but to their surprise and horror they didn't dissipate into the clouds of smoke that usually followed a heavy attack. "'Then fire fell from Heaven and consumed him and his men,'" Eran continued coldly as he watched them burn. "You've been made flesh by this Scripture, and just like the Word of God says, the flames won't stop until you've been consumed entirely." The sound of their suffering did little to satisfy him, and he even wished he could do more.

"Why?!" Legion screeched with ire in his eyes. Eran extended his hand again at the question.

"'On the wicked He will rain fiery coals and burning sulfur; a scorching wind will be their lot.'" The fire that engulfed their bodies intensified and the air itself began to burn with potency much greater than even Moloch's. "Burn out," was the last thing he said to the tortured demon as his skin began to turn to char and the hairs that lined his body singed before his melting eyes. Eran stood for a moment and watched the fire roar, and as the smoke filled the early morning sky he turned his attention on Aiden. "Let's move. Our location's been compromised. We can expect Moloch to be here at any minute." Aiden didn't protest and walked with his old friend towards the slope. He slapped a hand on his wingman's back as Legion screamed even louder in the background.

"You know," Aiden started playfully, "it was only compromised because *somebody* had to pull an Elijah and call fire down from Heaven." Eran brushed his hand off as another unwanted smirk crept across his countenance.

“Shut up,” he told him with a slight chuckle. It had been twelve years since their suffering began, twelve years since their separation, but as they drifted towards the end of the darkness of the subterranean construct, they strode into the light of day and the start of a brighter future.

Chapter Thirteen

Lucifer pounded his fist against the spiked arm of his throne as he watched from Tel Megiddo, and in a fit of rage black flames burst from his lips behind the line of curses he spewed into the atmosphere. The black monsters in the valley below cringed in terror as the earth beneath them shook, and though they bore no physical form they knew that pain would likely ensue. He stood from his throne and paced the sandy ruins of the Tel as he hoped against Heaven itself that Moloch would be enough to subdue his enemies. Still though… he felt as if something had been overlooked on his part, but decided it best to brush it off and focus on the problem at hand.

The Nabi'im emerged from the tunnel to find themselves in the slums of Edgehaven. The homeless and the thugs that lived in the area marched in an almost militant trance towards the center of the city where Moloch rampaged in his search for the Two. Aiden and Eran exchanged looks, and ducked into the crowd as their hooded cloaks dissipated into a combined purple cloud of mist.

"So," Eran started in a hushed tone. The loud moans and grunts of the zombified mob echoed through the area and discomforted them both, but despite that fact they pressed on with all seriousness. "What's the plan?" One of the entranced citizens brushed up against Aiden's shoulder, and the contact sent a tremor of disgust through his body that was quickly dispelled when he remembered the blood of the Seed as it splashed against the walls of the dark underground hall. *At least it's not that bad…*

"Standard tactics of fighting in Spirit Mode won't work," Aiden commented, and lowered his head as he pushed through an awkward congregation of the homeless. “He’s not a standard demon, just a human with demonic powers—”

“That can be extinguished, right? I mean it is possible to push him so far that it fades away and we’re left with a normal man,” Eran assessed as he moved closer to Aiden and walked in step with him.

“That’d be a lot easier said than done. His power and longevity both hinge on how many children were burned in sacrifice to him. The quickest way to throw him off his game would have been to intercept the tributes, but from what I saw before our little underground skirmish, we’re already a little too late for that,” Aiden explained, his voice infused with disappointment. Eran let out a huff of agitation and crossed his arms while he walked. The act caught Aiden’s attention and called to mind his Air Force training.

“Arms at your side,” he told him subconsciously. Eran looked at him as if he’d lost his mind, but Aiden only shrugged.

“Really?” He prodded in disbelief. Aiden couldn’t help but chuckle, but the smile that shot onto his face quickly vanished as he took in his surroundings. The air stung like it did the night before. Buildings and homes lay in ruins, cars and busses were turned over, and the ground itself cracked in the places where Moloch had once stepped. The broken sidewalks were spattered with the blood of the fallen, and it was all Aiden could do to keep his power under control.

“Sorry,” he said with a tinge of embarrassment amid his hushed displeasure. “It’s a force of habit. But back to the main issue—”

“Force,” Eran interrupted as a light bulb went on in his head. “Aiden, what is a force?” The azure Nabi flashed him a confused look, but contemplated the definition.

“A force is a push or pull on an object by another object, right?” He offered. Eran nodded with a foxlike smirk in place. Aiden paused for a moment, unsure how his companion could even think to smile as the Two gazed upon the destruction left in a monster’s wake.

“What if we used two separate forces to pressure him?” Aiden was well aware that his teammate’s mind was at work, but it did little to assuage his bewilderment.

“He’d stand still,” Aiden commented. “Look, I’m not entirely sure I understand what you want to do here.” Eran shook his head as they continued their march through the city.

“Moloch is a human with demonic power, right?”

“Yeah, so?” Aiden’s focus was rocked by the path of destruction, and more so by the monumental minotaur that came into view. It cried out the names of its targets over the entire city, and the Nabi’im cautiously slipped through the crowd of hypnotized residents.

“So, it’s likely that he’s incredibly protective of that power and will expect spiritual attempts to strip him of it. Thing is, if we can speak Scripture not at once, but back to back from two different directions, we may be able to overcome whatever defenses he’s built up,” Eran elaborated. Aiden’s eyes went wide as they ducked behind a building and out of Moloch’s line of sight.

“He’d be powerless to stop us from siphoning off his power and making him mortal again,” Aiden realized. While the sound of the word “mortal” failed to reach his ear, Moloch’s intense disdain for the word allowed him to feel it in his bones. The thunderous crash of falling buildings filled the air and deafened the Two, and thousands of the mindless drones that marched toward their demonic idol lost their lives as the

Nabi'im looked on in horror. "I think our time to strategize is over. We can't let any more of those people get hurt." Aiden darted towards a nearby fire escape and climbed until he reached the roof.

"I guess that means it's time to go," Eran murmured. He took to a building on the other side of the street and bolted up its crumbled stairwell. Aiden watched in wait for his wingman to take to a rooftop, and just as Moloch caught sight of him he started to pray the words of the Prophet Isaiah.

"'The Spirit of the Sovereign Lord is on me,'" he quoted as thoughts of the King's warm embrace crept into his mind, "'because the Lord has anointed me to proclaim good news to the poor.'" *Bear in mind that I am always with you.* Aiden heard His soothing voice call to him, and the alarm that he would have felt before washed away instantly. "'He has sent me to bind up the brokenhearted, to proclaim freedom for the captives and release from darkness for the prisoners.'" Aiden's standard jeans and t-shirt were replaced with the clerical garb and the blue hooded cloak that overlapped it. The flames on his shoulders lit with bright blue intensity that shot up at Moloch's colossal hand as it reached for the Nabi. One by one, the people of Edgehaven, who had, in only a day's time, become Moloch's mind-slaves awoke from their daze and found themselves immobilized by fear.

"I will make you pay for that!" Moloch screamed into the burning air, and as he shrank a few feet the people below scattered in confusion. Eran kicked down the door to the roof of the building he'd ventured into, and stood triumphantly in Moloch's line of sight. He extended his arm towards the false idol with a malicious grin.

"'Hail fell and lightning flashed back and forth. It was the worst storm in all the land of Egypt since it had become a nation,'" he quoted, and the glimmer of fresh sunlight was blotted out by the sudden manifestation of dark clouds. Hail poured out of the sky at the prophet's command and fired on the minotaur as lightning struck him in his chest. He stumbled back and grasped the spot where the blast had hit him, but as he charged for Eran, Aiden lifted his right hand and took to a Scripture of his own.

"'I will bring terror on you from all those around you, declares the Sovereign Lord,'" he spoke, and the terrified people below him became as ravenous as the monsters in the valley of the Tel. Moloch was stopped in his tracks, and though he fought to shake his former slaves off, they wouldn't fall.

"How dare you rebel against your god!?" Moloch inhaled deeply, and expelled upon the former drones a wave of crimson fire that drained the life from them instantaneously.

"'But your iniquities have separated you from your God; your sins have hidden His face from you, so that he will not hear you,'" Aiden started again. The mention of the True and Living God pulled even more power from the beast, and as his strength left him his features became distinctively more human. Aiden and Eran smiled deviously at each other as they noticed the pattern. He turned toward Aiden and rampaged through the streets, but Eran came up behind him with another Scripture just the same.

"'For the Lord your God is a consuming fire, a jealous God,'" Eran called into the atmosphere, and as more power was siphoned away a great flame ignited upon the false god's skin. As he lit up in a blaze, the people of the city backed away from him, but the Nabi'im descended from their rooftops and advanced. They casually strode towards the now average-sized Moloch as if the threat had passed, but the ancient Ammonite erupted with a rage that extinguished the flames that seared his flesh.

“How dare you assault me in such a manner,” Moloch asserted as the black flames on his still-present horns flared. His voice was deep and threatening, and the madder he became, the more the air around them stung. “You mangy dogs are not even worthy of standing in my presence!” He stared at them as his breathing intensified. Fire protruded from the pores on his bald head and his eyes became a solid red. Eran blinked, and when he reopened his eyes he was surprised to find that his enemy was now before him. Moloch drove his meaty fist into the young prophet’s sternum, and the wind came out of him like a deflated tire.

“Eran!” Aiden cried as he burned with hatred hotter than the atmosphere. Moloch turned to him with a sadistic grin plastered on his jaw.

“Oh, my apologies,” he poked. “Have I broken your toy?” Moloch picked up the limp arm of the now unconscious Eran. “Here,” he said as he threw him into his friend. “You can have him back.” The Nabi’im tumbled across the pavement and into the side of the 17th Street Bank. Aiden watched as the hulking Ammonite trudged his way towards them, and to his absolute terror magma emerged from the ground with each of his crushing steps. Aiden gently rolled his brother off of him and sat him against the sturdy brick wall. He dusted himself off, and tread towards his adversary.

“You bark so loud for such a small dog,” Aiden taunted to the face of the false god. “I think it’s far beyond time that someone taught you your place.” Moloch laughed as he arrogantly folded his arms across his chest.

“Who do you expect to teach Moloch the Incinerator such a lesson, little worm?” He feigned a retreat, but quickly attempted a near sonic strike at the Nabi’s face. Aiden immediately blocked the extended fist with one hand, and released it promptly when the idolatrous idol retracted. He unleashed another attack, but again he was easily blocked. Aiden kicked his inner thigh as penance for his assault, which prompted the cult figure to let loose a flurry of punches at break-neck speed. Moloch's fists ignited the air around them with every strike, but no matter how hard he tried he found it impossible to break past Aiden's iron defense.

"You seem a little frustrated," Eran called from his seat on the concrete slab that had once been a sidewalk. Aiden looked back at him and noticed a cut on the upper right-hand side of his head. Blood poured from the gash and filtered into his eye, but despite the discomfort he watched on and openly mocked the enraged monster. Aiden shook his head with as a cocky half-smile took to his jawline.

"Aren't you going to come help me with him," Aiden inquired, but Eran shook his head as he leaned comfortably against the wall.

"Nah, seems like you've got it covered. Besides, we only planned to weaken him, remember? Now that he's all flimsy I don't see a point to joining in." Aiden took his words into consideration as he easily deflected a cheap shot aimed for the back of his head.

"I mean I guess," he conceded as the taunting grin grew wider. "It's not like I'm fighting a *god* or anything." Moloch stood there appalled, as he'd never in all his millennia of living been disrespected in such a way. He jumped backwards sharply and extended his fist, and the friction of his body against the scorching air gave birth to an immense blast of fire. Aiden stood there and crossed his arms as the blast hurdled towards him. The fireball hit him dead on, and as the smoke covered the area Moloch erupted with laughter.

"Now you witness the power of a true god! Even in my weakened state I prove my unattainable might! Bow down before me, Nabi, and I will reconsider your destruction," Moloch proposed to Eran, but when Aiden emerged from the smoke cloud's shadow, the false idol was forced to shut his boisterous mouth.

"Is that so? Well, forgive me if I feel disinclined to acquiesce to your request, O Foolish One," Aiden mocked with a playful bow to the pagan deity. The Nabi charged him, and though Moloch launched a blast similar to the one before, Aiden easily spun out of the way and rapidly closed the distance between them. He threw a punch at Moloch, but was blocked with an elbow. Moloch delivered a rib-shattering kick to Aiden's midsection, and as the prophet gasped for air the demon followed up with an unforgiving elbow to the back of the head. The Nabi fell to the ground, and Moloch issued a kick to his side that made him slide scathingly across the pavement. Aiden smiled as he stood to his feet, and popped a few of his bones. He spat a little blood off to the side, but then licked his lips in excitement. "Well I can say this: when you *do* land a blow, you can pack quite the punch. But if you think that's enough to put you on the same level as God then you're more delusional than I thought." Moloch rushed him in the same way he had Eran and attempted a knee to Aiden's face. Aiden, however, sidestepped the blow and punched the mortally sensitive groin of his opponent. Moloch fell to his knees, outraged by this blasphemy, but as he opened his mouth, Aiden kicked him in the jaw and stomped on his esophagus as he fell. "You don't even know who God is. How can you ever hope to be like Him?"

The Ammonite king pressed his hands against Aiden's face, but as he thought to apply pressure a searing pain spread through his palms the likes of which he never imagined he would feel.

"What was that," he gasped barely as Aiden applied more pressure to his throat.

“I already told you. ‘The Spirit of the Sovereign Lord is on me.’ That pain you felt is His way of telling you the hard way that you aren’t allowed to touch me, and I can guarantee you that if you even try, His flames’ll burn a whole lot hotter than yours ever did,” Aiden clarified. He removed his foot from his enemy’s throat and turned to face Eran. “You sure you don’t want to get in on this? It’s actually a lot more fun than I thought it would be.” Eran shook his head with a smile on his face as Moloch sprang to his feet and threw a hard left at the seemingly unsuspecting Nabi. The flames that rested on Aiden’s shoulders flared up and consumed the monster’s hand until it burned away entirely. Moloch looked upon the bloody wound as he realized that his power was fading. He turned nervously to the people of Edgehaven, who watched from behind the ruins of their city as the half-demon king of Ammon battled the man known only to them as the Nabi. He cursed Aiden and Eran for restoring their minds. He desperately needed their acts of worship, and now more than ever he needed the lives of their children. *Where is that mongrel Legion,* he barked inwardly as he scanned the wreckage of downtown.

“If you’re looking for your buddy with the multiple personalities, I already took care of him,” Eran called from the side of the bank as he slowly drifted back to sleep.

“You *what*?!” screamed the irate Ammonite. Aiden’s eyes narrowed as he dealt a crushing blow to the idol’s abdomen. Moloch fell to his knees once again, but this time coughed up blood. “How could this happen,” he asked in disbelief. “I am a god!”

“You’re still going on about that, huh? Surprising, given that you’ve seen His power and how it crushed you like a gnat. How could *you* be a god if mere men were able to take you down so easily? You may as well give in, since 'every knee shall bow and every tongue will confess to God.'" Moloch, though he fought to raise himself from the ground, found that the feat was more than impossible. His lips began to move, and no matter how hard he tried to fight it, he gave glory to the God he'd opposed for generations.

"Jesus… is Lord," he spoke begrudgingly. He spat on the ground at Aiden's feet, which prompted a swift kick to the skull.

"You know, it doesn't have to be this way," Aiden stated with mild smugness. "You could side with us, help us defeat Lucifer, and live out the rest of your days as a normal man. Maybe even retire in the countryside, or with horns like that even join the circus."

"I would rather die!" Moloch spat. "No! Better! I would much rather kill you for what you made me do!" Aiden placed his hand on the subdued Moloch's head with steel in his eyes.

"I have a better idea," Aiden offered in return. "'I will give you a new heart and put a new spirit in you; I will remove from you your heart of stone and give you a heart of flesh.'" A brilliant light flashed before Moloch's eyes, and the sound that erupted from his throat proved more painful than any Aiden had ever heard. The many faces of the thousands of children he'd consumed as sacrifices flooded his vision and reached for him with eerie cold. He screamed as he tried to flee, but as the seconds ticked by, he realized that he would never be rid of them. His calloused nature had been utterly shattered, and all that remained was the pathetic shell of a man he had always been too afraid to see. His horns shattered like glass and disappeared, and in a moment of immense grief he fell at the prophet's feet as he embraced a humility that in his natural life he'd never known. He took to his feet and limped away from the Nabi who administered his ultimate defeat, and as he ran into the crowd, those grieving parents whose children he stole and slaughtered, they closed in on him with every intention to strike.

"Leave him alone," Eran yelled above the clamor of the mob. Aiden stood there, taken aback that Eran chose to act out of mercy in spite of everything this man had done. Every head in the crowd turned to face the two prophets, not a single one pleased.

"And who the hell are you to order us around?" shouted an angry man from deep within the pack.

"Our homes were destroyed because of this *thing*," came a woman's voice shortly thereafter.

"We still can't find our children," cried a desperate mother as she approached the Nabi'im. "We don't even really know what's going on. We just want our babies back!" The poor woman broke down in tears as she feared the worst over their lost kids. Her husband quickly came up behind her and took her in his arms as she slowly sank to her knees. He did his best to comfort her, but turned his attention to the Nabi'im as well.

"Tell us," he started humbly, "just what are you?" Aiden cautiously glanced over to Eran and then back at the grief-stricken families. He knew to an extent the pain they felt. He knew what it was like to lose someone precious to him, to feel like he'd lost his will to live and fight. Still, he had never been a parent who had lost their child. Even so, the Two explained everything about the history of the Nabi'im, the demons that they fought against, and the dangers of Lucifer's release. The crowd listened in silence as they recounted the major events of the last twelve years, and how the destruction of their city came as a result of Lucifer's vendetta against the Two. The eyes of every parent grew tearful as Aiden continued on.

“There isn’t much I can say about how you’re probably feeling or what you’re thinking other than we tried, more than we can say to protect you all.” Aiden recalled the horrific image of the enflamed bodies of the children as they lay in the idol’s furnace. His stomach twisted all over again, and he dropped to his knees and cried just the same. He wanted so badly to speak life into them, to leave them with something to help them cope with their loss, but he realized that no matter what he wanted to say, he would never be able to relate to them. But then it hit him. In every instance thus far the answer was always in the Scriptures, and that revelation spurred him to seek the pocket Bible he always kept on his person. He flipped to the last book, Revelation, and found the only thing he thought to read to them. He straightened up, stretched out his right hand with his eyes closed and spake. “‘They triumphed over him by the blood of the Lamb and the word of their testimony.’”

A flash of lightning struck the ground between the prophets and the couple that grieved aloud just a few yards away. Dust shot into the air and blanketed the area and the couple slid back out of shock. A great gust suddenly swept away the remnants of the blast to reveal a frail woman in ancient robes with hair as bushy as a young sheep. She took in the crowd, one person at a time, and saw the man that once was Moloch the Incinerator in their midst. She looked at Aiden quietly, as if she waited for some sense of introduction, and the young Nabi bowed to her out of reverence.

“I don’t have anything worth saying,” he told the crowd, “but she does. Listen to the testimony of Mary, the mother of Jesus.” Mary squeezed him gently on his shoulder and approached the crowd, and very softly she gave her account of the most heartbreaking moments of her life.

"You poor children," she began in a motherly tone. "I understand the pain you all must be experiencing, the pain of outliving your child. Just because mine was different does not make it hurt any less. I watched them from the background as they led him to the Place of the Skull. The cross on his back dug into the still-bleeding wounds from the torturous beating he endured before, and though they seized a man from the crowd to take up the cross for him, he still staggered from the pain. My eyes shifted to the criminals that followed behind him. They proved themselves to be liars and thieves, the dregs of our society who were more than deserving of this kind of punishment, and my sweet little one, the boy who for nine months dwelt within my body and bonded with my soul, the man who tended to the lost and sick throughout Israel, had been thrown in with them for nothing short of speaking the truth." Her eyes watered as the memory came back in wildest vividness, but still she knew what good the story would do and carried on despite her discomfort. "The soldiers stripped him of his clothes and exposed him to the crowd as they auctioned them off before his weary eyes, and to my shock he was not embarrassed as was expected, nor was he angry. 'Father, forgive them, for they know not what they do,' he whispered amid the screams of the crowd around him that spurred the soldiers and begged for his crucifixion. They stretched out his hands on either side of his body, and aligned his feet against the trunk of that horrible tree. Strained tears fell from my eyes when they hammered those nails into the hands of my firstborn baby." Her voice trembled as she spoke, and the broken citizens who watched her bawled in silence as they listened to her tale. "Blood flowed from these new wounds, these fresh holes in his body, and nobody seemed to notice the life that slowly trickled from the openings. But I did. A mother notices the pain of her child, even when others refuse to see it. I pressed forward with my sister to watch on. What else could I do? I could never bring myself to leave him. As a boy, when he cried in the night, I put him at ease. I fed him and clothed him, played with him and held him, and with every knock of the hammer against the nails I could see him grow before my eyes and feel my rage building. I stepped forward, prepared to tear my son's attackers to pieces in total animosity when I felt a gentle hand take my shoulder. I turned abruptly, and when I recognized who touched me my heart sank further. Mary Magdalene offered a smile of comfort through tears of her own, and John behind her stood in awe of the horror that our people found so enjoyable. I looked back at him, my Yeshua, and as they raised him on that cross I felt my heart break. There, above his thorn-crowned head hung a notice that read: JESUS OF NAZARETH, THE KING OF THE JEWS, and immediately I froze as the pain in my chest heightened. It was destined to be this way, and I knew that since the angel appeared before me. But why? Why did it have to hurt so much? I could hold it in no longer. The tears came like a flood and fell to the blood-soaked ground, and with a wail I tried to look away, but before I could turn, my sister Mary pointed at the cross and I knew, with more certainty than that Mary was my name, that this was God's work. Somehow, in my son's humiliation he looked princely. In his defeat, he looked victorious. And then his eyes met mine. I struggled to straighten up but failed, and it was in that moment that I could have sworn I saw him smile, of all things. He looked to my right, to John his disciple, and back to me. Comfortingly he told me, 'Woman, here is your son.' I wept all the more, and then listened as he told John, 'Here is your mother.' My sweet boy did for me in his final hour what he did for so many in the three years before this point. He took care of me. I understand what it feels like to lose the child you held in your arms, and like you I know how it feels to lose them unjustly. But in his death, my little boy taught me something. It is easy to focus on what we lose in times like these. But when you really think about it, would they not rather us remember what they left us?" As the crowd openly sobbed over her account and her wisdom, Aiden and Eran turned and left the scene with streams of their own tears.

The sun shone brightly overhead, and as they traversed the demolished city of Edgehaven, they knew that the time had come to make Lucifer pay for what he'd done.

Chapter Fourteen

Maya Hadarah stood there on the onyx floor, and stared at the edge of the star-sapphire tiles upon which her predecessors once tread. She recalled all of their painful memories, every one recreated in the dark clouds generated by this platform, but dared not shy away from the realization of her own. She knew beyond a shadow of a doubt that the fundament reason for her existence on this earth rested beyond the gem-encrusted double doors that stood mere feet away from her.

"You may begin at any time you wish," Michael told her. She marveled at his gentleness in comparison to his siblings'… interesting personalities, and with a deep breath she began her journey across the floor. The task seemed easy to Maya at first, but just as she expected, it wasn't long before her past caught up with her.

"My sweet Maya," came her father's voice from her left. She looked into his loving eyes, but noticed the younger form of herself as she stood before him with a hopeful expression. Maya's eyes widened with discomfort as she recalled exactly what moment this was. He pat the little girl on her head and took her into his arms. He smothered her cheeks in fatherly kisses and whispered into her ear, "You don't need to try to be a therapist. Women don't need to work like men do, sweetheart. One day, you'll meet a man who'll see just how special you are and he'll treat you like a queen. The only job you need to think about is how you'll take care of him." The moment had weighed down on her for her entire life, and she loathed how easily her father had undermined her aspirations. It was because of that that she even made the defiant move to pursue her education and career, but as much as she hated to admit it, he wasn't the only person who underestimated her abilities and determination.

The image faded as she moved forward with teary eyes. The next moment emerged, and she saw herself with her two best friends in high school. Both of them were prettier than her in her opinion, but for some reason Bethany and Michelle sought her company above everyone else. Maya was never exactly popular, though she was well known, and despite the overwhelming kindness she experienced on a daily basis from friends and family she never quite understood why she was always so closely observed. The girls sat in her bedroom and gawked over the boys in their teen magazines, and laughed at how wide the gaps in their interests proved to be. The present-day Maya cringed at the incredibly shallow things that she said in her efforts to sound deep, and was appalled at the way her friends acted around her.

"What do you guys want out of the future," asked the adolescent Maya, who rested in a supine position on the bed and sighed as she stared longingly at the image of a young boy she'd never seen before. "I really wanna land a guy like this, but if I get to work as a therapist I don't know if I'm gonna have time to deal with a whole other person." The mystery behind the eyes of the boy on the page filled her with an uncommon mix of intrigue and uncertainty that, for Maya, issued a new level of seriousness to the otherwise jovial atmosphere. Both of her friends, on the other hand, erupted in laughter. "What?" she asked defensively, which only made the duo laugh all the more.

"Stop, you're gonna kill us," Bethany pleaded as she literally slapped her knee in amusement, and then quietly reprimanded herself for being so lame. "But really, sweetie, what are you talking about?"

"What do you mean," Maya begged as she sat up with a furrow in her brow. Michelle brushed her light brown hair out of her almost mesmerizing sea green eyes, and playfully leaned against her friend's shoulder as she smiled into her luminous blues.

"Maya, you really can be clueless sometimes," she said with a sisterly smile. Bethany scooted closer to the others and gently ran her fingers through Maya's long, dark brown hair.

"You're so beautiful," she said flatly. "Like a princess."

"Yeah," Michelle confirmed. "With those looks you could land any man, and he'd be lucky to have you and hold you and take care of you for the rest of your life. Forget having to work, girl. Ride on the gravy train that your looks are driving!" The present-day Maya shook her head. She wanted nothing to do with that ideology then, and some fifteen years later she stood firm in her conviction. She pressed onward towards the doors with a greater sense of affirmation. In the next moment, she watched herself run through the crowded sidewalks of Edgehaven and relived the fear she felt in that instance. Her heart pumped as rapidly as her feet against the pavement, and frantically she looked back to check the progression of the deranged man that gave chase. He wasn't that close, but despite the distance she could see the sadistic twinkle in his eye as he perilously pursued her.

"Come here, Princess," he shouted over the crowd. "I only wanna talk to ya!" Maya looked around from person to person and desperately sought help, but all she received were the blank stares of passersby who, in the comfort of their daily habits, chose to look right through her frantic expression. As the man gained distance, she felt even more hopeless when it occurred to her that she might not even survive the encounter. She turned her head again as tears slid down her face, but despite the obvious distress of the lovely Maya Hadarah, she found herself utterly alone.

She lifted her hand to wipe her face of the tears, but when she regained her sights she only barely noticed the man who stood in her path. He casually walked the streets in jeans and t-shirt, seemingly without a care in the world, but when she noticed him it was only mere seconds before their collision.

"Get out of the way," she called to him, but her warning did little good. She knocked him over and his head bounced unremittingly against the concrete sidewalk. She paused for a moment in fear that the impact had damaged him in some way, but when he opened his eyes she was surprised to see his expression go from pained with a tinge of irritation to completely and utterly shocked. She felt drawn to him from the very beginning, and for a moment as she gazed into his deep brown eyes and observed his milk chocolate skin that so easily contrasted with the fairness of her own, she felt as if she could tell him anything. She opened her mouth to speak but looked behind her, and when she saw the manic man as he roared with speed she pushed herself off and further distanced herself from her pursuer.

"Sorry," she shouted to him as she departed and strained to find an out of that predicament. The present-day Maya cried at the utter terror of the memory as she pressed onward towards the door. The only images she saw now were of Aiden, who always seemed to come to her rescue when she needed him. He was there that day when she'd almost been raped. He was the one who took her to safety when Bloodsport attacked the shopping district, and powered up enough to fend him off while others in the area evacuated. The images from the last few hours seemed to swirl together, and the more she watched her life on repeat, the more she saw how she caused him pain.

Maya saw the way he cringed at his own memories as he all-too-willingly shared them with her, how he cried as he relived every moment that led him to lose the one person he'd ever known as a friend. She watched herself beg shamelessly for more detail, and cried in remorse of her own actions. The Maya of a few hours prior left his home, and even after she was attacked by Bloodsport, after all the trauma she caused her rescuer, he still cared for her and shielded her from harm as best he could.

The present Maya looked around at the glorious Hall that she'd only seen through the memories of another, and realized that it was most likely his doing that she was there in the first place. She paused for a moment as the tears streamed more profusely. She realized that she would never be able to repay him for all he'd done for her, and how she'd never be able to make it up to him for all the trouble that she caused. She was disgusted with who she'd allowed herself to become, this helpless creature born of the underestimation of her friends and family, who despite her advancements failed to restore her damaged self-esteem and apparently endangered the lives of others.

A black cloud washed over her just as it had Eran those many years ago, and Maya, overwhelmingly frustrated with herself bellowed into the Hall with enough fury as to scatter the fog around her. The Archangels stood in awe as she approached the door. There were no more visions now, no more doubts or feelings of helplessness and hopelessness. There was only resolve. *I'm done,* she spoke to herself as she reached for the door to the Grand Hall, *I'm done being seen as some delicate little princess. From here on out, I'm going to do what I can to make life easier on the others around me instead of harder. I'm going to be more than just the damsel in distress, and I won't allow anyone to underestimate me another second longer. The most they can do is hope they're ready for Maya Hadarah,* she reassured herself as she placed her hand on the door and watched it open. The radiant luminescence that she remembered from Aiden's memory shimmered through the crack and intensified as the door moved further out of her path.

It opened entirely, and though the light from the other side blasted forth she stared into it as she crossed the threshold. Elijah the Tishbite sat comfortably on his throne and leaned against one of the arms as he watched the young lady stride with unprecedented confidence. The Flame Prophet quickly noticed a power about her presence that Aiden and Eran lacked upon their initial entry to the pristine chamber.

The High King descended from his throne and approached Maya, who quickly abandoned her confidence in the presence of the prophet. She averted her eyes to the onyx floor of the Grand Hall and listened to the sound of his wooden sandals as they clicked against the tile. The closer Elijah came to her, the more he analyzed her, and the more apparent it became to him that she'd had a rather special encounter whilst she slept in the emerald room. She slowly picked up her head and took in the sight of the old man from before. He wore an ancient blue robe that proved too baggy for him, and though his gray beard rested thickly upon his face she could tell he smiled at her with a great excitement.

"You must not be so quick to abandon your confidence," he said to her in regard to her entrance. "You were chosen by the Most High for a very special purpose, and in order to fulfill that purpose you must have faith that transcends heaven and earth. You must be confident in not only yourself, but in the One who appointed you for this task. Tell me, child," his face intensified as he prepared to ask the question. Maya took a deep breath to brace herself, for what she had no idea, and locked eyes with the mysterious elder. "Do you know for what you have been called?"

Maya shook her head. She thought about the encounter from the odd dream that she'd had before, but somehow it didn't seem very relevant to the conversation at hand. Elijah paced around her just as he had the two young men twelve years prior. Her eyes followed him as he pulled a large green Bible out of thin air and flipped to the Book of Isaiah. He handed it to her, and directed her attention toward the page to reveal the 61st chapter. Maya's eyes met the page, and after a brief skim she looked back at the prophet.

"I'm sorry," she started with a confused wrinkle in her brow, "but what is it that you'd like me to do here?"

"Read the words on the page aloud until you are directed to stop. Everything pertaining to your purpose in this place will be revealed through this simple action," he explained. Reluctantly she returned her eyes to the book in her hands, and with a final exchange of looks between the young woman and the mysterious prophet, she started to read.

"'The Spirit of the Sovereign Lord is on me, because the Lord has anointed me to proclaim good news to the poor,'" she read with a shaky voice. Her stomach flipped as an overwhelming sense of power flowed from it. "'He has sent me to bind up the brokenhearted, to proclaim freedom for the captives and release from darkness for the prisoners,'" as she continued to read, the power surged throughout her body in a way that nearly dropped her to her knees, but she straightened up and endured its flow, "to proclaim the year of the Lord's favor and the day of vengeance of our God,'" her voice intensified now, and unbeknownst to her, her clothes began to morph. She no longer wore the green and ivory robe, but a green hooded cloak with bright green flames at the shoulders manifested over an ivory clerical shirt and collar with a matching set of ivory slacks. She continued to the end, and as the power erupted over her skin she softened in her speech and expression as the words took her back to that ethereal plane. Suddenly she locked eyes with the prophet Elijah as she uttered the words, "'to comfort all who mourn, and provide for those who grieve in Zion—"

"That is good enough," he told her joyfully before she could start again. She made an attempt to hand the Bible back to him, but he refused it and pointed downward. Her eyes followed his earthward finger and to her utter astonishment she noticed that a green variation of the Nabi'im robes had covered her body.

"What on earth is going on here," she managed with a bewildered expression. She glanced back at the Archangels that once protested her presence in the Hall, and was at least put at ease upon the realization that they were just as baffled as she.

"It would seem that the Two have now become the Three. Tell me, Ms. Maya," Elijah asked as his soft amber eyes locked on her with bright intensity, "have you any idea now?" Maya offered no answer, and refocused awkwardly on the garb that overshadowed her body. Elijah breathed deeply and closed his eyes as he walked away from her and Michael approached. "You are the third of the Nabi'im, matched evenly in spirit with Aiden Zane and Eran Hewer, and capable of all their abilities given the proper training."

"How… how is this possible," Michael asked, astonished and a bit unnerved, from behind the young woman. He glanced at her as he finally realized the reason for the pull her presence had on him. "Up until now there have only been two—"

"Up until now," Elijah interrupted patiently, "our greatest enemy was a manageable threat, but as the days drag on he grows in power." Michael walked around the awestricken Maya to meet the eyes of the elderly Nabi of days long past.

"My king," he spoke, "forgive me if I speak out of turn, but even if that is the case, I fail to see how that warrants the rise of a new Nabi." Elijah waved off the comment, and Maya focused intently on the conversation now.

"There are some things that the Master does that we are not meant to understand, Michael. Now, then, given the circumstances I think it best if you take Ms. Hadarah into the training chamber. There is much to cover with her, and I fear that this sudden lack of intensity with Lucifer is only the calm before the storm." Elijah walked back towards his massive throne once the order had been given, and Michael stared upon the lovely young Maya with an air of doubt.

Maya stared back into his strong gold and silver eyes, and though she instinctively thought to avert her gaze, she remembered the charge of the Flame Prophet to cling to her assertiveness and did just that.

"Problem?" She asked the chief Archangel with more force than intended. He refused to acknowledge her question, but led her out of the Grand Hall and into the same training area that Uriel had once taken her predecessors. As the two made their exit, Elijah wondered just how this newcomer would fare.

"Oriphiel, Uriel," he said as he continued to watch the door. They unfurled their massive silver wings and glided across the onyx floor to kneel at the foot of the great throne. "Return to your respective prophets. The greatest battle of the modern Nabi'im will take place within the next 24 hours, and what little time we have left should be spent developing strategy and unity amongst the Three."

"Understood," they said in unison, and in an instant they vanished without a trace. Elijah opened his palm, and a scroll dropped from heaven landed firmly within his grasp. He opened it with great joy, and a flash of light emanated that temporarily blinded him. Still, though, his heart beat intensely and his mind raced with anticipation for the training that he knew now took place. He refocused his vision on the portal that manifested in the center of the page, and saw the duo of Michael and Maya stand across from each other in the training room.

"So, this is where it all began for them," she muttered under her breath as she looked around at the cracks in the walls and the miniature craters in the floor. "I have the sneaking suspicion that I should be at least a little nervous about this." The flames on her shoulders lulled to a dull flicker in response to her timidity, which only lit a bigger flame in the pit of Michael's belly.

"That kind of weakness has no place here. I do not know if you realize what battle lies ahead of you, but if you head into it thinking like a scared child, then Lucifer will destroy you before you have time to breathe Scripture. Understood?" Maya's eyes narrowed on her trainer as her temper flared, and the flames on either side of her head burst to the ceiling. His eyes widened in surprise, as he thought that the little human before him was completely hopeless from the start.

"The only one getting destroyed around here will be you if you ever call me a child again. If you don't believe me, then let me show you," she offered, and the flames at her shoulders lunged for the Archangel in her path. Michael slapped his rock-solid hand against the floor, and a slab of earth protruded from the space in front of him to form a barrier. The flames, however, shifted around the makeshift blockade and struck him on both sides. Michael slid across the floor and the barrier he'd erected crumbled before his very eyes as Maya methodically strolled towards him. His eyebrows lifted in delighted surprise.

"Well, would you look at that," remarked the Archangel teasingly, "it would seem that you are not completely helpless after all." She smirked with a gleam in her eye that spoke of her voracious appetite for combat, and the glowing green script of "Nabi" flickered on the hood of her cloak. She charged him, but the experienced warrior angel unfurled his wings and pushed her back before he took to the air. He hovered above the room, and breathed a sigh of relief as he watched to see what she would do next. She angrily punched against the broken-tiled floor of the training chamber as she watched him fold his arms and flash a cocky grin. "You are aware of the Bible in your hands, yes? You may consider opening it and finding something that you might use to help you out here. Otherwise," he said as he flexed his muscular arms, and seven shimmering clouds formed in the air. Maya watched them as one by one the glimmering manifestations of mist gave way to brighter shining swords, each encrusted with a different colored jewel.

The previously enraged Maya now stood before the Archangel awestricken over the blades, and Michael, with more of a smile on his face than he could mask, extended his hand towards her. The first blade lurched at her at staggering speed, but the determined neophyte narrowly rolled out of the way and watched as it embedded itself in the floor. Michael deployed two more of the majestic brands in intersecting paths, and while Maya evaded the first of the projectiles, she landed in the way of the second. As it hurdled towards her face, she quickly bent backwards and allowed it to pass over her. Michael deployed another of the swords at her lower body, but the flexible girl flipped backwards on her hands. He launched yet another at her abdomen, but with what seemed to be the greatest of ease Maya sidestepped the sword with her eyes firmly locked on her eventual target.

Michael floated in the air with a blade on either side of him, utterly astonished that the weakling had the ability to predict where he would next fire. *Of course,* he thought as his eyes went wide with the realization, *the prophetic vision.* He lifted his hand and the two swords that remained at his sides ascended above his head. Maya quickly opened her Bible to the presumed middle and looked down at a random verse.

"'I have hidden your Word in my heart that I might not sin against you,'" she recited. The flames on her shoulders immediately flared with an intensity that sent a massive shockwave through the room and blasted Maya in her chest. She stood firmly in place, and watched as the room around her seemed to slow drastically. Pages upon pages of information filtered into her mind in Hebrew, Greek, Latin, and English, and to her astonishment she could read it all. She smiled excitedly, and within a moment she saw the words of Isaiah the Prophet come into view. Michael thrust his swords sharply downward towards her, and as they approached she quickly took to the verse in her sights. "'But those who hope in the Lord will renew their strength. They will soar on wings like eagles; they will run and not grow weary, they will walk and not be faint.'" As the words left her mouth, the flames that previously struck her heart unfurled into a pair of emerald green wings and lifted her into the air as the blades rained down.

Maya charged at him in midair with fist upraised, but the seasoned angelic commander easily sidestepped her and delivered a kick to the center of her upper back. She shook from the pain and almost fell, but with a single beat of her deep green wings she managed to stay aloft.

"I have to admit," Michael said with the same twinkle in his eye that Uriel had in Aiden's memory, "you are a lot more fun than the others."

"That's so sweet of you," she responded, her tone infused with sarcasm. "I wonder what you'll think of me after this: 'Let the land produce vegetation: seed-bearing plants and trees on the land that bear fruit with seed in it, according to their various kinds.'" The ground beneath the Hall of quaked below, and out of the floor of the training room came a full-grown forest. Michael cringed at the sight, but still applauded the young woman who proved more masterful than he'd ever imagined.

"So, you wisely decided to give yourself some cover," he mused. "No matter. It will not be long before the forest and its creator are devastated at my hand." His tone was almost as sadistic as his sister Uriel's, but Maya smiled from the shadows as he materialized yet another blade in his hand. He chopped at a nearby tree with enough force to demolish a small building, but the lush vegetation stood firmly in its place. Michael took another strike and applied much more force this time, but the result remained the same. "What is this?" The tree that he'd abused began to rattle, and before Maya could answer him, it buried one of its branches in his belly. The Archangel clutched his abdomen as he fought to retain air, when Maya descended from above and drove her foot into his face. The Archangel crashed to the grass-covered floor below, and Maya gently descended across from him.

"Who's the child now," she quipped as she made her way for the door. Maya Hadarah couldn't help but bask in her victory, more over herself than over the Archangel. For her entire life, she'd been treated like a helpless princess, talked down to and underestimated to the point where she had come to underestimate herself. But this, this battle with Michael of the Archangels and the victory she'd won out of sheer determination and luck, proved that nobody would ever underscore her again, and that she was finally able to make the difference in the world that she always knew she could.

Elijah sat comfortably in his throne with a brilliant smile emblazoned on his face from the duel's outcome. He listened silently as she walked down the corridor and back into the Grand Hall, and from sheer compulsion he jumped from his seat.

"My dear, no human being since Jacob the Patriarch has bested Michael like that in battle. Very well done," he praised. She blushed at his compliment and curtseyed before the High King. "It was very fortunate of you to land on the verse you did. I have to admit I questioned your ability to stand against Michael of the Clanging Steel even in training, but you proved your moxie in a way that neither of your predecessors could have imagined. Tell me," he asked her with smiling amber eyes, "what led you to open your Bible there?" Maya pensively placed a single finger on her chin and looked off into the atmosphere as she thought carefully about that moment.

"I really don't know," she told the old prophet honestly. Her eyes locked with his as the defeated Archangel strode back into the Grand Hall and took his place beside his king. "I just relied on the One who gave me the power. I figured that if I was really meant to be involved in this, then He would take care of me when I needed Him to and that's what I got." Maya's eyes shifted to Michael, who sported a fresh splash of green against his otherwise threatening silver, and it was all she could do to hold back the laughter.

Elijah watched as she approached her trainer and extended her hand in a gesture of good sportsmanship, and reluctantly the commander of the angels accepted her display of kindness. *Just as I thought,* Elijah mused with a subtle grin firmly in place. *So, this is what you had planned all along...*

Chapter Fifteen

The day pressed on, and as the citizens of Edgehaven started work on the reconstruction in their war-ravaged home, Aiden and Eran walked the streets in discomfort at the sudden calm. A few hours had passed since their battle with Moloch the Incinerator. Mary had since departed, and the chaos of the events that surrounded the siege on the city resonated with everyone who had seen it. Fear polluted the air, and the only saving grace those poor people had was the knowledge that the prophets walked among them. This calm, however, unearthed in Eran things he wasn't yet prepared to deal with.

"What are we supposed to do with this," Eran asked as his eyes shiftily observed the area as they marched onward. He marveled at the desolation left behind the Ammonite monster, and among the living that worked to repair the damage he was able to see the faces of lives he took. "Something doesn't feel right. After all that Lucifer's thrown at us, suddenly there's nothing."

"He's toying with us," Aiden stated flatly and broke Eran's focus on the ghosts of his past. "He wants to lure us into a false sense of security, so that when the time comes to put him back in his prison he'll have all the pieces in place to annihilate us all. On top of that, he doesn't want to risk giving away too much of his plan so that when he's ready to proceed, we won't have much time to prepare." Eran's brow furrowed. He couldn't help but think about the whispers and lies that the Seed of the Flesh had told him throughout the years and the separation that it caused between him and his best friend, nor could he forget the party responsible for its planting. For little more than a decade his life was so chaotic, even in the last few hours since the Seed's defeat, but now… this silence that he endured forced him to face his sins. His fists trembled and his body stiffened, and though Aiden hadn't turned to see him, he instinctively knew to ask, "Are you alright?" Eran's expression softened and he looked up at his wingman.

"What?" he asked, but in the next instance the question itself resonated in his mind's ear, and he offered a proper answer. Eran wanted desperately to cry out, to grieve the many terrible things that he'd done, but upon the emergence of his tears he forced them back with a slight choke and said, "No, I'm fine, just… thinking." Aiden looked away from him as he realized that despite their recent collaborations there was still a rift there. They fell silent for a while as they watched the city around them, and as they took in the broken windows and overturned cars, the shattered rooftops and demolished homes, Aiden thought about the endless torture that Eran must have endured for those twelve years, how he must have been abused with no hope for salvation. The image of the grotesque Seed flashed into his mind, and the rage he felt when he destroyed it pumped back into his veins.

He had thought Eran dead for so long, and up until now it hadn't resonated with him that he'd suffered much more than simple death in the time they'd been apart. Though he was helpless to do anything during that time, the realization of that fact only angered and saddened him all the more. He thought it funny that no matter how much of a hellion Eran had turned out to be, no matter what he'd done wrong, no matter how many times he tried to kill him, Aiden only thought of a way to save him. Even now, the only thing that crossed his mind was how to be there for Eran, because he knew that his old war buddy had seen enough isolation to last him a lifetime.

“What happened since that day,” Aiden asked him, and watched as Eran’s eyes rattled at the memory, “when you fell into the pit?” They continued to walk, and with every step Eran took shorter breaths. A barrage of heinous memories bombarded his mind, and as they flurried around inside his head, he placed a hand against his temple to stabilize himself. His pace slowed, and Aiden paused a moment to take in the sight of his emotionally broken wingman. “Are you alright?”

“I… I just need to… rest,” Eran breathed. The violence of his past, the innocent lives he’d destroyed, the destruction he’d caused for his own fictitious ambition of obtaining absolute power drained him of all strength, and the more he struggled with it, the more unbearable it became. Aiden placed a hand on his back and guided him over to a bench at the entrance to the park. They sat down, and for a moment Aiden recalled the former beauty of the place. The sound of birds as they sang in the fresh summer breeze echoed to him through time immemorial, but all that he heard in the present were the solemn sighs and quiet tears of a desolated city. He placed his hand comfortingly on Eran’s shoulder, and the action startled him to the point where he initially shied away, but inevitably grew more relaxed next to Aiden. “I’m sorry, I just…”

“Take your time,” Aiden told him as he retracted his hand. “I understand that you’ve been through a lot. I’m just here to help.” Eran placed his hand on Aiden’s shoulder and stared into his eyes. His face dripped with sweat, though the air was considerably cooler now that Moloch had lost his power. He was on the verge of tears as the memories flooded into his mind all at once.

“So many terrible things,” he said as he trembled. “I can’t…” he grabbed his head again as tears streamed. He was in pain, and for every second his friend suffered Aiden hated himself for how powerless he was to stop it.

"It's alright," Aiden assured him. He lifted his hand, placed it on top of Eran's blond head, and closed his eyes. The Scripture came clearly into his mind, and without any delay he uttered the words, "'Carry each other's burdens, and in this way you fulfill the law of Christ.'" At first there was calm, but then an overwhelming mass of faces long dead and cities thrown into chaos stormed his mind. He fought with the images and the noise of those disturbing thoughts in a desperate move to make sense of the turmoil, and though difficult, he managed to hone in on the sinister whispers that emanated from the pit of Tel Megiddo.

"I'm the one who will save your life," Aiden heard from within the black. It was an oddly childlike voice, and as he looked around at the darkness of the pit, he felt his other arm latch onto the wall from which he hung. His body lurched upward as whatever beast within him eagerly spurred onward towards its escape.

"Who are you?" Eran's voice came from his mouth. *So that's it,* Aiden thought, *I'm seeing the past through* his *eyes...* "What do you want with me?"

"Don't you recognize me," came the voice again, almost appalled. "I'm *you.* I'm the realization of your every dream and aspiration, I'm your ambition, your motivation, the thing that pushes you onward, and I just want you to be as powerful as you were destined to be." The words of the voice sounded so sweet and attractive, and though Eran was well aware that it wasn't in fact him who spoke those words, he found himself drawn more to the fantasies it spewed than the reality he was faced with. His body climbed further and further out of the pit, and the closer he got to the surface the more he realized that everyone was gone. *Aiden,* he whispered to himself, and the Seed laughed.

"Aiden isn't here anymore. He and the Archangels have abandoned you," the voice malevolently whispered into Eran's ear.

"No," Eran returned, almost sure that once they reached the top he would find his comrade there unshaken in his devotion, but a heartbroken Aiden knew the untainted truth in the words of the Seed. "You're wrong… Aiden would never do that," Eran protested as the many triumphs and failures of their days in basic training filtered into his mind. "There's a lot of heartless scum in this world who would turn on their brother and leave him for dead, but Aiden's different! Out of everyone in my life, he—"

"Waited until you became more powerful than he did and fled from you in fear," the Seed lied. "Did you really think that he would join you in the ultimate destiny? He loves to bask in the lie of selflessness and claims that he can teach the world a better way, but don't you think that if there was any truth behind that he'd start with the friend who in his eyes is lost? Don't you think it odd that he challenges your call to greatness? He's abandoned you, Eran, and like the rest of the humans, Aiden must die—"

"Shut up!" Eran bellowed into the vast darkness of the pit. He couldn't take any more. He couldn't listen to the twisted logic of the Seed and even refused to acknowledge its authenticity. He saw it for the lie that it really was, the ruse designed to separate him from the only person who had the potential to save him, but the fear of actuality pushed him onward in his own strength now. Curiosity outweighed denial as he dug his hands into the cleft of the rock and pulled himself from the pit to the surface, and as he crawled out of the ruins he realized that he was, in fact, all alone.

He stared into the sky as his knees descended to the earth, and as his heart crumbled slowly within him, the heavens wept to mask his tears. The tornado of Eran's memories continued to swirl before Aiden's eyes. He clutched his heart for a moment and looked to the man who sat beside him on the bench, and in that moment, he saw on Eran's face a look of relief he was suddenly desperate to recreate. Despite his own discomfort, Aiden narrowed in on another memory as it surged through the morning light.

The image of a preacher came into full view. He stood behind his pulpit as he emphatically commissioned them to expect magical gifts of cars and houses at the expense of their screams. Eran sat quietly on the back pew, and even though Aiden still saw through his eyes, he knew that there was something fundamentally different about the man he sought to help. Eran watched the vehement preacher continue to mock the doctrine he knew in his heart to be true, and trembled in anger as he felt his belt for the Desert Eagle he'd managed to tuck away.

"Remember, brothers and sisters that when the praises go up the blessings come down, and that all you have to do is seek Him first and He'll start dropping everything you need right in your lap! The word says that ALL these things will be added unto you—"

"What a sham!" Eran called out over the many praises of the congregation. Every head turned to look at him as he stood from his seat and proceeded to the center aisle, but he couldn't find the simplest reason to care about what they thought. "You know, it's people like you who sicken me the most; so quick to tell the people what they want to hear and not what they need. You fill them with the illusion of a genie-adjacent God, and send them back into the world with an entitled mentality that contradicts and disgusts the very One you claim to believe in."

The preacher shook in anger at his unbothered manner of speech as Eran methodically paced the center aisle of the dead-silent church.

"Who are you," the preacher demanded as he motioned for security to move in. They surrounded Eran, who smiled at their adorable attempt to put a stop to his advance.

"Simple; I'm the strongest one here." He smiled at the preacher as the three security guards moved in to apprehend him. With little hesitation, he jumped backwards with his elbow extended and met the face of the first guard with an unforgiving blow to his nose. Due to the angle of the hit, the cartilage was quickly shoved into the man's brain. The other two assaulted him as he rolled away from their dead coworker, and without delay he unleashed a spinning jump kick that handled them both at once. He moved towards the pulpit with fire in his eyes as he lightly ran his finger along the handle of his favorite .50 caliber Desert Eagle. He pulled it from his belt and aimed it point blank at the preacher's skull.

"Somebody help me," whimpered the terrified clergyman. A sadistic smile slid over the lips of Aiden's best friend as he placed his finger on the trigger. "Please," the minister begged, but the congregation watched on in horror as Eran laughed maniacally.

"I have an idea," he almost sang in excitement, "how about you send your empty praises upward and see what comes down? Test your blasphemous theology in the face of real danger! Give these entitled *sheep* an example of the power of your genie God!" The man remained silent and shuttered at the feet of his assailant. Eran's expression sobered as he lightly squeezed the trigger. "Those who are unable to lead by example are unfit to lead," was the last thing he said to his hostage, and as he discharged the bullet from the chamber of his weapon, the mass of people within the church clamored for the door. Eran stood for a moment and watched the blood flow from the hole in the preacher's head, but as the people screamed in panic over the situation he thought it best to slip out the back and into the casual commotion of the city.

He blended with the crowd that traveled the sidewalk until he'd come to the alley alongside the abandoned warehouse that — for the moment — he called his home. He followed it and came to the back door, which he left ajar just for the sake of slipping back in without a hassle. He looked through the murky glass window at the city around him and held his nauseated stomach. The image of that man's dead body upon the altar of a church was etched into his skull.

"How could I have…" the sudden urge to vomit interrupted his sentence, but with a single powerful swallow he continued, "done something like that? What is this *thing* I've become?"

"You've taken the first step, Eran," the twisted Seed responded with a slightly disturbed chuckle. Its voice proved more cunning now, deeper, as if like a plant it actually grew within him. "You've started down the path to achieving ultimate power." Eran withdrew his gun and shot at the wall across from him. His breathing was just as heavy in this memory as it was in the present day. He gripped his head, and stared at the gun in his hand as tears streamed down his cheeks.

"Waging war to obtain power…" he scoffed disdainfully at the idea as he tossed his weapon across the concrete floor of the lifeless shack. For a moment he questioned whether or not it was worth it, if he could take so many lives for the chance to rework the fabric of reality on Earth. "Nothing good could ever come of war," he resolved. "It breeds monsters, not heroes."

"That's why you have to become the strongest force in the world. It's the right of the strong to make the rules, Eran, and today you've proven to yourself that you can take the power that you need. By showing that you can take a life to get what you want, you shed your reservations and prove that no matter what happens, it'll end with you at the pinnacle of existence," the Seed misled him further, and with every word it spewed Aiden grew all the more furious.

"What I'm doing is wrong," Eran decided for himself as he shook his head against the will of the thing that spurred him onward into darkness. "I wanted power so that things would be different, so that I wouldn't have to deal with the pain of being weak. But tell me how I'm supposed to forget that when all I'm doing is projecting that weakness onto others and victimizing them for it?"

"Everything will make sense in time," the Seed told him soothingly. "It all gets easier for everyone as you just keep going." The moment in the warehouse transitioned into a vivid killing spree. There was timidity the first few times, but just as the Seed predicted it became easier for Eran to kill the more he did it. Aiden receded from the memories, and found that he breathed just as heavily as Eran had before. He slammed his fist against the bench, and his comrade looked at him through concerned eyes. Aiden stopped moving as he watched his wingman's descent. He watched him murder people left and right, pave a path of destruction throughout the United States, level entire cities with his appalling power and strategy. Aiden couldn't stand to hear how the cries of countless innocent children were drowned out by the sound of his twisted ideology, and watch how he'd come to Edgehaven to start anew.

Aiden looked at Eran, who silently sobbed as he watched his friend's face distort in anguish and fury at the actions of his past, but shortly returned to the ocean of memories. As he sifted through the gale of Eran's turmoil, he suddenly found himself perched atop the building across from his apartment, and it became incredibly clear that the Eran of this age was now the fully hardened madman known as Bloodsport. He watched through Eran's eyes as he himself exited the quaint domain, and minutes later appeared on the streets below. As Aiden moved, so did Eran.

He saw Aiden lift his head at the sound of the red car as it rumbled on the road, and saw that all too familiar look of nostalgia in his eyes. *What are you thinking about,* Eran pondered as they kept moving. He seemed lost in thought, and for a second it was almost as if the unsuspecting Aiden Zane smiled. It sickened Eran, and without warning he withdrew his M110 and aimed carefully for his "brother's" head. Aiden continued down his path only seconds from death and without any knowledge, and as Bloodsport moved his finger ever so slowly from the magazine well to the trigger he was stunned when his target had been knocked unceremoniously to the ground. He removed the rifle from his line of sight and noticed that a fair-skinned girl with blackish brown hair and blue eyes lay on top of him.

For a moment Bloodsport mulled over the possibility of killing her out of principle, but ultimately decided to see how things played out, as the game was much more fun if Aiden had something of value to lose. Before long, the woman returned to her feet and bolted in the opposite direction of his former comrade's travel, and a third element to the situation was produced: the chaser who, garbed in an old fedora and tattered black long coat, sprinted past Aiden in an effort to secure his prize. Bloodsport placed his sniper rifle back on his back, and casually sat down upon the ledge of the rooftop.

"What will you do now, Aiden?" he asked rhetorically as he watched the scene from above, but as his old ally donned the garb that he'd forsaken long ago, it sparked something within him. He felt something shatter in his very soul, and for the first time in little over a decade it was as if he heard Eran — the real Eran — roar from within him. The sensation pulsed through his body with the force of a thousand electrical volts. His heart beat like a wild beast against his ribcage, and in a futile attempt to stabilize it he grabbed his chest as if to rip it out himself. "What's going on here," he asked himself as remorse for his actions slowly filtered into his mind. "Why do I feel so… pathetic?"

"Because you are," Eran vocalized hazily from within. There was a certain fury about him that burned the innards of the creature that overtook his body. "Mark my words, I'm gonna get out of here, and when I do you'll pay for everything you've done." With that, the visions vanished. Aiden and Eran sat on the bench, and as the former breathed heavily the latter placed his hand upon his shoulder. Aiden looked into his wingman's eyes to see an immense amount of penitence.

"That was… a lot," Aiden breathed as he slammed his back against the bench and closed his eyes. Eran quickly redirected his gaze to the ground as he removed his hand, completely ashamed of the things that Aiden might have seen. His pulse accelerated as he wondered just how to address the issue. Still there remained so many insecurities within him, and for the love of God the silence of the city unnerved him so. Aiden opened his eyes and looked into the clear blue sky as he silently prayed for an opportunity to fix his mistake from all those years ago. "I'm so sorry."

Aiden leaned forward, his face stone, and clasped his hands together tightly as his arms slid between his open legs. "I realize that the only reason why you endured all of that suffering was because I didn't have the strength to hold onto you that day. I have to admit that I allowed my own fear of who I thought you were going to turn into influence the actions I took, and that only caused you more pain in the end."

"Was that what it felt like…" Eran asked as he attempted to choke back his sobs. Aiden looked up at him, and the tears of a man he'd known to be so strong shattered his heart all over again. Eran looked away as he wiped his face on his sleeve and then started over. "Was that what it felt like before? When you were alone?" Aiden took a moment of silence as he reminisced about his life in the orphanage. Every day he found himself surrounded by people who thought him a nuisance despite his best efforts to prove his worth, and though all he wanted was to be loved, he always managed to draw more hatred than affection. "I thought I understood," Eran continued as he thought back on their days in basic training, "I thought I knew what kind of loneliness you shouldered back then. I thought I knew how you felt in your heart, what it was like to have nobody on your side even though you had the world around you. But how could I have? My mother was there for me as much as possible until the day that she…" The pain of the memory of her passing prevented him from formulating the words, but nevertheless he continued. "Even then you were with me, and with each day that you stood by me and took care of me like the good friend you were, the less I knew about what kind of pain you experienced long before we even met. And then…" his voice trailed off, and he was forced to look at the splintered trees and broken bridge of the once tranquil park.

“And then I was gone,” Aiden finished with an air of remorse. Eran remained silent for a moment but then redirected his attention.

“I understand it now, having walked the path of Bloodsport’s darkness. I know what it’s like to push so hard for something and never have it realized. More than that, I know what it’s like to have someone there with you every second of every day and still feel alone. But the reason I know so much about it is that you let me fall, and then let me go. Please,” he asked flatly as his brow furrowed atop his intensely focused eyes, “don’t let me go like that again.” In that moment as Aiden met his Eran’s gaze, he didn’t see the established Airman that he’d known since basic training, the Nabi who had learned by his side, or even the grown man that he’d met in the airport in San Antonio. In that moment, Eran Hewer was the terrified child bound to a doorknob so many years ago.

“I promise I won’t,” Aiden confirmed as he pulled his comrade into a hug. For the first time since his mother’s passing Eran cried in the presence of his friend, and with no judgment or timidity Aiden sat by his side and offered his shoulder to make it easier. They sat there in the broken park and watched as the people around them slowly tried to piece their lives back together until Eran felt at ease. Once the water ceased to fall from his eyes, he straightened himself up and stood to his feet.

“We should probably find a way out of the city. It would probably be best to find an airplane as soon as possible,” Eran said with a cough. Aiden smiled as he watched his wingman fight off embarrassment as best he could as he stood up beside him.

“That would probably work,” Aiden started, mildly amused, “except we can’t fly a plane.” Eran glared at Aiden, but quickly regained his military bearing before he started down the broken path that ran through the park. Aiden started after him with a beaming smile plastered along his jawline, but the bright and warm glow of the sun was quickly drowned out by a cold and distressing darkness similar to that over Tel Megiddo twelve years prior. Lightning flashed and thunder roared as the clouds circled overhead, and suddenly the joy of the Nabi'im transformed into concern. The winds swept through the city with unparalleled force, and the rubble and battered cars began to tumble through the streets. The people who worked to repair their damaged city fought to evade the onslaught of inanimate objects, and all the while screamed into the eye of the storm that swirled overhead.

"Well that's not good," Eran stated as he looked around at the chaos that ensued on all sides. "The only buildings untouched by Moloch's attack are clear across the city. In conditions like this it would be impossible to move everyone to safety unharmed."

"Then we'll just have to create a barrier between the city and the storm," Aiden said as a bus rolled down the street and towards a family of four. The father and mother took their two young daughters in their arms as they feared that there was no time to escape a gruesome death. The flames on Aiden's shoulders spiraled around it from where he stood just moments before it flattened the quartet, and as the blue turned to white, the holy fire melted the vehicle until only the wheels remained. The father nodded in thanks to the young Nabi, and ducked behind the crumbling wall of a nearby building in a desperate attempt at taking cover. "Eran! Exodus 33!" Eran placed his hands upon the ground as the trees rattled in the wind, and Aiden extended his own hands towards his brother as he knelt.

"'When my glory passes by, I will put you in a cleft in the rock and cover you with my hand until I have passed by,'" they recited together. The broken trees of the park hurdled towards them, but the power of their combined flames incinerated the wooden projectiles as they came. Tremors surged through the ground, and to the surprise of Edgehaven's residents, their city was guarded to the east and to the west by mountainous formations that significantly disrupted the air current. The geological anomalies molded themselves around the city until they created a single opening to the northernmost position near enough to be within walking distance of the Nabi'im. The father of the family that Aiden saved rushed over to the Two, but before he could express the joy and relief that he felt, Aiden interrupted with a request of his own. "I hate to bother you, but I need you to spread word throughout the city that the Nabi'im are leaving for a little while." The man's eyes grew wide with shock and fear.

"What," he started to ask as Aiden and Eran moved towards their exit. Eran placed a hand on his shoulder before he passed him by.

"Don't worry," he told the man as he watched Aiden walk onward for the opening. "You're all safe within this barrier and no monsters are gonna get through to change that. Tell everyone you can, and have them spread it to everyone else. Also, tell them not to leave the barrier. For their own protection." The man nodded confusedly, but when Eran strode after Aiden he felt the man grab him by the wrist. Hewer turned to see the worry in his eyes.

"What will you do?" he asked. Eran smiled as Aiden stopped to see what held him.

"We're going to handle a little business." Without another word, Aiden and Eran marched for the opening and out into the open world.

Chapter Sixteen

The Nabi'im looked up at the black clouds that circled overhead, and the sickening memory of Tel Megiddo rang ever-presently in their minds. The road they followed was as empty as the desert that surrounded it, and the only signs of life were the sounds of the storm above. The flames that rested on their shoulders morphed into barriers that staved off the advances of the wind-blown sands.

"So, what's our next move?" Eran asked as they marched the path.

"Wait," Aiden responded. "Right now, our biggest concern is getting to the Hall, and since planes are out of the question at the moment we'll have to bide our time until the Archangels can get us to Israel. It isn't like that's a bad thing, though. They're much faster than modern transportation, so the minute they arrive it'll probably take all of five minutes to make the trip."

"How will we know when they're available," Eran felt compelled to ask. Aiden looked at him and then back at the sky as they veered slightly off the road and sat down at its edge. He picked up a smooth stone and rolled it around in his hand before he tossed it across the desert.

"A little while after you left, I started training more closely with Oriphiel and occasionally Uriel. We went on a few missions throughout Israel and fought demons that wreaked havoc in the area, and somewhere along the way it got to a point where I can just sense them," Aiden explained cautiously. Eran's face twisted a little more than he wanted it to, and though he couldn't blame Aiden for finding a suitable team to work with as he fulfilled his duty, the idea of his replacement still stung a little.

“I see,” Eran mumbled, but despite his obvious disappointment he had to admit that the ability to sense the Archangels was nothing short of impressive. Aiden looked at Eran apologetically, and when Eran took notice he quickly diffused whatever tension his comrade might have thought present. “Don’t worry, I’m more impressed than upset. I didn’t even know that was possible. But now the question is how do we use that when we fight with Lucifer, or do we even use it at all?” Aiden picked up another rock and fiddled with it for a while as he thought it over. The Archangels weren’t able to possess human bodies like their demonic counterparts, so an outright combination of their power would be impossible.

“I honestly don’t know. Based on the lack of distractions and the sudden weather change I’d say that Lucifer is fairly confident in his ability to beat us whether we use their help or not,” Aiden explained as he tossed the rock into the air and caught it. “That said, we’d need another strategy.”

“Pride,” Eran said flatly as he, too, picked up a rock, though his was jagged in comparison with the one Aiden toyed around with. Aiden looked at him with a smile that beamed with approval.

“Of course,” Aiden exclaimed with joy. “Lucifer’s Rebellion was only due in part to his inherent disdain for mankind. When God the Father refused to do away with His most precious creation on the whim of His then-chiefest Archangel, Lucifer became convinced that a new god was in order and promptly incited rebellion in Heaven.”

“Exactly. Pride was the foundation of his actions back then, and here we are eons later, only to find that he’s relatively unchanged. He wants to be in the spotlight so much that he’s even manufactured his own little apocalypse. So, all we have to do is exploit his arrogance and we shouldn’t have much of a problem sealing him away for a while to come," Eran proposed, but Aiden shook his head.

"That would be much easier said than done," he pointed out as he gave the smooth stone in his hand another toss and catch. "We still don't know the extent of his preparations. Demonic hoards are to be expected since our enemy thinks himself a king, and what's a king without his subjects?"

"But Lucifer knows that we can beat the demons that he's got at his disposal. Even his attempts to send some big names this way have backfired on him in a major way," Eran contested as he skipped his jagged rock across the sea of hardened sand.

"That may be true, but like I implied before, they were just distractions. Lucifer's been waging war against our kind for millennia. He wouldn't be so foolish as to give his best from the jump. Instead, he'd probably try to trick us with the delivery of those big names you mentioned to boost our confidence before he ultimately crushes us," Aiden hypothesized. He gave his stone another toss, and then rested his arms on his knees.

"So what then, we just sit here and calmly await our destruction?" Eran asked irritatedly as he skipped another rock. Aiden looked around at the cloud of dust that blasted towards the city and listened to the rumble of thunder as it passed through the overhanging clouds.

"No, I assure you we'll be taking the fight to him. I'm just saying that it would be better to expect trouble on all sides instead of a direct shot at Hell's Master himself," Aiden cautioned, and as the words left his mouth, he and Eran were imprisoned in a shell of solid rock at the side of the road.

“Well, speak of the—” Eran started since the opportunity presented itself, but Aiden, irritated as he was, quickly cupped his hand over his wingman’s mouth and glared at him.

“Don’t even think about finishing that statement,” he warned. He retracted his hand and analyzed the structure that appeared around them. “So, what do you think?” Eran lazily tossed his hands up into the air, but his mind ran wild with the possibilities.

“Looks like you were right on the money as usual. We’ve found trouble and we’ve only just stepped out of the city. And more than that…” Eran’s voice trailed off as he stared at the earthen shell. “Yeah, I see them. There’s about four demons on the outside holding this thing together. Signatures are pretty weak though, so I doubt they’d be very effective in terms of possession.”

“Which means that we’re dealing with a Mage,” Aiden presumed and Eran nodded. “Fantastic.” Eran looked at Aiden with a puzzled expression. “What?”

“Haven’t you fought a Mage before,” he asked, but Aiden looked away from his friend and stared at the wall. He pressed his hand against it in order to locate a weak point.

“I haven’t, but I don’t think it’d be very hard. They use demons to influence the people, objects, and circumstances around them and so their power is vastly limited, whereas ours comes from an unlimited source. Factor in the fact that they can’t see what they’re messing with, and we may just be able to open their eyes and scare them off,” Aiden contemplated. He retracted his hand and started to pace around the inside of the dome, and given the small space Eran was forced to do the same. Eran thought it a good idea for a moment, but then looked back at his war buddy as they continued to pace the shell.

"That doesn't sound like a bad strategy, but what happens if they aren't afraid by what they see," Eran asked, truly curious about the possibility. "People who turn to magic of any kind are driven by the Flesh, and I don't think I need to remind you how difficult it can be to break that kind of hold. So, what would be your strategy?" Aiden smiled, genuinely amused by the inquiry.

"What was my strategy with you?" The question provoked Eran to look down at the burn marks that spiraled on his arms. He struggled to hold back a grin. "We don't target the people under oppression, but the things that oppress them. That's what I did with Bloodsport and that's what we'll do here."

"Sounds good enough to me," Eran supposed. They kept moving in silence, and a smirk fell into place on Aiden's face as Eran asked, "How many times have we walked around this pitiful little dirt-bubble?"

"This last time will mark thirteen," Aiden responded as gleefully as his voice would allow. Eran lightly slapped his palm against his forehead.

"Of course," he groaned. "Joshua chapter six, the walls of Jericho!"

"Exactly," Aiden replied as they reached the end of their extremely confined trek. He looked at Eran as the sound of an angelic trumpet sounded in the stormy skies above. "You ready for the shouting part?" Eran nodded, and as the flames on their shoulders flickered with excitement, the Two closed their eyes and meditated on the words to be spoken.

"In the name of the Father, and of the Son, and of the Holy Spirit," they shouted together, and the ground outside the dome began to shake, "shatter and be destroyed!" The storm that raged on the outside grew more intense and violent, and the ground around their entrapment rumbled with enough force that the walls of the structure gave way despite the demons' attempt to keep it together. Aiden and Eran took notice of the monsters before them, who bore the shape of black dogs with human hands and dead white eyes. They snarled at the Nabi'im, but before they could pounce, a command in ancient Greek echoed from the distance and forced them to run into the swirling sands that blanketed the road. The prophets watched the cloud patiently, and before long the silhouette of a slender young woman appeared in the shadow of the storm.

She lifted her hand and the winds howled in response. She brought it down, and lightning flashed through the sand and solidified it in a spike of glass. Eran lifted his eyebrows, impressed that he'd only barely noticed the demons behind the displays.

"Hello, boys," she said in an almost seductive tone as she came into full view. Her long black hair billowed like a cape in the high winds, and the tattered robe she wore bore strange symbols in sequence along the hem. Her face was round and her skin smooth and dark, but the familiar blackness of her eyes sent a chill down the spines of the Nabi'im, who quickly clasped their hands together as a sign of war. "Did you miss me?"

"Why would we," Eran asked as his brow furrowed and his glare narrowed on her. "We don't even know who you are." The Mage cackled wildly as she strolled forward just a little bit more. They stared into her eyes for a moment longer when they realized that they were more than just familiar. Those eyes belonged to an enemy that they'd thought permanently disposed of. "Bloodsport," Eran gasped in shock, and the demented Mage before them flashed a serpentine smile.

"Took you long enough, Eran," she taunted as she spread her hands to either side, "but I think I'll be going by Bloodmage from here on out. You see, I've acquired a few new tricks since we last shared a body." A myriad of fireballs emerged in the surrounding area, and the dull white eyes of the hellhounds behind them sparked alive from the flames. They awaited their mistress's command, and as the fire burned before them the beasts salivated at the thought of freshly fried Nabi. Aiden and Eran took note of it all, and silently began to work out a way to counter them all with as little effort as possible.

"How are you here," Aiden questioned as he watched the dogs of death, which snarled threateningly at the Two in their sights. The sultry laugh of the deranged witch resounded in the darkening sky.

"Well it looks like I've been given a second chance at life," she sang excitedly over the bellow of the rushing air current, but her face immediately sobered as she took in the sight of the man who'd expelled the Seed of the Flesh from its most ideal host. "And just like I said before, Aiden, I'm never gonna stop destroying everything you love. I think I'll start with my former host before I work my way around to you. You'll endure much more slowly the same kind of pain you inflicted upon me a few hours ago." Without further delay, she clasped her hands together and uttered another incantation. The feral beasts under her charge blasted at the Nabi'im from all directions, and before they had the chance to speak Scripture into power a brilliant wall of flames erupted from the ground around them and diffused the onslaught.

A flash of white light broke through the blustering winds and raging flames, and upon its dissolution Aiden and Eran were stunned to see Oriphiel and Uriel before them and aglow with bursting rage.

“That wouldn’t be a very good idea,” Oriphiel warned as lightning pulsed around his hulking frame. Uriel’s fists were alight with fire and her face donned an all-too-familiar mask of pyromaniacal joy that put the vengeful Mage on edge.

“I’m going to enjoy this,” she said as her eyes narrowed, but Eran marched in front of them and flashed them a look that instantly made them back down.

“No, you’re not,” he said flatly, and the Mage across from him smirked with twisted delight. He turned his attention back to her as he continued to speak. “Aiden, would you mind helping me take on the witch?”

“It’d be my pleasure,” Aiden replied before Eran even finished the question. He quickly approached the proverbial front line and stared down the witch just the same.

“Oriphiel, Uriel, you two will be on demon duty. Take out any of her little pets that try anything cheap.” The Archangels nodded and took their positions on either side of the Nabi’im who stood ready for a cataclysmic battle that was sure to shake the foundations of the city behind them. “It would have been better for you to have stayed dead. After all the hell you put us through, my whole body is screaming at the chance to wreck you myself.” The sickening smile of the witch vanished as she cast another spell. The endless sea of sand that rested on either side of the smoothed-out road rose at her command, and as the massive mounds drifted further into the sky, the two Archangels tossed their Nabi’im into the air before Oriphiel extended his hands.

The electricity that surged around him channeled into his fingertips, and with a loud yell it discharged into the two massive mounds of sand. In an instant they were solidified into glass platforms, and as the airborne prophets descended they landed squarely atop the colossal sculptures. They clasped their hands in unison, and to the horror of the Mage they began to pray.

"Greatest Elohim, creator of the heavens and the earth, I ask that you give me control of the storm as you gave your Son millennia ago so that your will might be accomplished," Aiden pleaded with his eyes firmly locked on the malefactor below.

"Jehovah Mephalti, my Deliverer, I beg you to light a fire in me that will never burn out," Eran added as the flames on his shoulders doubled in intensity.

"Make with us an everlasting covenant, establish your righteous rule through us, and snuff out evil with our hands in the Name of Jesus," the Two shouted in unison. The demonic dogs jumped into the raging air current at the Mage's command, and to her displeasure a massive fireball devoured a vast majority of them.

"I'll destroy you all," screamed the witch into the atmosphere. The Bloodmage began to chant, and the slick pavement upon which she stood breathed out more of the predatory hellhounds. She shouted a command and slammed her fists against the concrete road. A tremor pulsed through the ground and the Archangels leaped into the air, but as the ground rattled, the glass pillars upon which the prophets stood burst into thousands of tiny shards. Aiden quickly extended his arms to either side, and as the flames on his shoulders intensified, he and Eran were suspended by the clouds themselves. Eran looked at him, completely satisfied at the awesome display of power whereas the witch below stood dumbfounded.

“What *is* this,” she hissed, and the ravenous beasts that aided her roared angrily alongside her. “How could you do something like that without Scripture?” Aiden smiled as he lifted a hand into the air.

“Be still,” he whispered to the storm, and to the surprise of the angels, demons, and witch it obeyed. “You may have spent the last twelve years inside Eran’s body, but judging from your shocked expression it seems you haven’t learned all the tricks we Nabi’im have.”

“They’ve taken a step in their lives as Nabi’im that few ever do. They’ve made a covenant with the Lord God in Heaven. Once a contract has been issued, they are bound by it until the day of death,” Oriphiel explained with a smug look on his face. One of the hellhounds covered the girl with its own body, and as she chanted another ancient curse, she jumped into the air with superhuman force. Her arm extended towards Eran, but as she made an attempt to grab him, the flames on his shoulders blasted her away.

She growled like a jungle cat as she cursed him once more, and this time the clouds that kept him suspended dispersed and reemerged beneath her. She smiled satisfactorily as she drifted away and he started to descend, but quickly flared with rage when he flexed his arms and was engulfed in the bright red flames he’d long been without.

“Fool,” Eran taunted outright as he extended his arm. A fireball twice the size of Uriel’s manifested in the palm of his hand, and grew in immensity until it rested mere inches from her face. “Did you really think it would be that easy to screw with us a second time?” He deployed the infernal sphere, and before the vicious sorceress had a chance to dodge she was consumed. The demons below bounded into the air in a hopeful attempt to save their mistress, but the intensity of the holy fire burned them away just as Uriel's had their predecessors.

The body hit the ground with a loud crash, and the road beneath her cracked from the impact. Aiden and Eran watched carefully, as they could feel that the battle was far from over. Their eyes narrowed as they caught sight of the girl's twitching arm, and though Uriel and Oriphiel closed in on her, Aiden urged them to stand down. The sorceress, now heavily charred and covered in blackened streams of her own blood, spread her hands wide and allowed the monsters at her command to overtake her in their shadowy aura. She laughed uncontrollably as her body repaired the damage that Eran had done, and with a single hand lifted she blasted pure darkness into the air.

Aiden smirked, fully confident in his God and the covenant power behind his prayer, and directed a single finger towards her.

"Rage," he said, and the storm that was quelled before ignited with a relentless fury that disrupted the flow of her attack. She lunged for them and spat fire from her mouth, but with his finger still upraised Aiden issued a single command: "Burst," and a flash of lightning erupted from the sky that shot through the fire blast and scattered the flames until they were no more. The girl narrowly evaded electrocution and retreated into a ball of shadows that slipped between the cracks of the broken pavement below.

"You may have gotten the best of me this time," her voice echoed threateningly, "but we'll meet on the battlefield again *very* soon." As her sickly cackle faded, the Nabi'im descended upon the road and approached the Archangels, who at this point awaited the conclusion of the battle in sheer boredom. Their cloaks immediately vanished into a cloud of purple mist, and much to their surprise the Nabi'im staggered as soon as they did.

"Well now that that's settled, we need to go," Uriel informed them. "The High King says that whatever Lucifer has planned is scheduled to occur within the next 24 hours, so we need to get you back to the Hall, work out a strategy, and make our way for Tel Megiddo." The mere mention of that name made the hairs on Eran's arms stand on end. Even though it made him uncomfortable, he knew that there was no way that he could avoid that abominable place. Aiden noticed his friend tense up, and comfortingly placed a hand on his shoulder to reassure him that he wasn't alone anymore.

"It'll be alright," he told Eran with a warm smile despite his own discomfort. His face quickly sobered as he looked back at the Archangels. "Let's go."

"Very well," Oriphiel agreed as he and Uriel turned back towards the city. "Grab on," he urged the young prophets, and without any hesitation Aiden placed his hand on Oriphiel's back in the space between his mighty silver wings. Uriel looked back at Eran, who stood there pensively as he mulled over the darkness of his past.

"Lord Eran," she called to him. He snapped out of his trance and braced her in the same manner, and in a matter of seconds they shimmered away in a flash of light.

Within a five-minute time frame, the Two and their Archangel companions manifested within the glimmering lobby of the Hall of Nabi'im. They immediately started for the Grand Hall, and as they climbed the black onyx stairs that led to that majestic chamber they were overcome with bittersweet nostalgia. It all started for them right there, where they gained power, where they grew closer, where they fought both with and against each other, and where their hopelessly repetitive lives were given a much higher purpose. It was there in the Hall that they saw into each other's souls for the very first time, and it was there that they would prepare for the biggest battle they'd ever faced. They reached the top, and as they tread, the star-sapphire tiles that once caused them so much grief remained inactive. They pushed the double doors open and that familiar light shone right in their faces, but despite the discomfort they walked in with their eyes fully open.

"Welcome back," Elijah the Tishbite greeted as they walked in. His old heart jumped with joy over the fact that Eran had indeed come back to them, fully restored as he had foreseen. "It certainly has been a long time." His eyes glistened with joyous tears, but given the situation he quickly wiped them away. Eran gave a passive chuckle as he reflected upon the arrogant child that first appeared in this room, but quickly dismissed the thought.

"It certainly has been," Eran responded. "About twelve years. Looks like you guys have gotten into quite the mess without me. Can't say I'm surprised." Uriel slapped her searing hand across the back of his neck.

"Enough with the jokes, you idiot," she barked at him. "Lucifer's on the rampage and you want to act the comedian." Her anger lit her flowing red hair ablaze just as it did in the past.

"Now, now, Uriel," Elijah interjected soothingly. "You still have to train with the Nabi'im to prepare them for the battle. How would it look if you just smote them here and now out of burning hot anger?"

"You have to admit," Oriphiel chimed in, "it wouldn't be a very good idea. My lord," he said as he redirected his attention to the old man with the soothing amber eyes, "what is the status of our enemy?"

"Lucifer's power has increased steadily over the course of the last twelve years, but very recently it hit an all-time high that dwarfs even

Michael on his own. In a matter of hours, he will make his move, and in that same amount of time we have to be ready," Elijah explained, but as he opened his mouth to continue, the sound of footsteps echoed through the Grand Hall. Aiden and Eran turned their attention to the left side of the throne, and much to Aiden's surprise he saw Maya there in perfect health. He was taken aback by the green robe she wore in the place of the white and black gown he'd seen her in the day before, and marveled at how well it suited her. It was when their eyes met, though, that a shockwave fired through his body that he'd never experienced before.

She watched him with tearful eyes as she slowly approached, and much to Aiden's surprise she wrapped her arms around his waist and gently rested her head on his chest. She listened to his heartbeat as the water from her eyes dripped against the t-shirt he'd worn since the day before. He was alive.

"Thank God," Maya said as she pulled back. "I woke up here and I didn't know what happened to you. I thought…" her voice trailed off as she caught sight of Eran, who waved and smiled at her in response to the shocked expression she sported. Maya shoved Aiden aside and mouthed a quick prayer, and as her green robe transformed into the ivory-colored collared shirt and slacks with a green hooded cloak on her shoulders, Aiden and Eran both stood in utter surprise. She moved to attack, eager to repay the former Bloodsport for all he'd done to them.

"Maya," Elijah called from the comfort of his throne. She looked at him with the same fiery passion as she had before, but stopped nonetheless. The old prophet smiled as he gestured to an adjacent hallway. "There is much to discuss."

Chapter Seventeen

They traversed the hallway in painfully awkward silence. Maya refused to walk in front of Eran, who failed to earn her trust despite his best efforts. Elijah led them into a stunning room with walls of white and gray marble and four spiraled pillars of solid gold to support the roof. The Three stood in wonder of the remarkable craftsmanship, the complimentary colors of the cream, white, gray and gold, and the monumental cedar table that rested squarely between the four pillars.

"Please," Elijah offered as he took his place at the head of the table. "Sit. The time has come to discuss our plan of action as we endeavor to deal with Lucifer." Maya's gaze shifted from the High King to Eran, and in a burst of uncontrollable anger she slammed her fists against the table.

"Alright, then," she began, "why don't we start by getting the *killer* out of this meeting?" Eran's eyes, which were noticeably softer than they'd been in ages, quickly averted to the ground. The shame he felt for his actions under the duress of Bloodsport couldn't be expressed, but he knew that for the sake of their success he had to make the effort to perpetuate peace between himself and the others. He looked at Maya, who sat irately with furrowed brow and relentless scowl, and then at Aiden, his longtime friend who carefully observed the tension between the two as if it were a person.

"Eran is necessary for our fight against the Devil whether you like to admit it or not. If we stand any chance against the Prince Demon it's only because we have him on our side," Aiden explained before Elijah had the opportunity. The elderly prophet looked at his younger with a sense of concession in his soft amber eyes as he closed his mouth.

“He shot me!” Maya’s voice elevated to a point where the Archangels manifested in the room and pointed their various swords at her throat. She shoved them away with a single swipe of her hands, and Eran’s pained expression intensified.

“That wasn’t his fault, he was—” Aiden started but was quickly interrupted by another fist to the hard wooden table.

“I don’t want to hear any excuses,” she barked as animosity towards them both took to her eyes. Over and over that moment played back in her mind, and each time it did she trembled with an overwhelming sense of fear and disgust.

“Listen to me,” Aiden spoke from a place of irritated calm. She calmed down, surprised that he could even assert himself in such a way. He took a deep breath and calmly collected his thoughts as he prepared to address the issue. “Eran was under the influence of a being known primarily as the Seed of the Flesh. It takes root in your own hidden sins and feeds off of them until it controls you. Eran was the slave of the Seed for twelve years unbeknownst to us, so it wasn’t *him* that shot you but the Seed itself.” Maya’s watch shifted between the two of them as she grew angrier still.

“So what, I’m supposed to trust him because he wasn’t in his right mind when he punched a hole in my flesh,” she demanded as her nostrils flared like an enraged bull.

“No,” Aiden spoke, his irritation more apparent now. “You’re supposed to trust him because he’s no longer bound by the thing that did you harm. I personally saw to that just a few hours ago.” She was caught off guard, and given her loss of words she quietly sank back into her seat. “The Seed isn’t dead, however,” he continued as he addressed the elder prophet and the two youngers in the room. “While we handled a little extra business in Edgehaven, we had the misfortune of meeting a female Mage whose captor was none other than Bloodsport." Aiden looked to Eran for additional input but he said nothing, and shook with regret as he clasped his hands together so tightly that Aiden feared they might bleed. "From what we saw, she looks to be pretty masterful and is actually capable of summoning more demons for her magic spells." Elijah tilted his head to the side and ran his fingers through his long gray beard out of intrigue.

"Were you able to bring her down?" Asked the elder, but Aiden shook his head in denial. He interlocked his fingers just in front of his mouth and stared at the centermost point of the long table.

"She managed to slip away, but she did say that we'd meet on the battlefield again so I doubt our business with her is finished. I'm under the persuasion that she's just a pawn in Lucifer's game, but if there are others like her then she could pose a legitimate threat to our plans to stop demonic rule from entering this world any more than it already has." Maya held up her hands in surprise.

"A Mage," she asked him. "As in a witch? You've got to be kidding me…"

"No," Aiden denied. "They can be cunning and manipulative, and no offense, but I don't think a new Nabi like you is well equipped to charge into danger like this." Maya's eyes went wide as she recalled the day he'd saved her from that rapist in the alley. She remembered the helplessness that she felt and remembered the path of her life that led her to believe that she was just that.

"Excuse you?" She asked with attitude. "While you may be my predecessor, I don't think you have a say in my part of this battle." Aiden looked at her, captivated by her challenge.

“He’s right,” Eran finally spoke with his head focused aimlessly in front of him. “It wouldn’t be safe for you to go out there just yet. If you do, then there’s the possibility that you’ll fall into one of Lucifer’s traps like I did.” Maya’s right eye twitched angrily as he dared address her after all he’d done.

“Oh yeah? And what could you possibly know about me, huh, *Bloodsport*?” She all but spat the name at him, which made his eyes quickly meet hers. His brow furrowed and his eyes glistened with a fiery intensity that she’d never known before.

“Let me take a wild guess. You were raised all your life as some posh little princess, and when you grew up and stepped into the real world you realized that you’re nothing but a helpless, overgrown child who has about as much chance taking care of herself as a snowball in the summertime. You may have been granted the power of a Nabi, but until you learn how to use it and master yourself in addition, you’ll still be the selfish little girl you’ve always been.”

“Alright that is more than enough,” Elijah interjected before another word could be uttered. “We do not have time for this little game that the two of you are playing. Lucifer plans to implement his own Armageddon and you two sit here creating division over issues of the past.” His soft eyes sharpened as a gray robe manifested and pure white flames erupted from his shoulders. The three young Nabi’im instantaneously straightened up, and the Archangels who now stood in the background shielded their eyes for fear of what may come.

“Forgive us, Master Elijah,” Aiden quickly interceded, and the old prophet crossed his arms and settled down. He hummed as his eyes quickly passed from face to face.

“You make the case of a lack of power,” he uttered after a moment, “so rather than Uriel, the task will rest on the two of you to take Maya under your wing.” Maya cringed at the very idea of working with Eran, but it was beyond her control. Elijah picked up on her discomfort almost as soon as her face contorted with disgust, and without hesitation his eyes narrowed on her. “Problem,” he asked, but she quickly did her best to adopt a grin and promptly shook her head. “Very well. As far as the Mage problem is concerned, the chances of more are slim given that the one you faced was enough to match the two of you simultaneously. Lucifer does not suspect the awakening of a Third, which gives us a clear advantage. All things considered, the witch should be a simple matter to dispose of. The biggest concern out of the whole thing is the Devil himself.”

“It is difficult to work out a decent strategy to use against him when you consider that we hardly know what we’re up against,” Aiden commented, and Elijah nodded.

“This is very true,” he responded with an almost uncharacteristic irritation in his tone. “Even I do not fully understand the power he has amassed in all this time, and so the only logical thing we could do is increase what power we have on our side.”

“That’s a step that Aiden and I have already taken,” Eran informed him. “The covenants have already been established with the King of Kings, and as a result of our relationship with Him strengthening, we’ve been given a greater power to wield as we combat demon-kind.” Elijah’s eyes went wide with surprise as he took his seat.

“Ah, what a splendid idea,” he had to admit. “Perhaps it would be wise to teach the newest among you the true extent of that power.” His eyes shifted to the angry woman at the table, who kept her gaze fixed on Eran.

“It would be good for us to blow off some steam,” Maya thought out loud.

“Too bad,” Aiden asserted much to her disdain. “As much as I’d like to get in a good warm up, we can’t afford to forget that we’re on the clock here. The most we can do is teach you the basics of our lifestyle and hope that you can adapt it to the battlefield.” Maya looked taken aback and raised an eyebrow as a smug grin crossed her face.

“I thought it wasn’t a good idea for me to go into the battle with you boys,” she playfully challenged.

“The girl brings up a valid point,” Eran contended as he abandoned his attempts at showing kindness to the spitfire that was Maya, but Aiden shook his head as he clasped his hands together again.

“The more I think about it, the more I realize that what Master Elijah said is absolutely right. Lucifer wouldn’t expect there to be three of us. Adding Maya to the equation, assuming we can get her trained well enough in the little time we have, could prove to be the difference maker in this battle,” Aiden suggested. Eran and Maya crossed their arms as they reclined in their respective chairs.

“You’re right,” Eran admitted in a more rational tone than his previous outburst. “And in addition to that we have no clue when Lucifer’s gonna try and kill us all. If she’s gonna be on the battlefield with us, then she needs to be brought up to our level of warfare in the next about the next hour so we can move out and get the jump on our little friend...” Maya huffed as she adjusted to lean on the arm of the chair.

“Lucky for you I’ve already been training since I woke up,” she shot back. Aiden and Eran quietly looked at her, and Elijah smiled.

"I can attest to this," he said proudly. "The lovely Maya has already defeated Gabriel, Raphael, and Michael on her own, and has utilized the Scriptures expertly as she did so. I have to say, boys, she has proven to be a much more promising candidate than you two heathens were those many years ago." Aiden adjusted in a similar fashion to the neophyte Maya and carefully looked her over.

"Then this should be much less time-consuming than I originally thought. Now there's just the matter of how to get to the Tel and settle this once Maya's been properly trained," Aiden said in a partial attempt to change the subject. The Archangel Uriel stepped forward and addressed the Court of Nabi'im.

"The only accessible route is the Passage of Nasah that Lord Aiden and Lord Eran used twelve years ago to join the Battle of Tel Megiddo," she spoke with an air of uncharacteristically controlled irritation. "It seems that Lucifer has erected a barrier against us just outside the valley, and the only opening is the demon-infested corridor that left Lord Eran corrupted in the first place. I'd steal Oriphiel's line and say it wouldn't be a good idea to send them through that passage, but it seems like there isn't any other choice."

"Very well," Elijah conceded as he brought his arms down to the table before him. He looked between the faces of his Nabi'im with all severity in his expression. "For the time being, however, you three are to spend what little time you have left working out battle strategies and perfecting your unity." Maya rolled her eyes at the notion, but a quick glare from her elder made her stiffen out of respect.

"We will take them right away, my king," Oriphiel assured him. He turned his penetrating gaze to the Three who sat all too comfortably in his opinion. “Time to get moving,” he ordered, and without question the team of prophets made for the hall. The idea of Eran within reach of her was enough to make Maya’s skin crawl, but despite her discomfort she knew better than to question the orders of a man who had a history of calling down fire from Heaven. Still, she wanted him dead, and he felt every bit of it.

Eran wasn’t aware of the actions the Seed had taken against her when he first reawakened, but with each passing second, he was reminded of a new horror from his past. A part of him wished that he could have done something to make up for his sins, but he knew that in most of the cases of the people he’d hurt over the years, nothing could have been done. But here was Maya, who not only stood beside him but had to work in tandem with him in order to survive, and finally, after years of ineptitude and quiet sobs of remorse, he thought himself capable of restitution.

The tension between them made Aiden particularly uneasy as he paced hastily behind the two of them. Maya’s determination to hold that grudge was, to Lucifer at least, an exploitable weakness that could be used to corrupt her as he had Eran years prior. She was much more volatile towards his best friend than Aiden even thought she could be, and each time she glanced back at her frequent savior it was as if that feeling intensified. He had to figure out a way to get them on the same page, and the more he thought about the amount of work that would take, the more frustrated he became with the both of them. They tread across the threshold of the training room, and much to the surprise of the two veterans it retained the trees first planted at Maya’s behest.

“Wow,” was all Eran could say at first as he moved around the miniature forest. Maya crossed her arms, instantly irritated at the shock on his face. She carefully watched him as he moved, like a lioness watches a gazelle, and waited in all eagerness for the opportunity to strike.

"It definitely beats the plain cracked floors and crumbling walls from when we first got here," Aiden commented as he looked around. He walked calmly through the trees and observed his two teammates.

"Well, we're on the clock," Maya abruptly stated. Aiden looked at her with deep concern in his eyes as she walked into the artificial wilderness a few feet from him.

"She's right, Aiden," Eran agreed as he quickly sobered and placed his hands at his sides. "We need to get to work on bringing Maya up to speed." Aiden sighed at the unnecessary amount of force in his voice, but carefully monitored the both of them in the event that anyone issued a cheap shot.

"So then what's first?" Maya asked in obvious irritation. Aiden crossed his arms and held his fingertips to his forehead in an attempt to soothe the headache that his two comrades provoked. Eran shook his head at her tone and tossed his hands up in the air as a smile of disbelief crept onto his face. Maya cocked her head to the side as her eyes narrowed on her former adversary. "What? You have a problem with me?"

"You know what, I do," Eran fired as he turned back to face her. "I understand the grudge you have against me. I welcome it, to be totally honest with you, because I've done a lot of terrible things that I can't make up for, and with every passing second I'm reminded of something new. But right now, we have a war to fight and we're severely outnumbered and with you helping us out, we may as well be outgunned too. So why don't you just get over your hatred of me for all of a day and when this is all over with we can revisit it?" Eran was oddly serious as he shifted his eyes periodically from the nuisance of a girl to his old colleague. For an instant, the terrified girl that lay dormant in Maya emerged, but she quickly returned to her offensive state as she stepped to Eran just the same.

"Don't you dare try and make it seem like I don't understand what's at stake here! It's because this is such a crucial battle that I don't want you anywhere near it! After all, your track record when it comes to stuff like this isn't exactly stellar." The words plunged into his heart like daggers, but he knew exactly what she referred to. He again glanced at Aiden. All he wanted since he came back from the control of his dark side was peace for the one friend that for so long sought him. Aiden's eyes went wide as she dared press on. "You're a murderer and a traitor, and for the last twelve years all you've done is create more chaos than you've fixed. Even in Edgehaven, the only reason you saved me was so you could kill me yourself and make Aiden watch!"

"You don't know the first thing about the kind of hell I've been through in that time!" Eran balled his fists and trembled as he screamed, but as Maya shrunk back from him he lowered his voice and turned his eyes to the trees that pressed against the walls and ceiling of the room. "Do you know what it's like to be a slave to the darkness that lives inside of you? Do you have any idea what it feels like not to be able to control yourself and watch from the back of your mind as the thing that took over your body kills people for sport? Tell me, Maya, help me understand, when has a spoiled princess like you ever experienced anything like that?" He turned away from her, but she pulled his shoulder in an effort to turn him around.

"Don't you walk away from me," she demanded shakily. "You think that just because you—"

“Rage,” Aiden whispered, and to their utter shock the air in the room circulated with the force of a hurricane. My and Eran both cast their gaze upon the only Nabi who abstained from the argument, and saw naught but disgust on his face as his hooded cloak formed over his clothes.

“Aiden,” Maya whispered, and the thought of the deeply pained man from the apartment in Edgehaven crept into her mind.

“Like I said,” Eran grumbled over the howl of the powerful winds, “this isn’t the time to behave like children.” A vein popped out of Aiden’s forehead as he allowed the wounds of his past to resonate in the present, and he wondered as tears streaked his face just how his teammates would handle the situation.

“I’m so sick of this,” he growled in faux aggression, and the winds intensified. Maya braced herself against a nearby tree as she looked on in shame. She knew that since they met, she was the reason he relived all of the misfortunes of his past. She was the one who dug deeper and deeper into his trauma, and sat there with wonder in her eyes as he was forced to watch it all in striking vividness. She looked over to Eran, who stood unshaken as he watched Aiden. “I’m so sick of the insults and the arguments! I’m sick of having to go through the pain of the last twelve years over and over again as if it was some sick sense of entertainment!”

“Aiden,” Eran shouted over the gale, but a flash of lightning struck the ground in front of him and caused him to stumble backward.

“Just shut up,” he commanded them both. He clutched his chest in his hand as if to shield his heart. “Just shut up…” The lightning flashed again as he flexed his muscles. Maya stood petrified, and to her horror the enraged Aiden turned his attention to her. “Flash,” he uttered remorselessly, and another bolt of lightning descended from the air above. Before it could strike her, Eran extended his arm behind him and blasted a massive wave of flames that were only intensified by the swirl of the winds. He shot forward, and managed to take Maya into his open arm to narrowly evade immediate electrocution.

"What's happening to him," Maya asked, stunned that he'd ever act this way.

"I'm not entirely sure," Eran admitted. He extended his hand towards the front of the room and unleashed another blast of flames that rocketed the two of them backwards. He directed the roaring flames toward the ground and launched himself and the girl into the canopy of the trees. Aiden roared in undeniable anger over the howl of the winds he created. Eran let Maya go, and the two of them jumped from branch to branch in an effort to distance themselves from him further.

"I don't understand," Maya whimpered in despair as she stopped on a shaky tree branch. Eran stopped alongside her and quietly marveled at the fact that even now she wasn't arguing with him. She turned to face him, and tightened her grip on the tree when a flash of lightning struck only a few feet away from her. "How is he able to do this?"

"We need to keep moving," Eran told her as the flames on his shoulders molded into a barrier that blocked a sudden burst of celestial electricity. They were quiet for a moment, and though Eran had little trust for Maya and even less affection for her, he thought it best to confess the source of their power and come up with some sort of strategy. "You already know that our power is dependent on our reliance on the Holy Spirit, don't you?" Maya's eyes fixed on Eran as he spoke and she silently nodded. They started to circle around along the edge of the faux forest, but stopped when the rampaging Zane came into view. "There are three stages in which

Nabi'im use the power they've been given. The first is one that we all know and that's reliance on Scripture, standing on the Word of God and speaking the Scriptures into power. The next," he paused for a moment and watched as Aiden drew closer to their position, and silently mouthed a prayer. A ball of fire formed in the air over the back of the forest and plummeted to the ground with enough force to attract Aiden's attention. "Prayer," he continued aloud. "Prayer opens the lines of communication between you and God, and more than that it nurtures a relationship between you. The closer you get to Him, the stronger you become because it isn't just you operating under His power. You actually become more of a conduit for it."

"And the third?" Maya couldn't help but ask. Based on the flashes of lightning that Aiden so freely tossed around the area, she knew that she wouldn't be able to quote or pray fast enough to defend herself, and it was in that that she realized how much more it would take to defeat Lucifer. Eran met her gaze for a moment but then watched as Aiden forced his way through the trees towards the point of impact.

"The third, and by far the most powerful, is the covenant. When you make a covenant with the Lord, you agree to live for Him and work towards His Will here on earth. It is the ultimate acknowledgement of your relationship and it's somewhat like a marriage, but I'd argue that what you gain from a relationship with Him dwarfs the benefits of any relationship you get yourself into with another human."

"And so you and Aiden have—" Maya started, but was interrupted by the ravenous bellow of Aiden's voice in the distant end of the tree-filled chamber.

"Established covenants, yes," Eran confirmed as they kept moving. They watched as Aiden froze and listened. The air around the room continued to swirl faster and faster by his command, and to their horror he lifted up his hand.

"Flash!" He shouted the word, and in the next moment the branch upon which they landed shattered into splinters. Eran and Maya were knocked to the ground, and Aiden had them within his sights.

"Maya, I'll do what I can to hold him back while you get to a safe distance," Eran offered. The suggestion caught the young woman off guard, and she stood frozen as more streams of lightning collided with Eran's bright red flames. Sparks flew, and the semi-sentient trees that filled the room attacked the young men blindly. "Get going!"

"R-right," she stuttered and quickly ran in the opposite direction in a zigzag pattern. Aiden had no opportunity to monitor her movements, as he was preoccupied with the flame-engulfed fist of his best friend as it hurdled towards his face.

"I won't make it that easy for you," Aiden said with a genuine smile on his face as he ducked the blow. "Rain." An egregious amount of water poured from the atmosphere of the room and extinguished the fire-punch without issue. Aiden delivered a blow of us own laced with bluish currents of electricity. Eran was launched upward from the contact and Aiden stood upright with a devilish grin. Maya watched on, and as her body shook from nerves, she felt disgust wash over herself. She was weak, almost pathetically so, and as the two warriors continued to trade attacks it became increasingly more apparent.

"Lord God, origin of my faith, please hear me," the frightened woman whispered as the clash of the elements waged before her very eyes. "Empower me to make a difference in the earth." The words of the prayer filtered into her heart, and the flames on her shoulders flickered with unimaginable power. “Make with me an everlasting covenant, establish your righteous rule through me, and snuff out evil with my hands in the name of Jesus.” She felt a mighty pulse flow through her, and as Eran fell to the ground, Maya issued an immediate command. “Bind!”

Chapter Eighteen

The earth beneath the floor expelled a quartet of solid stone shackles that linked around Aiden's arms and legs to hold him in place, and the branches of the trees around him angled themselves towards the ground and crossed over each other on each side to add an extra barrier of restraint. Maya breathed a sigh of relief and ducked to the ground.

"Eran!" As she called his name, the Scarlet Nabi launched himself into the air with a jet of bright red flames and his free hand extended towards his comrade. His face fell expressionless at this point, as Aiden's sudden attempts to kill them baffled him to say the least. He closed his eyes and formed a massive orb of flames, and without much delay he fired.

"Flash," Aiden uttered with a grin. Azure lightning fell from above once more, and the bonds that swallowed his limbs shattered. The blue flames on his shoulders extended before him and kept the infernal sphere at bay until a massive blast shot through the entire area. The trees were incinerated in an instant, and the unlikely team of Maya and Eran was hurled backward with crippling force. Smoke filled the room and the crumbling walls cracked all the more, but there was quiet. The winds of the storm, the water that mysteriously rained from heavens that weren't present, and even the creaks of the splintering trees ceased in an instant. All that remained was the eerie sound of methodical footsteps as they approached from the darkness of the smoke.

Little by little the massive cloud of black gave way, and the figure of an unscathed Aiden filled Maya's vision. She trembled in terror, as even with her sudden burst of power and the liberal use thereof she was still substandard at best. He came into clear focus, and Eran and Maya staggered back to their feet, determined to fight on despite their now numerous injuries. Aiden waved a hand and the smoke cloud gave way to reveal the total destruction of the trees. He stopped just a few feet away from them and surveyed their tattered clothes now spotted in their blood, as well as the pained and confused expressions they wore on their faces.

"You both did well," Aiden stated calmly as he brushed some dust off of his sleeve. "I'd say that the only part that needs improvement is your ability to follow up. You were completely unprepared for me to break free, and because of that you got hurt." Their jaws dropped, and the massive frame of Oriphiel appeared in the hallway just outside the training room. "Looks like we're out of time," he continued as he walked for the door. Oriphiel waved his hand and healed the two injured Nabi'im as Aiden addressed him. "I think it's safe to say that I should take the lead on this one, but while we're on the move, be thinking of ways that you can better complement each other's plays in combat. Maya, you got to watch my memories like a movie, so I expect you to be thinking about what it was you saw." Oriphiel's eyes widened in surprise, and he couldn't help but look at the two, mouth ajar, as they filed out of the room behind Aiden.

"So you found a way to convince them to cooperate with one another," he asked as he folded his arms in disbelief.

"Yes, and even better than that, Maya's established a covenant just the same as us. She's capable of tapping into that power and she has a lot of potential, but she still needs practice. She's good, but the girl's no master just yet," Aiden admitted. Oriphiel's eyes shifted to her, but nevertheless he shrugged and ushered the Three down the corridor.

"So what, that was just some horrible trick to get us on the same page," Maya demanded as she stormed in front of the smiling Aiden. He pushed past her, much to her displeasure, but was pulled back by the strong arm of his wingman.

"We thought that you'd turned on us," he said solemnly with a hint of worry in his tone. "I thought you were trying to kill us. Was your little show that necessary that you had to worry us to death like that?"

"It was absolutely necessary," Aiden shot back as his smile vanished. "Which would do us more good in our battle with Lucifer and his forces: fighting together or fighting each other?" The question struck Eran and Maya into stern silence, and the disgruntled Zane continued. "You both acted like children, and in case you haven't noticed we don't have the luxury of disliking one another right now. If you want to know why I did what I did, it was because talking to you about it wasn't getting us anywhere. I needed a way to remind you that there are no choices right now, and by the looks of things, it did us a world of good. So, if you don't mind, try and keep it that way until all this is over."

Maya and Eran stared at him as he turned around and strode after Oriphiel once again. They marched back into the Grand Hall and towards the massive double doors that served as the entrance.

"Please, this way," Oriphiel urged and started down the stairs. Aiden and Eran followed without hesitation, and Maya cautiously paced herself behind them. "It would be a good idea to keep up, Lady Maya." She hastened after her comrades as they reached the bottom, and the Archangel took the trio around the staircase and into a disturbingly familiar dimly lit passage. The bricks and pillars that comprised it seemed older than the Hall of Nabi'im itself, and at the end rested a circular door with a large stone seal at its center. Their Archangel guide approached and gently laid his hand upon it, and with a faint glimmer of light it receded into the door.

The stone before Oriphiel rumbled, and the passageway they stood in shook at its very foundations. Maya looked around nervously, but Aiden placed a hand on her shoulder to reassure her that everything would be fine. She pushed his hand away as her concern became anger, and Aiden shrugged in indifference.

"Like I said, Maya," Aiden reminded her. "We don't have that luxury right now. You may not have liked what I did, but in the next few minutes you'll thank me." Maya stepped forward and stood by Oriphiel as she watched the door to the Passage of Nasah roll away, and as she moved to take the first step, Oriphiel extended a hand to block the path.

"The time has come for you to face the greatest evil the universe has ever known. It would be a good idea if you kept your guard up. My brother Lucifer preys upon the weak, and the slightest hint of insecurity within your mind will open the door for temptations far worse than what you could experience here on this path. Be careful." Without another word he retracted his hand, and Maya entered the Passage. The warmth she felt from the Hall of Nabi'im was immediately snuffed out by a wave of cold she never would have thought imaginable in Israel. It was subarctic and empty, but despite the events that transpired years before in this very place, Maya staved off her trepidation and watched the path carefully while the men joined her on either side. The door to the Hall rolled shut, and all they were left with was the darkness ahead.

"Let's move," Eran ordered, completely disquieted by the whispers in the darkness. "The faster we get out of this place the better." Without a word, they stepped through the passage and carefully monitored the path for any signs of disturbance. The flames on their shoulders provided the only source of light, and the Nabi'im made every effort to remain close to one another. The shadows around them shifted, and from the moment they stepped into the Passage, Aiden and Eran felt as if they were under strict surveillance.

"Shouldn't we run," Maya questioned. "We don't have a lot of time, and just walking the path will put us dangerously behind schedule."

"Now isn't the time for that," Aiden told her as his eyes shifted in the light of his blue flames. "If we take off down the path we'll most likely trigger any traps they've set for us." Maya tilted her head in uneasy confusion.

"They?" she asked. Eran turned his head to face her.

"Someone's here," he said casually.

"Right you are, Eran," called a devilish yet familiar alto from the darkness beyond. The shadows that filled the Passage pulsed and groaned at the sound of her voice, and as a multitude of bright red eyes shone through the black she cackled like the witch they knew she was. "We had such a good time just a few hours ago I thought we'd move up our second date. That's not so bad, is it?" Aiden lunged for her, but Eran lifted his hand to keep him back. He looked at the girl, clad in black clothing that matched her surroundings and complimented her chocolate skin, and to her surprise his lips curled into a malevolent grin.

"Actually, no," the Scarlet One said with a hint of excitement. Her head tilted to the side in intrigue with a flare of girlish charm.

"Oh really?" Bloodmage asked.

"I was wondering when I would be able to make you suffer," Eran replied as his voice reached an intimidating depth. "I'm gonna enjoy this." He licked his lips as he lifted his hand by his side and watched it ignite.

“Mmm, I love it when a man wants to play rough,” she said seductively. Maya folded her arms and stared her down.

“Bind,” she uttered, and watched the ground beneath the perverted Mage swallow her legs and wrap around her arms. “You know, girl to girl, there are just some things better left unsaid. For instance… everything that comes out of your mouth.”

“Ooh, I like you too. Maybe after I’m done with the boys, you’d like to go for a spin,” Bloodmage cooed to Maya. The Earthen Nabi burned as hot as the flames of her comrade, and with a snap of her fingers the stone bonds tightened around the Mage’s limbs. She gasped from a strange mixture of pain and pleasure as her body trembled with excitement.

“Let her go,” Eran demanded. Maya shot him a look, but the intensity of his gaze caused a near instant break in Maya’s will.

“Release,” she commanded reluctantly. She took a step back and watched in awe as the demons materialized at the witch’s side. They bore the bodies of men but the heads of jackals, and with a glimmer of hunger in their eyes they snarled at the prophetess and the prophets with her. Bloodmage lifted her hand, and a sinister red light manifested in her palm. The cave revealed the Nabi’im to be surrounded by her dog-faced minions, each with the same sadistic starved stare. Eran smiled as his eyes narrowed on the sorceress, and in the time it took her to blink, he stood miraculously in front of her with his burning fist in her stomach.

She fell to her knees in an instant, and as she started to recite some ancient curse, Eran interrupted her with a kick to the face. The creature rolled across the floor of the cave and into the brawny legs of one of her slaves.

"Not bad," Bloodmage praised as she picked herself up and spat a mouthful of blood onto the ground. The shadows of the cave swept over her body as the downpour of a waterfall, and the burns and bruises she suffered were immediately healed. "But if that's all you've got, I'm afraid you'll never get the job done, sweetheart."

"Don't you *dare* call me that again," Eran shouted in a burst of anger. The deranged woman before him lifted her hand and Eran was assaulted by demons one by one. With a single flex of his muscles the flames on his shoulders spread outward until all that opposed him were instantly incinerated. Bloodmage's face contorted in anger, but rather than summon more monsters as she had in their last encounter, she thought it best to charge at him herself. She opened up with a high knee, but Eran ducked below her and grabbed her ankle as she passed through the air. The sudden resistance to her flow caused her upper body to jerk downward, but before her face met the stone of the cave floor she extended her hands. She caught herself easily, and followed up with a sharp kick to Eran's jaw that sent him to his back.

He rolled a few feet, but ultimately pushed himself back onto his legs and tossed a massive fireball in her direction as she flipped back onto her own. She evaded the blast with the execution of a leg sweep, and much to everyone's surprise a wave of solid shadow discharged in pursuit of Eran. He quickly blasted himself up into the air and flipped so that his feet would touch the ceiling. In the split second he paused there, the demoness kicked another shadow blast in his direction.

He kicked off to narrowly dodge the shot, and as he came downward he ignited his fist yet again. Bloodmage smirked as her hands became engulfed in the darkness. He punched at her face, but was easily blocked by her own extended palm. Though he crashed against her with inhuman momentum she stood firmly in place, and even had the audacity to smile at him through those sickening red and black eyes.

"How is this possible," Eran asked as his gaze shifted to the black mass that gripped his fiery fist, and his legs descended to the ground beneath him. He pulled his fist away from her, but the monster before him tightened her grip and dealt him a crippling kick to the ribs. He gasped for air as he coughed up blood. Bloodmage's eyes lit with delight, and in an act of unmitigated malice she slowly bent his fist backward. He screamed in agony as he gave his all in an effort to resist, but when he found that it would be impossible he shakily moved to kick her in the side of her head. She blocked it, but was taken by surprise when he followed up with a solid fire punch to the center of her forehead. She slid back, and the resistance of her heels in the dirt left streaks along the path. The burn on her face bled profusely, and the sadistic witch licked her lips as the blood dripped upon them. In the next instant, the shadows of the cave washed over her again and her injuries vanished without a trace.

"What's going on here," Aiden demanded. By all logic her magic was supposed to be limited to the demons under her command, but because of Eran's earlier attack there were none left.

"This is pretty fun, isn't it sweetie?" Bloodmage taunted with a sick cackle that echoed in the vast emptiness of the cave. "You were so tightly wound last time, and I thought I'd do you a favor and treat you to a very special night." The Nabi'im grimaced simultaneously at her unnerving seductive tone.

"You shouldn't be able to use any magic without the help of demons," Eran growled. "How are you doing this?" A sickening serpentine smirk slithered across the lips of Eran's greatest adversary.

"That's simple, honey," she teased some more, "I just made a little… business transaction with Lucifer. At the cost of one human soul, I've got all the magic I need wrapped up into this hot little body of mine." Aiden's eyes grew wide in anger, and though he rushed for the creature that dared war against them, Eran shot a fireball at his feet. Aiden jumped back just in time, and trembled in agitation at his inability to join the fray.

"You stay back," Eran demanded as he fixed his eyes on the monster. "This is my fight."

"Yes," said the iniquitous vixen. "Let's see if the power of your God can hold up against my magic." She jumped backwards with her hand extended as she chanted a curse at him. The shadows that surrounded him swept over him like a wave, and though he did his best to fight out of it he was powerless to do so.

"What did you do to him," Maya asked in a furious tone that shocked her more than anything. Bloodmage locked eyes with the stunning Maya and flashed a toothy grin.

"I've taken him prisoner with a memory curse," she informed them with sultry rhythm. "Any minute now the panic and pain of his past will lock him in my world of shadows for eternity, and I'll get to do with him whatever I want." Aiden charged his hand with an electrical current, but before he could take his first step towards her, she wagged her finger before her demonic red and black eyes. "I wouldn't do that if I were you. The only way for him to get out of there is if I let him out. You kill me, he dies right along with me." The two Nabi'im trembled with fury, but watched the pool of shadows carefully in the hope that their comrade would return.

Eran felt a burning sensation sweep over his body, and the added strain of his rigorous offensive against the shadows only aggravated the bruised ribs he'd suffered before. He dropped to his knees and closed his eyes for a moment as the sounds of the world around him slipped away into the black. For a moment it was nice, and it offered him the opportunity to mouth a silent prayer for healing. Nothing happened. He prayed again, louder and more fervently than before, but still the pain in his side persisted.

"How dare you speak prayers to God here," challenged a voice all too familiar to him. Footsteps approached the Nabi, and he opened his eyes to see that he kneeled on the hardwood floors of a moderately large church. To his dismay, the one who approached him was none other than the preacher he'd shot in the head. The bullet hole remained just as fresh now as it had been twelve years before, and with every step taken more blood ran down his face.

"No," Eran protested as he shook his head. He staggered as he stood, and a tremor of excruciating pain rippled through his body. "This isn't real. You're not here!" As he vehemently rejected the sights before him the pews of the church began to fill with the faces of all those he'd killed since that fateful day, and with dead eyes they watched him as his first continued to advance.

"I am," spoke the dead man with uplifted hand as he approached at unhurried pace. "We all are, and it was you, Eran, who put us here." His eyes widened as the burn of the shadows returned. "You were the one who tortured us, mutilated us, and slaughtered us." Eran looked to the furious souls that lined the pews as tears of remorse fell from his eyes. "You enjoyed it didn't you; how easy it was, or how our spouses and children cried over our bleeding corpses if you were gracious enough to leave them alive?" He shook his head, mortified by his past actions and angry with himself for the way he embraced the hellish beast of Flesh at the beginning. "Well now it's our turn. *You* get to die, and we get to savor the experience of making it happen."

"No, this can't be happening," he shouted into the infernal air. He grabbed the sides of his head as the veins in his hands pressed against his skin. The preacher of the past reached behind a pew and pulled out a gun. Eran heard the click, and his head jolted upward. He stared into the blackness of the barrel, but what he saw in the chamber struck him with a combination of disgust and rage. Bloodmage's face smiled at him from within the firearm, and the undead minister snickered wildly as he pulled the trigger. Eran's blood boiled over, and by the sheer force of his will he stepped back into the power he'd been given. The hooded cloak returned and the red flames that graced his shoulders burned brighter than they ever had. He slapped the gun out of his face just as the dead man shot, and the witch-faced bullet blasted into the floorboard. The enraged prophet dealt a crushing push kick to the chest of the man before him, and watched as he rolled onto his back.

"How dare you!" The priest barked from his downed position as he looked up at Eran. The Nabi spread his hands apart, and the assembly of lost souls watched as the flames on his shoulders took the form of Uriel's majestic silver wings and lifted him into the air. Seven orbs of fire, much larger than the ones he'd dealt with in his training, formed in a triangle before him. "We own you!"

"No," Eran asserted, "I will not be bound by this anymore. Incinerate." He pushed his hand forward, just as Uriel had in distant memory, and the fireballs crushed the sanctuary in a literal blaze of glory. Eran blinked, and upon the reopening of his eyes he found himself surrounded by the stone and shadow of the Passage of Nasah. Aiden and Maya smiled upon his return to their realm, but the indignant sorceress screamed.

"How did you break through my curse," she howled as she launched another blast of solid black at him. He exhaled lightly as it approached and smiled when a ball of fire materialized in midair that devoured the shadows.

"Maya," Eran called, and instinctively the prophetess knew just what he wanted her to do.

"Bind," she spoke, and the ground around Bloodmage's feet began to shift again. The witch jumped into the air in an attempt to evade the humiliation of bondage but was shocked when the stone ceiling warped around her arms. She found herself suspended above her targets, and as they smiled at her out of joy for the first time, she struggled and screamed profanities at them.

"'Forget the former things;'" Eran quoted of the prophet Isaiah, "'do not dwell on the past.'" He lifted his hand with an ineffable intensity in his eyes as an orb of flame appeared before him. The fire that rested on his shoulders molded around the ball, and the subarctic chill within the Passage of Nasah gave way to near Saharan heat. "Burn away," he told her, and with a remorseless grin Eran tossed the ball towards his greatest enemy and the shades of his past all the same. The monstrous shell that once housed the Seed of the Flesh screamed in agony until nothing but ash remained.

Eran stood there with his eyes lifted towards the ceiling as Aiden approached him. He pat his Eran's shoulder and stared at the ceiling along with him, and in that moment, he realized that in the last twelve years this was the first time their eyes had been focused on the same path. Eran, whose eyes always looked to the troubles of his past and Aiden, whose vision honed in on the possibility of a brighter future, finally walked in the same direction.

"You did well," Aiden told him as he took him into a tight hug. Maya held a hand on her chest as she approached the brothers in arms, and offered a smile of approval to her one-time attacker. Aiden backed off and turned his attention to the length of the passage.

"I—" she paused for a second as she recalled everything she knew about this man and his relationship with Aiden. For the first time since their official meeting, Maya felt as if she could understand him, and because of that she wrapped her arms around him just as well. "I'm sorry."

"Well, be sorry later," Aiden urged her before Eran had the opportunity to respond. "We wasted a lot of time with the Mage and we really do need to get going." Maya rolled her eyes as she crossed her arms in her best attempt to hide her uncontrollable nervousness. *Oh joy,* she thought sarcastically, *the Devil awaits.*

"Will we at least be able to run now," she asked.

"I don't see why not," Aiden responded flatly. "We are on a time schedule, after all. However…" he took a few paces away from the others as he stretched out both of his hands. The flames on his shoulders danced as a breeze filtered in from the distance. "Arrow Wave," he commanded, and a colossal wave of successive lightning strikes ripped through the length of the ceiling all the way to the exit. The light that shined through the newly created rift burned at what demons lay in wait for them. “Now we don’t have to worry about anything jumping out at us to slow us down. Let’s move.” Without another word, Aiden darted down the path and Maya followed suit. Eran stood there for a moment longer and glanced back at the spot on the ceiling. He struggled with the guilt of his past and the memory of his possession for twelve years, but now he pressed onward after his comrades knowing that that past was at last behind him.

Chapter Nineteen

The Nabi'im came upon the halfway point and watched as the once luminescent sky blackened. Thunder sounded and lightning flashed, and as the rains poured through the fissure above, Aiden couldn't help but be reminded of twelve years ago. Even then, he could see the saddening image of his brother Eran bloodied for Lucifer's sake. He could still feel the sting of Evil's glare, but despite that he thought it best to refocus on the present rather than fall into the snare of the past. The ground beneath them shook under the crack of thunder, and the sound of shifting rocks filled their ears.

"That doesn't sound too good," Aiden shouted over the sound as the rocky walls of the Passage of Nasah crumbled as they passed.

"It wouldn't be this bad if *someone* hadn't destroyed the ceiling," Eran commented in all smugness. Aiden slapped the back of his head as they ran side by side and quickly upped his own speed before Eran could return the favor.

"It isn't like it was a bad idea to lighten the path though. There are less obstacles that stand between us and Lucifer, and if anything, the fact that the walls are crumbling around us only pushes us further down the path," Maya rebutted. Aiden smiled and Eran rolled his eyes.

"Way to look on the bright side, Princess," Eran teased, but when Maya chuckled at the comment he looked over to her out of obligation. She smirked, and given the situation it disturbed her onlookers.

"We'll see who the princess is when I beat you to the end of the tunnel," she told him. For the first time since she became a Nabi, she felt as if she could overcome anything. Eran assured her of that in his victory over his former master. She caught sight of Aiden, who flashed her a look of disbelief.

"You… you can't possibly be serious right now," he challenged, but it was no use. Aiden shook his head as she passed them by, and Eran couldn't help but laugh at her determination.

"That girl really has no perception of danger, does she?" he asked Aiden with an expression of amusement firmly in place. Aiden rolled his eyes as he looked back on all the times he'd rescued her.

"You have no earthly idea…" he responded with a humored smirk. The rock walls on either side of them crumbled faster and faster as they sped down the channel. Their hearts beat with the ferocity of wild beasts, and the beads of sweat that formed on their faces became streams. Minute by minute, it felt as though their legs grew closer to their breaking point. "Looks like we don't have much of a choice in the matter. You down to dust the female?" Eran's smile grew all the wider.

"Aren't I always," Aiden asked cockily as they sprinted after Maya. She looked on in competitive angst as the boys passed her and ran in front of her to block her path.

"Really guys?" Maya huffed. She smirked as a brilliant idea crept into her mind. The Scriptures once again flashed in her vision, and as she focused her mind she found one apt for the situation. "'I will hasten and not delay to obey your commands,'" she quoted with utmost sincerity, and as green flames engulfed her feet she ran along the crumbling wall to get around them. The two men watched her gracefully tread upon the highly unstable partition, jaws agape but resolution stirred.

"If that's how you want to play it," Eran shrugged as he went to one of his signature Scriptures. "'Do you not know that in a race all the runners run, but only one gets the prize? Run in such a way as to get the prize.'" The red flames on Eran's shoulders trickled down his back, and erupted in a sudden burst to propel him forward on the ground. He passed by Aiden with relative ease, and shot ahead of Maya as she dismounted the wall. Aiden laughed, because just like before it seemed as though the worries of the world melted into the background. His heart pumped with indescribable excitement, and he balled his fists as he searched his mind for a Scripture that would keep him in the game.

"'They charge like warriors; they scale walls like soldiers. They all march in line, not swerving from their course.'" As Aiden quoted the Scripture, his body surged with blue sparks of lightning and in an instant, he blasted ahead of the others. Maya and Eran stared on behind him, and to their dissatisfaction they found that they were incapable of altering their course.

"Alright, now that's just playing dirty," Eran shouted after him, but Aiden laughed as the end of the tunnel drew nearer and nearer.

"How can it be playing dirty? I'm just standing on the Word of God like you two," he disputed. Eran shook his head at his wingman, but sobered up as they neared their exit. "Do you guys feel that?" The storm overhead intensified as they drew closer to the outside, and with a flash of lightning and subsequent pulse of thunder, they felt a foreboding chill despite the raised temperature of the Passage.

"Yeah," Maya confirmed. Her mind filled with the images of the vision from the day before, and as the glowing red and black eyes stood at the forefront, she quivered in her uneasiness. "I've definitely felt that before. If I'm not mistaken it was the first vision I ever had, and if we don't hurry then the world itself will cease to exist." The severity of the statement stunned the others to silence, and the three pushed through the exit as the Passage of Nasah crumbled away to dust.

Nothing could have prepared the Nabi'im for what they saw in the valley below the hills of Megiddo. The bodies of Israelis and Palestinians alike lay mutilated upon the roads and grass, and fire burst from the ground as jackal-headed and snake-skinned demons fed upon the corpses. Their mouths gushed with the blood of their victims as they snarled into the stormy skies, and atop the Tel across the way, Lucifer sat comfortably upon his spike-covered throne. Maya's heart jumped into her throat as she took in the scene, and with tears in her eyes she gazed upon the king of nightmares.

He lifted his hand, and with a unified roar, the multitude of demons that populated the valley below shifted to more humanoid figures and teleported away, scattered throughout the corners of the world. Lucifer stood from his throne and folded his arms as he watched his nemeses move from the hillside into the corpse-laden valley. He laughed at their expressions of pain and horror, and the dark aura that shrouded him polluted the very air. The thunder roared and the winds howled like a wounded beast, and the flames on the shoulders of the Nabi'im flared in the presence of their enemy.

Lucifer lifted his eyebrows as they tread towards the Tel through the fire and the blood, and as the rain showered down from the heavens he clasped his clawed hands together with great anticipation. Aiden led the trio up the side and to the top of Tel Megiddo, and couldn't help but gaze upon the great divide that ran through the hill as they climbed. This was the moment, the only opportunity to rectify the wrongs of the past and preserve hope for the future. He glanced back at Eran, the best friend that for so long he'd fought for, even before they became the Two, and as his brow furrowed he resolved to protect him at all costs.

They both thought of that day twelve years ago, and both of them hated just how weak they were back then, how they failed to protect each other, and how their actions only gave life to a situation that never should have arisen. Though Maya had only seen those horrific events through memories, she knew of a tumultuous future should they fail, and resolved just as they did to fight with everything she had. Their flames burned brighter than the surrounding darkness could dim, and as they reached the top of Tel Megiddo the Hebrew script on their hoods that read "Nabi" glowed with affirming intensity. Lucifer looked upon the Three who now stood across from him with a sinister delight in his eyes.

"So, you decided to come after all," spoke the Devil as lightning flashed overhead and darkened his already malevolent appearance. "I was beginning to wonder if I had lost your interest. Reassure me, you do like the decorations, do you not?" He spread his hands as thunder rolled, and flames jetted from the ground on all sides. Aiden glared at him with unparalleled animosity as Lucifer grinned from ear to ear. "I rather enjoy the living kind. They tend to flock to this place like flies to manure, which leaves me to do with them as I please." The demon's eyes flickered with joy at the sight of blood and fire.

"Lucifer," Aiden growled with a brief glance back to the valley, but then took a moment to calm himself. "I suppose it shouldn't surprise me that you'd be this twisted and arrogant. Still, I would have expected much better from someone who fancies himself a king. Don't you think it's ironic, though, that the hell you put us through for all these years in a desperate grab at victory would ultimately lead to a crushing defeat?" Lucifer laughed at the very notion as he flexed his jet-black wings.

"Hell?! You know nothing of Hell, you worthless mongrel. It was because of *you* that I was debased from my position in Heaven, because of *you* that I was disowned as a son, and because of *you* that my name is even synonymous with that word you use so lightly. Your pitiful sufferings are of no consequence to me. In fact, I relish in them. The screams of pain and agony sing to me in my own anguish, and sooth the very core of my being. The way your kind so willingly marches along the beaten path to Hell itself sends a chill of euphoria down my spine the likes of which cannot be described, because in all of that you finally get what you deserve for what you did to me!" His voice deepened as his anger escalated, the thunder and lightning ensued overhead.

"You did it to yourself," Eran shot back as he came to his colleague's defense. "You allowed yourself to become so blind to your hatred towards our kind that you openly rejected what love you received. You betrayed God Himself and tried to usurp Him as King, and *that's* why you fell. Our part to play wasn't all that great, Lucy." Lucifer's eyes widened in the purest form of hatred at the sound of the nickname, and with a volatile roar he shook the foundation of the entire region. Aiden, Eran, and Maya struggled to maintain their ground against the shockwave and braced themselves against the nearby stone wall. Much of the ancient city crumbled from the attack, but in a moment's time the Nabi'im stood on still ground.

"How dare you, of all people, mention *His* name in my presence when you yourself are just as treacherous as I am," Lucifer challenged. Eran's eyes remained fixed on him and stood strong in their conviction.

"You murdered hundreds of people for the sake of pleasure, all under the pretense of becoming the most powerful person in the world. You embraced the Seed of—"

"It was a Seed that *you* planted in me! The actions I took are mine, yeah, but it was you who manipulated me into following my own selfishness just so you could get out of jail free and use me to help you spark your own personal Apocalypse. Don't you dare try and play innocent with me," Eran snapped. Lucifer's dark aura flickered as he clenched his fists tighter and dug the metal claws that decorated his fingertips into his palms. His blood poured out from the wounds onto the ground, and much to the deep concern of the Nabi'im that watched, it melted away the stone upon which it fell.

"You…" Lucifer breathed heavily, and growled like a hungry lion with every exhalation. "You dare interrupt me? I…" he caught himself, and placed a hand on his forehead as he started to laugh. "I need not sully myself with indignation on account of lowly filth. Yes, I confess, it was indeed my plan to have you fall to your own insecurity, and for a time you served as a splendid distraction while I made the preparations for my Apocalypse. It seems now, though, that I should have ended you that night I infiltrated the Hall of Nabi'im. So now, I will simply grind your bones into dust with my teeth."

"I've been waiting twelve years to see you try," Aiden snapped back as he bared his teeth like a dog.

"Such insolence," Lucifer taunted. "And from someone of such high esteem."

"Funny," Maya chimed in with a hand on her hip as she brushed the long side of her bob-cut hair out of her face and tucked it behind her ear.

"For someone who always seems to lose, you seem awfully confident. How does the Scripture go? 'Pride goes before destruction, a haughty spirit before a fall?' Allow us to personally teach you what that means." In an act of blind fury, the Devil charged at the young woman with his clawed hand outstretched. She stood there, perfectly immobile as the vision she'd seen in her unconsciousness manifested before her very eyes.

"You're mine," Lucifer shouted venomously. Maya closed her eyes as she felt his darkness drift towards her, and crossed her arms in front of her face in a hopeless effort to block him.

"You don't have permission," Aiden countered as he dealt a sharp kick to the side of Lucifer's skull. The Prince of Flies rocketed off to the side in a spiral. He landed on his feet and smiled at the Nabi'im who gawked at him in awe.

"Whatever is the matter? Did you think your little attack would cause me harm? You are nothing but gnats to me just begging to be crushed," Lucifer said with a laugh. He lifted his hand and urged them to charge him, and with a brief exchange of looks, Aiden assailed. He started things off with a high kick, but Lucifer carelessly lifted his hand and grabbed the leg. His sinister eyes lit with perverted delight as he grabbed for Aiden's face, but before Satan's pointed nails found their place in his eyes, Aiden twisted his body downward and kicked him in the ribs. He managed to break the hold and roll away from the demon, and as he pulled to a stop Eran vaulted over him to deliver a kick of his own. Lucifer blocked, this time only narrowly, and as Aiden charged him, the demon tossed Eran back into the oncoming Nabi as if he were no heavier than an average rock.

The two of them rolled across the sandy foundation of the ancient city until they stopped at Maya's feet. Lucifer flashed a toothy grin at her as he paced the ground like a starved jungle cat.

"Care to try your hand, my dear," he inquired of her. She met his demonic gaze as the boys pushed back to their feet.

"What's the rush, Lucy," Eran mocked as he spat blood on the ground. Aiden smirked as he wiped the sweat from his brow.

"Tired of us already?" The two of them charged Lucifer simultaneously, and as they came he braced himself for their assaults.

"Not at all," he admitted. Eran punched at his face as Aiden went for a leg sweep, but to their astonishment he bounded away with a single beat of his colossal black wings. "Your feeble attempts at combat are the equivalent of an ant biting down on a shoe." He extended a single finger and discharged a gargantuan wave of darkness. Both Aiden and Eran were knocked back by the blast, and as Lucifer laughed, so did they. Maya stood confused by their amusement and eyed the rips in their dust-covered clothes and the cuts that bled beneath them with increasing concern. Lucifer fell silent and serious, but the boys continued to chortle as they regained their legs.

"Well if this is substandard, then why don't we take things up a level?" Aiden proposed. Lucifer shrugged with a smile on his face.

"It makes no difference to me, little fly. I shall swat you down all the same."

"We'll see about that," Eran started as the flames on his shoulders danced with greater life. Aiden extended his hand with a devilish smirk emblazoned on his face.

"'The earth trembled and quaked, the foundations of the Heavens shook; they trembled because He was angry,'" Aiden quoted with fervor, and as the words crossed his lips, the ground beneath them started to shake. The tremble of the Tel rocked Lucifer to his knees, and he was forced to watch as the foundation of the timeworn city steadily broke apart beneath his touch. "Maya," he yelled, and Maya stepped up with a relieved expression as she extended both of her arms.

"'He split the rocks in the wilderness and gave them water as abundant as the seas;'" she quoted. The sensitive rock upon which the Devil sat began to rumble even more, and before he had the opportunity to speak on the subject, water erupted from the cracks and thrust him high into the air. Lucifer parted his wings and hovered in the sky, and as he joined his hands together and formed a mammoth ball of solidified shadows between them, the young prophetess smirked. "Eran," she called behind her, and watched Eran step up to the plate and extend his left arm as the flames on his shoulders burst with life on either side.

"'Smoke rose from His nostrils; consuming fire came from his mouth, burning coals blazed out of it,'" he added in a joyous tone. The black sky up above parted, and like a happy child Eran watched with a smile firmly in place as thousands of birds made of pure flame descended upon the airborne King of Demons. The sound of their cries filled the black sky, and when Lucifer turned around he was struck with the full force of their onslaught. He stumbled back in the air but maintained altitude as he fired multiple shadow blasts at the seemingly endless flock of igneous avifauna.

"My turn," Aiden asserted as he lifted his hand into the sky. "'He made darkness His canopy around Him — the dark rain clouds of the sky."

As Aiden quoted the Scripture, the black clouds that parted upon the arrival of the fire flock converged once again. "'Out of the brightness of His presence bolts of lightning blazed forth." The thunder returned with a deafening roar, and from all directions lightning discharged and struck the dark lord.

Lucifer was blasted from the sky, and the Nabi'im rejoiced as they watched him plummet to the earth below. The sounds of their cheers and laughter awakened an uncontrollable rage deep within the core of the monster, and with another beat of his majestic black wings he returned to an upright position. The black energy that surrounded him expanded and shifted to a dull scarlet. The Three stood and watched him as he unleashed a beastly roar, and the aura around him exuded a wave of raw dark power.

"Well, this doesn't look good," Maya observed. She closed her eyes, and the Hebrew script that lined her forehead glowed with new intensity as she took up a Scripture in her heart. "'But those who hope in the Lord will renew their strength. They will soar on wings like eagles; they will run and not grow weary, they will walk and not be faint.'" The green flames that burned bright on her shoulders spread into wings and carried her shakily into the air. The demon caught sight of this, and as he bellowed into the darkness, a beam of solid shadow rocketed out of his mouth. Maya narrowly managed to evade the attack but quickly corrected herself in the air. She clasped her hands together as she soared about in an evasive pattern and openly began to pray. "Father God, the Righteous Judge, fill me with your power so that the Enemy would see defeat and savor it!" The force behind her words provoked Satan to action, and he flew after her as swiftly as his wings would carry him.

“You will die here,” Lucifer hissed to her as he attempted to run his jagged claws along her back. She felt his darkness once again, and though he reached for her she quickly dove closer to the earth and scooped up an even mixture of rock and sand. She looked back at him with a smile on her face, because it was in that moment that she realized that he might be right. Still, she knew she had to give this battle her all. She refused to let even Satan underestimate her.

“Use what you have put in me,” she continued in her most earnest petition of the Most High. “The clay from which I was sculpted and the bone from which I was made are your tools, my God. Use them as you see fit and subdue my enemy.” The sand and stone molded around her arm and created an extended blade with the Hebrew inscription “Emeth” written along the edge. Lucifer swooped down on her like a falcon on a field mouse, but to his surprise his clawed hands were met with the miracle blade. They became locked in a struggle for power as they continued to drift in the air, but with a sinister smile on his face, Lucifer vanished from her sights and rematerialized on the ground below.

Before Aiden and Eran could warn her, Lucifer had already thrust himself back into the air and dug his pointed fingertips into the flesh of her back. She howled in pain, and as her vision blurred from the agony the mighty wings upon which she flew receded into the flames on her shoulders.

“Maya,” Eran yelled, his jaw agape, and Lucifer smiled down at him with delight. As his best friend launched himself into the air to catch her, Aiden dropped to his knees at Lucifer’s daunting power. His blood ran as hot as Eran’s fire, but he knew better than to lose his temper as the dark lord had. Eran raced through the air to save Maya from a horrible death, but despite his staggering speed Lucifer still intercepted him.

"Going somewhere," the demon inquired as he let out a sinister laugh. Eran watched as Maya continued to fall, and the flightless Aiden felt only helpless to watch. *No,* he thought, *I reject that.*

"Brilliant Flash!" The sound of Aiden's voice boomed through the Tel like the thunder above, and a colossal burst of bright blue lightning blasted Lucifer to the ground. Eran quickly rushed after Maya, who rapidly continued her descent. The Scarlet Nabi intensified his flames in an effort to speed up just enough to catch her comfortably, but quickly realized that on his own he was useless. "Rage," Aiden commanded, and a blast of air fed into his wingman's fire to push him forward. He caught Maya as carefully as he could and drifted back around towards their azure companion. He landed at Aiden's side and gently laid Maya down on the ground. He mouthed a quick healing prayer, and as she slowly regained mobility they watched Lucifer pick himself off the ground.

"What's the plan," Eran asked Aiden with his eyes still focused on the Devil. "We need to get Lucifer back in his prison before this goes any further." Aiden tightened his fists and looked at the ground for a moment as his thoughts raced.

"I have an idea," he told his teammate. Eran looked at him earnestly.

"Let's hear it," he urged. Aiden hesitated for a moment, but as Lucifer charged his fist with an obscene amount of those shadows he loved so much, Aiden realized that this wasn't the time. He looked into his friend's eyes as a tear trickled out of his own.

"When I tell you, I want you to establish the seal," Aiden said gravely. Eran's eyes widened as they filled with water.

"No," he protested despite Aiden's best effort to calm him down. "No, it's too dangerous for you to hold him back alone. There has to be another way—"

"Eran!" The force with which Aiden yelled his name instantly provoked him to silence. "There isn't another way. I'll hold him in place, and you invoke the power of the Blood to seal him up again." Aiden and Eran turned their gaze to the Enemy, and Aiden in all sobriety asked his wingman a simple question. "You ready?" Eran froze at the sound of those two words, and though they rattled him to his very core he smiled through the pain.

"Aren't I always," he uttered. Aiden couldn't help but show a bittersweet smile as they stood to their feet. The Azure Nabi took a deep breath and savored the rush that came with standing alongside a brother on the battlefield. He felt the wind press against his face and the rain pour downward upon his hood, and even though he fought a demon, he knew that this would be the greatest fight of his entire life.

"Flash," Aiden commanded with an unexpected calm that expertly masked the deep sadness in his heart. Eran watched with the greatest sense of fear he'd ever felt, but did his best to fight it off just as Aiden did their aggressor. Lucifer heard the command and monitored the heavens with an unimpressed expression on his face.

"You really think that that little trick will do you some good," he asked with his eyes trained on the sky. Aiden shook his head as a spark emerged from his hand.

"Strike," he continued. Lightning from heaven struck the palm of his hand, and the unrestrained celestial power flashed around the whole of it. Lucifer's eyes widened, as the intensity of the blue lightning rivaled that of his own shadows, but his surprise quickly gave way to intrigue as he motioned with his hand once again. The Prophet of God and the Devil himself charged one another in one last battle of light and darkness. They lifted their hands as they moved inward, and without a second's delay, Aiden drove his lightning charged hand straight through Lucifer's silver. Lucifer released a horrid groan.

"Let… me… go…" he demanded as he now wheezed. Eran and Maya looked on in overjoyed surprise as Satan himself bled at the hands of a prophet.

"Eran, do it now!" Aiden called urgently behind him. He turned his head back towards Lucifer and stared into those red and black eyes hot with anger.

"'They triumphed over him by the blood of the Lamb and by the word of their testimony,'" Eran quoted in the face of the Devil. Blood rushed into the ancient ruins of Tel Megiddo from all directions as he spoke, and in confidence he continued with haste. "'They did not love their lives so much as to shrink away from death.'" Lucifer flashed a sinister smile as the blood slowly overtook his body.

"How convenient," said the emperor of darkness, and with that sickening smile on his face he drove his hand through Aiden's abdomen. The blood overcame him and dragged him down into the well from whence he came, but despite the retraction of the talons of the demon, the gaping wound remained. Tears welled up in Eran's eyes, and Maya clasped her hands around her mouth as Aiden fell lifelessly to the ground. Eran ran to him and took his brother's head in his arms as the rain continued to pour, and with a flash of lightning, the prophets wept.

Chapter Twenty

He sat in the sanctuary silently as the preacher spoke. He watched the people carefully, but couldn't help but allow the Word that was being spoken in his hearing to minister to his Spirit. He needed it, that empowering message, that reassurance that he was on the right path, that restoration to his soul. The sermon, though powerful and inspiring, did little to sooth his troubled mind, and even less to make him forget about that horrible night twelve years ago. His mind returned to Tel Megiddo, and no matter how hard he fought against it, the image of Lucifer's eyes remained ever present. He lowered his head as his body trembled at the memory, but suddenly the hand of the person next to him gently massaged his forearm. He looked up at her, and despite her years of loyalty to him he could never understand just what he did to deserve it.

She gave him her best attempt at a reassuring smile, but in all reality she suffered just the same. Nothing felt right after their war with Lucifer, and even though they'd managed to save the world, it came with such a terrible cost that she wondered if it was worth it. Still, she supposed that her ideas were without foundation, as it was her husband who suffered the most after Aiden's death.

"The second thing we see is that in order to Hope in Heaven While Going Through Hell, we have to challenge our conditions by crying out in faith," the preacher spoke passionately into the microphone. The many people of the church shouted in agreement, but Eran and Maya choked back tears at the repetition of the title. All they could see at that moment was Aiden's smiling face as blood ran from his mouth and the wound that the Enemy left in his body. They desperately grasped each other's hand as silent tears fell, but still they dared hear the words of the minister in the pulpit. "The Bible says in Exodus chapter 5 verses 22-23, 'Moses returned to the Lord and said, 'Why, Lord, why have you brought trouble on this people? Is this why you sent me? Ever since I went to Pharaoh to speak in your name, he has brought trouble on this people, and you have not rescued your people at all.' What we see here is Moses struggling with his faith. Pharaoh doesn't like him, the Israelites don't like him, his people are worse off than before, and from what he's seen, God has not acted on His promise just yet. But in this seemingly dark situation," the preacher paused as he reached beneath the podium and pulled out a glass of water. He took a sip and caught his breath, but nevertheless continued, "Moses doesn't follow the example of his people and storm off cursing. The Bible says right there that, 'Moses returned to the Lord.' Moses, God's most celebrated prophet second only to Jesus, in the face of adversity and at the mercy of hostility, went *into* the presence of God Most High and cried out his circumstantial concerns to God."

"Alright," someone in the congregation shouted with enthusiasm as a means of pushing the preacher onward. Eran, though he wept, was reminded of Aiden's faithfulness despite all the hell he'd been through. He couldn't help but think of how lonely his dear friend felt in the earlier parts of his life. Eran hated himself for the events that surrounded Lucifer's release, how he betrayed Aiden without so much as a second thought, and how he spent every second of his life after that putting others, including his wingman, through unimaginable torment. He intensified Aiden's loneliness, forced him to wallow in it and meditate on the taste of it, but still, Eran couldn't help but marvel at how Aiden had still tried to save him. It was because of Aiden that he even walked the streets of Edgehaven uninhibited, that he was given pardon for his crimes because of their victory over Moloch. In a somewhat twisted way, it was because of Aiden that he met the love of his life and even had the possibility for a future spent with her. The more Eran thought of his wingman's genuine spirit and open devotion to what proved to be his only family in this world, the more he just wanted him back.

"That almost doesn't sound right, I know," the preacher continued with elevated passion, "but Moses remembered the promise and how it didn't make anything easier when he acted on it. He needed clarity, and instead of going to those hopeless, curse-spouting people, he went to God and asked, 'What's up?' He had the audacity to look at God and say, 'why are we in trouble,' and 'you have not saved your people at all.' In saying those things, Moses was challenging God to challenge the conditions that challenged his people."

The crowd shouted at the revelation of God's Word, and a still-quiet Eran lifted his tearful eyes toward the heavens.

"The situation made Moses uneasy, so he challenged it. The workers of the Underground Railroad were uncomfortable with slavery, and they cried out in faith to God and each other and they challenged it. The workers of the Civil Rights movement were sick of being judged by the color of their skin rather than the content of their character, so they cried out in faith to God and each other and they challenged it! Jesus was sick and tired of sin enslaving His people, so He came from Heaven to Earth to cry out in faith to His Father God from a rugged cross and He challenged it! Don't allow people to tell you what you can and can't do when you walk in the will of God! Challenge them! Don't sit there in a financial or relational crisis as if all hope is lost! Challenge it! Don't wallow in that sorrow and depression for a minute more! Speak a word over your life right now, cry out to God and challenge it! I don't know about you, but the Bible that I read tells me, 'Weeping may remain for a night, but rejoicing comes in the morning!' Quit acting like you don't have God-given authority and start Hoping in Heaven While Going through Hell!"

The crowd of people cheered wildly as many stood all across the building. Eran was among them, and as he wiped his eyes he moved towards the center aisle. Maya grabbed his hand, and when he looked back at her he saw clearly the concern in her eyes.

"Don't worry," he reassured her, "everything's fine. I just need a little bit of fresh air. I'll see you at home." She reluctantly released her husband, and watched as he walked down the aisle and out the door. His body still trembled as people waved at him as he passed by, but regardless of his discomfort with the social interaction he waved back and kept on his way. The city buildings of Edgehaven had grown taller since Moloch's attack twelve years prior, and the protective barrier remained in place on all sides.

The birds chirped overhead as a light breeze brushed against his skin. His black suit and dark red shirt quickly heated in the summer sun, but to Eran it was the loving embrace of friends and family long gone. He passed by a pair of teens who teased each other as they marched down the sidewalk. They were both tall, and though one was considerably thinner than the other, the family resemblance was still there. As much as Eran wanted to smile, he couldn't.

His mind wandered back over a decade to the aftermath of the battle, and he watched again as Lucifer pierced Aiden's gut with a mighty thrust. The blood summoned by the Scripture washed over him, and as he was dragged down into the depths of Tel Megiddo Eran rushed to the impaled Aiden's side.

"Aiden," he said shakily as his wingman, his comrade, the only brother he'd ever known struggled to breathe. "Aiden, stay with me!" He opened his eyes just a little, and to Eran's alarm the light therein had already grown so dim. He started to cry as he looked down at the Azure Prophet, who smiled as he slowly lifted his hand.

"Well…" he grunted in pain as the word left his mouth, but Aiden knew that the time would soon come where he would breathe his last. His smile remained in place as he continued to speak. "This kinda sucks. I fought so hard… to save you, only to… die in the end." Eran rapidly shook his head in firm denial as his wingman continually struggled to breathe.

"No," he grasped Aiden's uplifted hand and trembled as the heat in his body started to fade. "No, you can't… you can't die." Maya slowly approached and kneeled next to them.

"It's alright," Aiden told his war buddy through a much wider smile. "I got… to spend my last moments… with the only family I've ever known, and my best…" his body convulsed as the flowing wind blasted sand into his open wound, but still he felt as if he had to press towards the finish. "My best friend… in the world." He looked at Maya, who cried just as heavily as Eran as they watched him slowly slip away from them. "It wasn't ideal… but you sealed away the Devil… nobody can ever question your strength." Eran burst into heavy sobs as the volume of Aiden's voice steadily decreased.

"This isn't what I wanted," he shouted as his wingman gripped his hand tightly. "I don't want to lose you again!" He couldn't help but think back to his emergence from the pit twelve years prior, and how he endured that entire time without his best friend at his side. His heart sank as the thunder overhead boomed throughout Israel.

"Eran," Aiden started hazily, his voice softer and fading by the second, "please… just live. Maya… take care… of my brother." The light in his eyes faded away as a tear streamed down the side of his face, but still he smiled all the same. The rain fell from heaven, and as his heart gave a final beat, Aiden Zane found his peace surrounded by all he cared about.

In the present day, Eran still felt his old partner's cold hand go limp in his grasp. He was praised as a hero, but over time he grew to despise it.

"I really wish you were here, Zane," he whispered to himself as he continued to walk the streets of the city.

"Hey," whispered a quiet feminine voice from behind him. He stopped and turned to see his wife, the lovely Maya Hewer, who stared at him lovingly and placed a gentle hand upon his cheek. "You alright?" Eran took a moment to truly contemplate the question, and as he looked around he quietly nodded. They walked across the street and further through the city in silence, and though she had already received Eran's answer she was smart enough to know that he wasn't as well off as he implied. She clung to him, and as they passed by the corner of Norville Avenue, she watched Aiden save her all over again.

To think if that hadn't happened, she thought as she leaned her head against her husband's shoulder and gazed up at his scarred face. All the memories flooded back, and she couldn't help but cry. *Thank you, Aiden.* The pensive couple continued to walk in silence, and Maya came to understand the mood of her companion despite the lack of verbal exchange. They neared the rebuilt apartment complex that Aiden had once called home, and as they climbed the stairs a wave of unconventional nostalgia swept over her. They came to a door and clasped hands as Eran lightly tapped it.

"Just a minute," called a female voice from the other side. The sound of a baby cooed in the background as she rushed to straighten up, and once she thought her living room tidy enough she opened the door to Eran and Maya. They came in upon request with smiles on their faces to mask the bittersweet thoughts that even then circled in their minds.

"He wasn't any trouble, was he," Eran asked as he turned to face the woman. She wore blue pajamas with purple accents, and her hair was tied up neatly in a bun. Her face was a gentle mahogany, and something about her smile reminded him of his mother. She shook her head and clasped her hands together in adoration.

"Oh no," she told them as she strolled across the room and picked up the child wrapped snugly in a baby blue blanket. She looked down at him with as much tender affection as his own mother did as she handed him back to Eran. "As always, he was a little angel."

"God, I hope not," Eran muttered involuntarily as the image of an enraged Uriel crept into the back of his mind.

"I'm sorry?" Eran looked up at the confused babysitter, but smiled and shook his head.

"It's nothing, really," he responded as he rocked the little boy back and forth. As Maya and the sitter followed his gaze to the little bundle of joy, they couldn't help but feel the strangest sensation, as if they were being watched.

"We are so blessed to have you," Eran whispered to the baby as his little hand grasped the end of his father's nose. Eran stayed his tears as he took in the sight of the little boy's curly hair and chocolate skin. His big brown eyes were full of hope, and the sweet smile of the infant melted his heart.

"You two are such wonderful parents. It's almost hard to believe you adopted this little guy with as much love as you shower him with," the babysitter said as she took the child's hand in her fingers and massaged his incredibly soft skin.

They both smiled in agreement as they bid the nanny farewell and took their leave. As they traveled back into the open, Eran held the baby close as the words of Mary reentered his mind. *It is easy to focus on what we lose in times like these. But when you really think about it, would they not rather us remember what they left us?*

Eran looked at his beloved son as the sun began to set, and with a tearful smile he whispered as the child drifted off to sleep, "I love you, my little Zane."

www.ingramcontent.com/pod-product-compliance
Lightning Source LLC
Chambersburg PA
CBHW060807310726
48980CB00002B/269

* 9 7 8 0 6 9 2 6 8 3 2 8 6 *